THE
HISTORY
of THINGS
TO COME

BOOK ONE OF THE *DARK HORIZON* TRILOGY

THE
HISTORY
of THINGS
TO COME

THE MIND OF A GENIUS CAN HOLD
THE DARKEST OF SECRETS

DUNCAN SIMPSON

Whitefort Publishing
London

Whitefort Publishing

First Whitefort Publishing edition published in 2015.

ISBN: 978-0-9932063-0-6

Printed in the United Kingdom.

Edited by Katie Simpson, Gale Winskill & Amy Butcher.
Cover design by Derek Murphy.

For Katie, Tamsin, Louis and Finley, with all my love.

PROLOGUE

The sound of the auctioneer's gavel echoed through the large hall like a rifle shot. With the tension in the proceedings momentarily released, the assembled group of private collectors, dealers and museum representatives shuffled in their seats, ready for the next sales lot. The auctioneer peered over his wireframe spectacles at the packed audience before him. Squinting slightly in the afternoon sunlight, he looked around the room for a second and then back to the sales catalogue perched on the lectern.

'Ladies and gentlemen, now we come to Lot 249: a miscellaneous collection of Isaac Newton's papers concerning the history of the Early Church. This unusual lot also includes a volume from Newton's own personal library.'

As the auctioneer read aloud from the sales brochure, a man wearing brown overalls placed an open wooden box on the table beside the lectern. Its contents, several large bundles of paper tied together by loops of brown string, shifted inside the box as the man tilted it to afford the audience a better view. Resting against the largest bundle was a small book whose vivid crimson cover seemed to illuminate the bottom of the box.

'Let us start the bidding at £500.'

The exchange of bids was immediate, and within a minute the auctioneer's starting price doubled. Soon, the bidders were reduced to two men sitting uncomfortably close to each other in the centre of the hall. The room looked on in silence, as the men batted offer and then counter-offer back and forwards.

Suddenly, the auctioneer's attention was drawn to the back of the hall. After a pause, he nodded and announced a bid of £3,000. A chorus of gasps was accompanied by the sound of shifting seats on the wooden floor, as the audience swung round to follow the auctioneer's sightline. A man, his face slatted in light and shadow, stood alone against the back wall.

'I have £3,000. Thank you, sir. Do I have any more bids?'

The auctioneer's request was met by the resigned shaking of heads from the previous two bidders.

'Thank you, sir. £3,000. Going once ... Going twice ... Sold to the gentleman at the back of the room.'

The strike of the gavel sounded once again through the auction hall.

'Let us move on. Lot 250: parts 1 and 2 of Newton's unpublished treatise on the transmutation of metals. Let's start the bidding at say £300.'

The buyer of the previous lot was approached from the side by a man with ink-black hair carrying a clipboard. 'Congratulations, sir, on your purchase,' he said in a hushed, respectful tone. 'I am the auction clerk for today's sale. Please may I take some details from you?'

The man nodded and, from the inside pocket of his exquisitely tailored jacket, retrieved a silver business-card holder. He opened it and handed the auction clerk a printed card.

Dr Roberto Martinelli
Books & Manuscript Broker
Representative of the Vatican

PART 1

THE FIRST LAW
OF MOTION

Every body perseveres in its state of being at rest or of moving uniformly straight forward, except insofar as it is compelled to change its state by forces impressed.

CHAPTER 1

Monday 1 December

Bullets don't fly through the air in straight lines: they progress in an arc according to Newton's laws of motion. Many factors can influence the arc of travel, but at the relative short flight distance of 330 metres, the Drakon could ignore the bullet's marginal gravitational drop. Tonight, the most significant influence on the flight of the projectile would be the southwesterly wind gusting down Marshall Street.

All was quiet in the vacant fourth-floor Soho flat except for the discordant sound of a glass cutter working against the windowpane. With a careful twist of the suction handle, the Drakon freed a small circle of glass from the window base, and with it came a sudden rush of cold air from the street below. Moments later, the bipod legs of the Soviet-made SVD Dragunov sniper rifle were opened out, and a curved ten-round box magazine clicked into place. It was nearly eight o'clock. It was time. Things had got sloppy. There would be no more mistakes.

The Drakon quickly drew the bolt in and out, moving a single round into the firing chamber. Nuzzling into the stock, the Drakon breathed in the distinctive odour of factory gun oil. The weapon smelt new. A magnified eye blinked down the length of the telescopic sight as a pair of crosshairs focused on the head of a stone lion. Forming part of the coat of arms carved into the limestone façade of the restaurant below, its outline was now crystal clear. Soon the head of a beast would be replaced with the head of a man.

The Faversham was popular with London's hip wealthy set. Its fortunes had been turned around by a Danish chef, who transformed the tired inner-city pub into a buzzing modern restaurant. The once-cramped drinking rooms and dark snugs had been replaced by a large expanse of whitewashed walls, stripped-down floors, and salvaged art deco lamps. Although it was the start of a new working week, the large, high-ceilinged dining space was packed with customers. A cacophony of accents vied for dominance over the electronic music orchestrated by a cool-looking black DJ, a pair of earphones appearing permanently balanced between his shoulder and right ear.

A bearded man with a blunt, square face sat alone at a table. He looked up to the clock above the bar and checked the time with his watch. After repositioning himself in his chair, he tilted his head to the side and with his finger, opened up a small gap between his neck and the collar of his red lumberjack shirt. As he did so, the lines on his forehead intensified into a deep frown. Touching his earpiece with his other hand, he whispered into the microphone taped to his wrist.

'Any sign?'

His question was met swiftly by an annoyed voice in his ear.

'Stop touching your ear with your fucking hand! You're going to blow the whole operation.' A pause. 'Just sit tight. The message said eight o'clock at the Faversham. They'll be here. Just stay cool.'

The large Afro-Caribbean police officer threw down the headset onto the bank of controls in the back of the surveillance van and let out a long deep sigh. Detective Chief Inspector Lukas Milton didn't like it one bit: too many people, too many guns. He slowly shook his head, returned the plastic smoking inhalator to his lips, and bit down hard onto the end of the white tube. His teeth ached. He tried to stretch out his legs in his chair, but his shins quickly hit the underside of the instrument desk. The van wasn't big enough to comfortably accommodate a man of Milton's size plus the racks of cameras and recording equipment installed in the back of the vehicle. Milton raised his binoculars to peer through the one-way privacy glass. From the van's parallel position to the restaurant, he had an unobstructed view through the large window that ran down the length of The Faversham's crowded dining room. Milton repositioned himself in his chair and focused the binoculars on the cloakroom next to a large green statue of a Buddha at the far end of the restaurant.

Behind the open hatch to the cloakroom sat a female attendant on a bar stool, her arms folded over her mid-section and her shoulders hunched over the counter. In front of her lay an open paperback book. Even though she had opened the book over thirty minutes ago she hadn't read a word.

Outside The Faversham, a black Mercedes came to a halt. Tarek Vinka reached over to the small canvas bag on the passenger's seat and hauled it onto his lap. After studying the street's reflection in the side mirrors for several seconds, he opened the door and stepped out into the cold London night. Vinka placed the bag by his feet, straightened his back and pulled up his collar against the wind. He closed and locked the car door and as he did so noticed a single snowflake land on the roof. Almost instantly, its delicate structure began to dissolve. With a finger, he went to touch where the snowflake had been, but all trace had disappeared, as if it had never existed. Vinka pulled down his baseball cap, picked up the bag and began to cross the street.

The surveillance van driver whispered over his shoulder. Milton quickly turned round in his chair.

'Yeah, I see him. This could be our man,' Milton followed his every step. 'So, Mr whatever your name is, what's in that bag?'

Vinka pushed open The Faversham's front door and stepped into the small reception area, letting the door close slowly behind him. He looked unkempt and unwashed, and his face was dark and weathered like a gypsy's. However, his clothes were expensive and recently pressed. Despite appearing in his late forties, his physique was strong and showed no signs of middle-aged spread.

On seeing the man's arrival, a waiter smiled a welcome and shouted for his colleague's attention. Vinka nodded. Several seconds later, a woman emerged from behind an espresso machine. She collected an oversized menu from the bar and headed over to him. After they exchanged several words, the waitress directed Vinka to the cloakroom.

The sound of street traffic was all but drowned out by the wind whistling through the small hole in the window of the fourth-floor flat.

The strength and direction of the crosswind was visible by the Union Jack flag billowing on the roof of the restaurant. The crosshairs of the telescopic sight centred onto the head of the man walking from the foyer of the restaurant. At this range, the 0.50-calibre bullet would not only tear up the contents of the skull but also rip the back of the head clean off. After making a small adjustment to the sight's magnification ring, the Drakon followed Vinka as he progressed towards the cloakroom, bag in hand. The Drakon dropped a finger down onto the steel arc of the trigger. The rifle's scope rapidly found the back of Vinka's head. The Drakon took a breath and held it.

As the cloakroom attendant rose to her feet, she could feel her heart racing. She tried not to meet the eyes of the man in front of her. He stood there impassively as she forced a smile and ripped off a numbered ticket from a small book. Not taking his eyes off the attendant, Vinka carefully placed the canvas bag on the countertop and picked up the ticket. The attendant shot a glance over Vinka's shoulder that lasted only a fraction of a second. Just long enough to establish a line of sight with the man in the dining room wearing the red-checked shirt. Somewhere in his subconscious, Vinka perceived the minute flicker in her eyes.

As she hauled the bag off the counter and turned to place it in the numbered storage rack, Vinka's gaze rose to the angled mirror on the wall behind the counter. Instinctively, his eyes were drawn to the reflection of the man in the scarlet plaid shirt. He appeared to be mouthing words to an invisible companion, but what he said was lost in the din of the dining room. Vinka's brow narrowed. The man touched his ear and then did it again. Time slowed. In a moment of dreadful recognition, the man in the red shirt looked up and stared directly at Vinka's reflection. His cover had been blown.

Before Vinka's line of vision snapped back to eye level, the cloakroom attendant had dropped the bag and reached for her service pistol hidden in the racking. She turned on her heels and came face to face with Vinka's raised Glock 17 pointing directly at her temple. A dark shadow had fallen across his face.

'Mistake, bitch,' he whispered, as his finger tightened around the curve of the trigger.

In the back of the surveillance van, Detective Milton bit down on his inhalator. The plastic tube flexed between his teeth and snapped.

The steel-cored sniper round erupted from the rifle barrel. By the time the crack of the high-powered weapon sounded from the opposite side of the street, the projectile had already gained a velocity of 830 metres per second. It was designed to spin in flight. Set in motion by the four right-handed helical grooves tooled into the rifle's barrel, the spin served to gyroscopically stabilise the projectile in the air. As a result, the bullet's flight was only marginally degraded by its impact with the front window of the restaurant. The same was also true of its flight through Vinka's head. The bullet entered through the back of his skull and punched a track through his brain, macerating all soft tissue in its wake. After exiting through his eye socket in a cloud of red mist and skull fragments, the bullet whistled past the shoulder of the cloakroom attendant before slamming into a marble pillar behind her.

The back doors of the surveillance van swung open, and Milton's huge frame suddenly appeared. Seconds later, he was running at full speed towards the restaurant. As he ran, he shouted into his handheld radio.

'What the hell just happened? I need a situation update now.'

Voices crackled back. Next came the call signs from the unmarked patrol cars parked at either end of Marshall Street.

'Situation update!' Milton's voice reverberated down the earpiece of the female officer stationed at the cloakroom.

Her back pinned against the wall, she tried to verbalise the scene at her feet. 'Suspect ... down. Suspect down. He pulled his weapon and ...' Her voice faltered, her throat clamped solid by the carnage at her feet.

'Condition? The suspect's condition?' said Milton. 'The ambulance is on its way.'

'It won't be needed,' she said slowly. 'Half his head is missing.'

As she spoke, the policewoman became aware of something on her cheek.

'Who discharged their weapon? Who took the shot?' Milton's voice was getting breathless.

'No one in here. The shooter must have been outside.' As she spoke, she stared down at her hand and the red grit she had just brushed from her face. She took a moment to realise what it was and began to cry.

With his police badge raised high above his head, Milton burst through the front door of The Faversham and was quickly followed by four armed uniformed officers. A hundred terrified faces stared at Milton in complete silence. After nodding his orders, two of the policemen headed towards the swing doors at the back of the restaurant leading to the kitchen, and the others took positions in the centre of the dining hall. Half-walking, half-running, Milton ran over to the undercover cloakroom attendant.

She stood there shaking, her wide eyes staring into empty space. Slowly, the detective unpeeled her fingers from the handle grip of her firearm and dropped the gun into his coat pocket. Then he lowered her trembling hands, waved over to the police officer wearing the red lumberjack shirt and directed him to look after her.

At his feet was the body of a dead man whose face had been cloven in two by a spike of molten metal travelling at twice the speed of sound. The effects had been catastrophic.

Milton's eyes tracked over the body to the canvas bag lying on the floor. He walked over to it while snapping on a pair of surgical gloves. The bag was about the size of a laptop case; light green, almost military. He thought for a second and then pulled back the zip. For a long while, he stood there staring at the bag's contents. It just didn't make sense. None of it made sense.

The sound of screeching tyres from a police car arriving outside shook Milton from his thoughts. Mumbling to himself, he searched the inside pocket of his coat for his mobile phone and dialled a number. It only took two rings to get an answer.

'Vincent, its Lukas. There's been another shooting.'

'Jesus, where?'

The detective whispered into his handset. 'Soho, in a packed bloody restaurant. Vincent, I'll explain later. Now I need your help.'

The detective picked up the canvas bag and placed it the counter. 'I need you to tell me why people are being killed because of these fucking books.'

CHAPTER 2

Wednesday 10 December

Vincent Blake waited patiently for DCI Milton to finish reading the final page of the forensics report. In that moment, two things separated the men: the first was an unremarkable office table, its well-worn exterior a testament to the years it had stood in Milton's office; the second was certainty as to the provenance of the small leather-bound book sitting proudly on the table top.

The policeman gave out a deep sigh, dropped the report nonchalantly onto the floor and leant back in his chair. It creaked back disapprovingly. Milton was an ox of a man who stood over six feet five inches tall. His skin was dark from his Caribbean ancestry, and his face wore a prominent scar from a knife attack during a drugs bust south of the river. He looked over to Blake, and the crack forming at the side of his mouth stayed around long enough to form a transitory grin.

'Vincent, all this lab stuff means nothing to me. What can you tell me? Is it genuine?' Blake leant forward and slid the volume carefully across the table to his old friend.

In contrast to the detective's imposing frame, Blake was a lean man. He was dressed smartly in an open white shirt, a pressed grey suit and a pair of gleaming black boots. He dragged his chair behind him and quickly positioned himself at Milton's side, as if he were there to turn the sheets of music for a concert pianist.

'This one's a puzzle, it really is.' Blake's eyes were now locked onto the small, dark-tanned volume finished with gilt decorations. 'The cover is good. I initially thought it might have been aged chemically, but you can usually smell if it's been done that way.' Blake leant over the book and gave the cover an exaggerated sniff. 'There's absolutely no trace of chemical tampering. It's in fabulous condition.'

He opened the antique book and continued. 'I've done isotopic testing to confirm the age of the paper and the type of parchment glues used in the bindings, and they all check out.'

He rotated the volume ninety degrees so that the policeman could get a clear view of the first page. It was blank apart from a signature in neat lettering in its top right-hand corner.

Isaac Newton

'The handwriting is consistent with the originals in the British Library. See the sweep in the tail of the letter *I* and the forward leaning letter *S*? These are all very characteristic.'

Blake paused and again rearranged his chair position. 'The answer to your question—whether the volume is a fake or not—is actually contained within the forensics report.' A smile spread slowly across Blake's face as he recovered the abandoned report from the floor. 'I asked the forensics team to run a full spectroscopy analysis of the coloured inks used throughout the book.' After quickly finding the appropriate place in the report, he read aloud the list of inks that most closely matched the atomic profiles revealed by the laboratory analysis. 'Orpiment, yellow ochre, madder, azur d'Allemagne, vermillion, malachite green, ivory black, red ochre, vert azur—'

'Okay, Vincent, enough, enough!' the policeman protested. 'What's your point?'

'My point is that all these colours were commonly available in London in Newton's time, but getting hold of these colours today, blending them and artificially ageing them to produce these shades would be very difficult to do.' A frown fleetingly passed over Blake's brow. 'Every part of my analysis indicates that it's genuine.' He paused. 'The bigger mystery is what does it all mean?'

Blake thumbed carefully through the yellowing pages and then let the volume fall open. For a long moment, the two men just stared at the revealed writing. Both sides were alike, as if the book's spine were a mirror producing a reflection of itself. The entire surface area of each page was filled with handwritten numbers neatly tabulated into columns, with ten columns to a side. At certain points down the length of each column, a particular number was stained with a spot of translucent coloured paint. Finally, Blake broke the silence.

'Every page of the notebook is the same. Newton wrote hundreds of notebooks during his lifetime, but not like this one.'

Milton gave a quiet grunt and nodded.

'They could be tables of results from his experiments, but the numbers and colours appear to follow no discernible pattern. More likely that it's code.'

'Code?' said the detective.

'Code to protect his research from prying eyes,' said Blake. 'Lots of the old scientists did it, and some modern ones still do. It's all about being the first to go public with a discovery. Until you go public, you protect what you've discovered. Reputations depend on it.'

'So you've got no idea what it means?' asked Milton.

'No idea at all.' Blake shrugged and gave out a long sigh. 'Leave it with me and I'll see what I can come up with.'

Milton checked the date on his watch. 'Two weeks. You've got two weeks and then it will need to be returned to its owner,' said Milton.

Blake nodded.

The policeman retrieved a sheet of folded paper from his jacket pocket, along with a shiny silver foil bag, and smoothed both out on the table top. Milton picked up his pen and signed the bottom of the *Evidence Appropriation Form* with a casual squiggle before sliding it and the silver evidence bag over to Blake. The detective waited until Blake had signed before continuing.

'Two weeks, no longer,' said Milton.

'Right you are. What about the courier who was shot? You get an ID on him?'

'There wasn't much left of his face, but his fingerprints came up with a match. Hold on.' Blake waited as Milton retrieved his briefcase from underneath the table with his feet. He picked it up, laid it flat next to the book and flipped open the locks. From inside he located a photograph and handed it to Blake.

'Tarek Vinka. A grade-one hard bastard. Bosnian, ex-army, turned mercenary. Interpol has been after his hide for years.'

Blake stared at the police mug shot of a man standing against a background of horizontal lines indicating the man's height. He looked like a bare-knuckle boxer.

'He's been linked to a number of armed robberies in France and Luxembourg, and a kidnapping in Milan. I don't think he's going to be missed anytime soon.' The detective gave a half-smile that died fast. 'So we have another robbery.' Milton started rubbing his forehead with the back of his hand. 'And a Bosnian mercenary gunned down in a busy restaurant. The only clue we have is this bloody book.'

Simultaneously, the two men gazed back at the book.

'There is one thing,' said Blake. 'The last page is different.'

Before the policeman had time to ask why, Blake was busy locating the page.

'There,' said Blake.

'And what the hell is that?'

The page staring back at the two men couldn't have been more unlike the previous ones. Instead of having columns of numbers, the page was given over to a drawing, expertly executed in black ink. The design was circular, and its circumference almost touched the edges of the page. It was divided into twelve equal quadrants, like the spokes of a wheel. Where the end of each spoke intersected the circle's perimeter, the same small peculiar motif had been copied.

'They look like bees,' said Milton, his eyes scanning around the face of the illustration.

'I thought that too. Bees,' agreed Blake.

'And this?' The detective pointed at the word written at the centre of the circle.

'*Clavis*? It's Latin,' said Blake. 'It means "the key".'

CHAPTER 3

Saturday 13 December

The early evening flurry of light snow hung in the air like a fog. Through the lens of suspended snowflakes, the lights from the constant stream of traffic moving along Clerkenwell Road were transformed into a wash of diffuse orange and reds.

Abruptly, Vincent Blake stopped on the pavement, bringing his wife and daughter to a sudden halt beside him. Blake gently squeezed the hand that had just arrived in the large pocket of his tailored overcoat. The gloved hand felt warm and caused a big smile to crinkle across his face.

'Searching for sweets, Sarah?'

Sarah gave her dad's finger a pinch in response.

'You know me, Dad. Always searching for sweets.'

The pretty girl of ten years looked up expectantly at her father, her face beaming. Without looking down, Blake tugged the front of the girl's baseball cap covering her eyes. His daughter's hand quickly recoiled from Blake's pocket, and she went about resetting the tight curls dislodged by the movement of the hat.

'Dad, the hair. Don't touch the hair!'

The child's feigned annoyance dissolved as a small chocolate bar appeared before her eyes.

'You are very welcome,' said Blake, wiping away the single snowflake that had just landed on his lips.

A man in his mid-thirties, Blake spoke in a quiet measured way that hinted at a public school education. Nomsa had often teased him that he spoke like an English diplomat, which he secretly enjoyed. His face was strong-featured without being conventionally handsome, and even under the street lights, his skin still bore the remnants of an incongruous tan. His slightly thinning hair was swept dramatically backwards, and his chin was hidden under a purple scarf. Trying to keep warm, Blake began to rock from side to side, his polished boots glistening on the damp pavement.

'It's time to head home.' His breath condensed in the cold air as he spoke. Smiling over the folds of his scarf, Blake looked affectionately over to his wife.

Dr Nomsa Blake was an elegant woman. She was tall, of an equal height to her husband. Apart from a simple fringe swept back across her forehead, her sleek, straightened hair was neatly tucked under a white woollen ski hat. She was pretty, with a clear café-latte complexion, which made her look younger than her thirty-nine years. Originally from Zimbabwe and educated at Cambridge, Nomsa Blake had carved out a successful career as a human rights lawyer. She gently took her husband's arm.

'Sarah wants me to help her choose a nail varnish at the chemists,' she said. 'On the way home, we'll pop to the deli and pick up something for dinner. You head back and get the fire going.' Nestling into Blake's neck, Nomsa stared down at Sarah unwrapping the chocolate bar. Blake pulled his wife and daughter in close to himself, as if protecting them from the cold wind. Several seconds later, a muffled voice came from within the folds of his overcoat.

'Dad, I can't breathe.'

Chuckling, he released his captive from his forced embrace. He crouched down and whispered in Sarah's ear.

'Princess, make sure Mum gets something nice for dinner,' he said.

Sarah returned her father a reassuring wink. 'Don't worry, Dad, I'll make sure.'

A chilled blast of wind blew down Clerkenwell Road.

'It's freezing. Get the kettle on, love. We'll only be a few minutes.'

Blake hauled himself upright and kissed his wife's cheek. He lingered for a moment and kissed her again, this time on the lips.

'Oh please! Do you have to? In public and everything? You two are so embarrassing.'

'What you can't see won't hurt you,' said Blake.

He gave a second tug at the peak of Sarah's cap, and then, with a long lazy rub of his hand, further dislodged the cap from its fashionable position.

'I'll see you both in a couple of minutes, and remember ... something nice for dinner.'

With that, Vincent Blake turned up the collar of his overcoat and made his way through the lines of parked cars in the direction of home.

'Okay Dad, see you later,' waved Sarah.

Vincent Blake didn't hear the words of his daughter above the din of the loud London traffic.

CHAPTER 4

The ground-floor study of Blake's Victorian home was silent but for the sounds emerging from a large boxer dog sleeping next to the glowing embers of an open coal fire. The animal snored soundly, its body stretched out parallel to the ceramic tiled hearth. Abruptly the dog let out a long laboured breath, sending its oversized jowls spluttering against the oak floor.

Apart from the fire, the only other illumination in the room came from the lights of a Christmas tree, its branches heavily laden with decorations and long tracks of silver and red tinsel. The lights had been set to gently build in intensity over the course of several minutes to gradually impart the room with a rich ruby glow before dimming again.

The dog gave a shudder and opened its eyes wide. Within seconds the animal was on its feet, ears upright and alert. Sensing vibrations in the air, the dog's nostrils twitched, its compact but powerful body standing on perfectly straightened front legs. The dog waited, its eyes glistening from the lights of the Christmas tree. A sound came from behind the door, quickly followed by another, this time louder. The boxer's strong muscular neck turned, its short blunt muzzle tracking something on the other side of the wall. Slowly, the door handle began to move. Backing away from the door, the dog's white fangs began to bite at the air. The door creaked open.

The Drakon stood tall, barely clearing the top of the doorframe. Dressed in black, features hidden under a ski mask, the Drakon watched the snarling dog standing bolt upright in the corner of the room, a long strand of saliva trailing from its exposed fangs. The Drakon's eyes burned into the centre of the dog's skull like laser beams.

Do not fight,
Feel my shadow surround you.

Do not struggle against me.
Yield to me.

The animal attempted to shake its head to free itself from an invisible force tightening around its skull. The dog grappled to retain a foothold on the polished oak floor. The Drakon moved forwards. An impenetrable gaze locked onto the whimpering animal. Cold hands quickly surrounded the dog's head, enveloping it like a dark shroud. Long fingers stretched out, fingertips moving quickly over the ridges of the animal's heavy, compact skull.

Do not struggle.
Yield to me.

The dog's fur grew crimson in the intensifying lights of the Christmas tree as if the animal's body had started to glow with heat.

Feel my shadow surround you.
Yield to me.

With its head tilted upwards and cupped in the Drakon's hands, the dog stared back in terror.

Feel my shadow surround you.

A tremor shook along the animal's backbone before its back legs gave way underneath it. Then it was still.

The Drakon loosened the grip, and the dog's body fell to floor with a heavy thump. A dark line of blood began to trickle from the dog's left ear along the wooden floor. Stepping back from the discarded corpse, the Drakon now focused on the room layout.

The study was large, its original function probably that of a sitting room. It was tidy and ordered, and two of its walls were given over to a series of densely packed but well-organised bookshelves. Moving quickly, the Drakon scanned their contents. Each shelf was labelled with a handwritten sticker identifying a particular subject area: issues of modern academic journals on renaissance art, archaeology, material science, and architecture rubbed shoulders with old and obscure leather-bound volumes.

At regular gaps along the shelves were pictures, ornaments and curios of all different types. One such space was dedicated to a small collection of astronomical instruments: gilded brass sundials, quadrants of various sizes, a large brass astrolabe with Arabic lettering stamped down one of its sides, and a celestial globe representing a three-dimensional map of the night sky.

A loud popping sound came from the open fire. A pile of glowing coals collapsed into each other, sending a long single flame upwards into the chimney. The movement in the fire drew the intruder's gaze from the astronomical objects to a photo frame positioned in between two stacks of dog-eared papers.

The Drakon picked up the silver frame from the shelf. The picture was of three people balancing in close formation on a surfboard. The corner of the photograph had been slightly overexposed, as if the camera had been pointing directly into the sun. Each person was crouching and pretending to ride a wave with arms outstretched, though the board itself was firmly planted on a stretch of golden sand. All three were dressed in shortie wetsuits, and wide smiles beamed from each of their faces.

The front position of the surfboard was occupied by a pretty girl of around ten years of age. Her face was darkly tanned and her hair swept back into a loose ponytail except for a single multi-coloured braid that dangled in front of her nose. Behind the girl posed a man and a woman. The man was Caucasian, tall and slim and had one arm fastened securely around a woman's waist. His other arm extended out behind him like a rodeo rider, counterbalancing the force of the imaginary wave. His face was sun-bronzed and happy. At the centre of the group was a strikingly beautiful woman of mixed race, her full black hair forming a natural Afro style. The photograph had captured the woman staring directly into the camera, her wide eyes forming a natural focal point to the picture. In the background was a 4-x-4 vehicle painted in a bright red livery with the words '*Cornish Life Guard*' stencilled in large yellow lettering on its bonnet.

After returning the picture to the shelf, the Drakon crouched down and continued the systematic inspection of the shelves, pausing every so often over a particular volume before moving on. After several minutes of unfruitful searching, the intruder let out a long hiss of frustration.

The Drakon stepped away from the bookshelves and eyed the large writing desk at the centre of the room. It was of a sturdy wooden construction and painted in a dark lacquer, giving the impression that it was antique. A single manila card folder rested on its green leather-bound top. The Drakon opened the folder and tugged at the short cord of a marble desk light. A circle of bright light illuminated the desktop. The tip of a gloved finger dragged the police report free from the file. For several minutes the Drakon pored over the contents, quickly turning the pages before finally discarding the weighty file back to the desk.

The Drakon's gaze was now fixed upon the drawer at the centre of the desk. A concerted pull on the handle confirmed that it was locked. Soon the Drakon's full bodyweight was brought down upon the blade of a paper knife, its metal edge wedged in the gap between the drawer and the lock. All of a sudden, the knife shifted forwards and the room was filled with the sound of splintering wood. With a final yank of the knife, the drawer was set free, sending wood fragments showering down onto the carpet beneath.

Impatiently, the Drakon pulled open the drawer. A single object stared up from within: a silver foil bag measuring some twelve inches in length by ten inches across. Carefully, the Drakon removed the bag from the drawer and placed it on the desktop next to the folder. One end of the bag was open; the white sticker bearing the words '*Police Evidence*' once sealing its end had been cleanly cut in two by a sharp blade. The Drakon raised the closed end, and a small book effortlessly slid out.

CHAPTER 5

Blake thought of Sarah and chuckled to himself. She was a good kid. A metallic ping announced the arrival of a message on Blake's mobile phone. He stopped walking and fought through the folds of his coat to retrieve the device from his pocket. The screen shone in the gathering gloom of the London evening. The message was from Detective Milton. It was much longer than the detective's usual stripped-down messages. Blake quickly scrolled:

> AUTOPSY REPORT FOR TAREK VINKA JUST COME IN. CORONER FOUND REMNANTS OF AN INK STAMP ON HIS HAND ... ENTRY STAMP TO THE KOKO CLUB IN CAMDEN. MUST HAVE PAID EIGHT BALL A VISIT?

Blake and Eight Ball had history. Originally from Haiti, Eight Ball wasn't a man to be messed with. He was like a fight dog: dangerous and unpredictable.

Their paths had crossed several times before and most recently during the recovery of a stash of stolen Anglo-Saxon gold coins. It had been the usual story. A prestigious London museum, anxious to protect its reputation, had contacted Blake under conditions of complete confidentiality. The museum had suffered another break-in, this time in broad daylight, and a prized collection of twenty-seven gold coins had gone missing.

A museum's survival depended on the quality of its exhibits. Significant numbers of exhibits were loaned or donated to a museum for display or safe keeping. Any suspicions that a museum's security systems were a soft touch would result in the flow of exhibits from generous benefactors being shut off like a tap. That's where Blake came in. His business card read, *Dr Vincent Blake, Independent Art Recovery Investigator.* He was independent, discreet and probably the best in London. Over the last decade, he had carved out an enviable reputation amongst London's museums and auction houses. His methods were often unconventional, but his results spoke for themselves.

After several weeks of intense detective work, Blake tracked the stolen coins to a lock-up in Muswell Hill rented by Eight Ball. Whilst not directly implicated in the robbery, Eight Ball was a fence for the artefacts. Following Blake's tip-off, the police successfully recovered the coins, and Eight Ball was sent down for a nine-month stretch.

According to local folklore, Eight Ball had acquired his name after an infamous bar fight. An ex-crew member had made it known that his business partner had turned police informer. He tracked him down to a Brixton bar, where his business associate was shooting pool. Consumed with rage, Eight Ball pinned his former friend down on the pool table and smashed in his skull with a pool ball. Whether it was actually the eight ball or not was immaterial; the name stuck. No one would testify against him.

Recently, Eight Ball had reinvented himself as a music promoter and the manager of the Koko Club in Camden. But word on the streets was that he was back to his old games.

Blake sneezed loudly. The sound echoed down the deserted street. He waited for an imminent second sneeze, but none came. After first rubbing the end of his nose, he went back to composing a reply to Detective Milton's text. He turned the corner into Phoenix Place and, not looking up from the phone, stumbled over the legs of a woman sitting directly in his path. Her back was square up against the wall, and although her chin rested on her knees, her legs spanned the full width of the pavement. Blake reached out to the wall and hopped to a stop.

Both the dishevelled woman and the black mongrel dog lying by her side appeared quite unperturbed by the collision. She sat there like an apparition under the pale illumination of a streetlight. By the large clumps of greasy matted hair and the thick blanket around her shoulders, it looked like she was sleeping rough.

Blake raised his hands and fumbled an apology.

'I'm sorry. I wasn't paying attention. You okay?'

Before he had finished speaking, Blake had registered two details. The first was that the dog wasn't on a leash and the second was that on the pavement under the woman's legs was an open book. It looked like a bible.

At first, the shivering woman didn't respond to Blake's apology. She just stared blankly back at him. He returned his phone to his pocket. After a moment, his hand reappeared with a ten-pound note. With his eyes half-fixed on the dog, he stepped forward.

'What's your name?' he said.

'Mary,' she replied in a quiet, hollow voice.

'Look Mary, here's a tenner. Get yourself something hot to eat. You'll freeze out here tonight.'

Carefully, he crouched down and placed the bank note on the open page of the book. As he hauled himself to his feet, Blake noticed something familiar and yet totally unexpected about the book, like he was meeting an acquaintance in a completely incongruous setting.

The book was indeed a bible, but it was written in Aramaic, the language Jesus had spoken.

CHAPTER 6

A sudden gust of wind slammed the front door shut behind him. After recoiling from the loud noise, Blake shook the thoughts of his recent encounter with the curious vagrant woman from his head. Half-expecting to be greeted enthusiastically by Plato, the family pet dog, he hovered in the hallway listening out for the familiar sound of paws scampering on the stripped oak flooring. Standing perfectly still, he strained to listen for the tell-tale sounds, but all was silent apart from the loud ticking of the grandfather clock at the end of the corridor.

Lazy dog. Probably fast asleep in front of the fire, he thought, as he deposited his house keys on the sideboard next to the door.

Blake looked at his reflection in the hallway mirror and began to slowly unwind the scarf from around his neck. His winter holiday tan was still visible. The reflection smiled contently back. Shopping at Smithfield Market had left his muscles feeling heavy, and Blake gave into the large yawn developing in his jaws. After hanging up his coat on the hat stand, he remembered the fire in the study. With a bit of luck, he could revive it with a few prods from the poker. Blake raised his hands to his lips and breathed warm air between them. As he moved along the hallway towards the study, he could feel his frozen finger tips begin to thaw. Still blowing into his hands, Blake awkwardly pushed down on the door handle with his elbow. Helped by a gentle nudge of his shoulder, the door slowly opened.

In the doorway, Blake was met by a wall of stuffy warm air. His eyes tried to readjust to the relative darkness of the room. In the shadows, the lights of the Christmas tree gave out a pulse of red light. Lying on the floor next to the hearth was Plato's familiar profile. For a moment, Blake tilted his head and studied the twisted contours of the animal's outline. Something about the way its legs were spread out under its body was at odds with the position of its spine. The thought hung unreconciled in Blake's mind as a shape burst out from the darkness.

An intense jab of pain shot through Blake's shoulder, his vision exploding into shards of intense white light. He lurched forwards, his legs unable to keep his body upright. Blake dropped to the ground like a felled tree.

Seeing the effect of the blow, the Drakon let go of the heavy marble base of the desk light. It crashed to the floor only a foot away from Blake's head, the sharp edge of the stand cutting out a deep triangular wedge in the wooden floorboard.

Gradually, the splinters of light firing in Blake's optic nerve coalesced. Fighting for breath, Blake willed his mind to make sense of what he was seeing. He could make out a dark silhouette. Biting hard, he concentrated on the shadowy profile hovering over the desk that appeared to be gathering something into its hands and moving towards the door.

Blake reached out to touch his throbbing shoulder. He groaned as a piercing pain reverberated through his neck. His shoulder was wet with blood. The jolt of pain seemed to temporarily clear his blurred vision. Through blinking eyes, he could now make out the intruder: tall, dressed in black, features hidden under a ski mask. As the figure came closer, Blake could make out an object in the person's hand: it was Newton's notebook.

He closed his eyes and instinctively kicked out into space. The toe of his boot made hard contact with the burglar's ankle. Knocked off-course, the Drakon slammed into the side of the doorframe. Blake kicked out again, but this time his boot met thin air. Expecting another blow from above, his limbs drew back into a protective foetal position. He waited for the inevitable impact, his muscles stiffening in anticipation. Nothing came. Blake's eyes widened as the study door slammed shut.

Straining every muscle in his body, Blake tried to haul himself to his feet. The room horizon shifted in front of him, and he reached out to the bookshelf in an attempt regain his balance. Stumbling forwards, he struck his hand on the shelf, causing a collection of small Japanese ceramics to clatter in all directions. He lost his balance, and his shoulder pounded into the wall, sending a shockwave of pain blazing across his chest.

The sound of his heartbeat pulsed loudly in his head as Blake slammed his hand down onto the door handle. The door swung open, and a cold blast of air hit his face. Looking down the hallway, Blake could see the intruder sprinting towards the road, Newton's notebook in hand.

The air was suddenly filled with the nearby sound of a screaming car engine revving hard. At the far end of the road, a black Jaguar XJ saloon accelerated at speed towards the fleeing intruder. Blake stumbled down the hallway, using the walls to balance. Plumes of tyre smoke billowed from the wheel arches of the blacked-out car as it screeched to a halt outside Blake's house. Holding Newton's book like a running baton, the intruder sprinted towards the waiting vehicle. The Jaguar twitched forward, its brakes straining against the massive torque of its engine.

Blake willed himself forward, adrenalin surging through his bloodstream. He made it outside just in time to see the intruder disappear into the car's back seat. The rear wheels of the Jaguar spun as they fought to gain traction on the wet tarmac. In the blink of an eye, the Jaguar's sleek chassis gained momentum. Propelled by the acceleration of the vehicle, the car door slammed shut, enclosing the passenger behind tinted glass. By the time Blake reached the pavement, the car was gunning up the road at full speed. With every step, Blake's pace quickened. Soon he was pursuing the car up Phoenix Place in a desperate attempt to make out its registration number before it vanished.

CHAPTER 7

After visiting the Italian Deli and the chemist shop on Farringdon Road, Nomsa and Sarah turned into Mount Pleasant Street. Before the junction with Phoenix Place, the road performed a tight zigzag bend, the strange by-product of centuries of haphazard town planning. Knowing that the pavement disappeared on one end of the street before reappearing on the opposite side a little way up, Nomsa took hold of Sarah's hand. She was surprised how cold her daughter's fingers felt.

'Darling, where's your glove?'

Sarah gave her mother a sideways glance, her mouth breaking out in a cheeky grin.

'Mum, I think I left it in Dad's pocket.'

Nomsa's face dissolved into a warm smile. 'Well then, we'd better get home before you lose anything else.' Nomsa's words were muffled in the large woollen scarf around her neck. Glancing left and right, mother and daughter crossed the road.

The Jaguar accelerated hard out of the bend, shooting the needle of the rev gauge into the red. Suddenly, the driver saw the two figures marooned in the centre of the road ahead. In the back of the car, the passenger had a brief flash of recognition: the faces from the photograph in the study, the faces on the beach.

'Drive! Drive!'

Frozen in the middle of the road, Nomsa and Sarah could only watch as the high-performance car careered towards them. Without thinking, Nomsa pushed her daughter to the side, but it was too late. The leading edge of the car's bumper acted like the blade of an axe.

Nomsa's body jack-knifed in on itself. First her head slammed down onto the bonnet with the force of a hammer before being whipped backwards as her legs were pulled violently underneath the vehicle.

The moment the back of her skull hit the tarmac it fractured into three pieces, driving shards of bone deep into her brain.

The Jaguar's sophisticated on-board computer tried to make sense of the data from the traction sensors in the front wheels. A light on the dashboard momentarily flashed a warning, alerting the driver that the front wheels had temporarily lost grip on the road. Equating the frictional coefficient data with a road surface covered in wet leaves, the computer instantly sent back a cascade of electronic instructions to the Jaguar's front wheels. Instead of wet leaves, the tyres were spinning on human flesh and the squashed contents of a shopping bag.

The mother's raw instinct to push her daughter a fraction of a second before the impact changed the young girl's centre of gravity. That, combined with the colossal shearing forces of the Jaguar's curved bumper, tossed Sarah into the air like a rag doll. With limbs flailing at her side, her body cart-wheeled in empty space. Below her, the front of the Jaguar reared up off the road, running over an unseen obstacle. Sarah was soon caught by the irresistible pull of gravity, and her body hit the road with a force that seemed too big for her small frame. Sarah rolled forward and came to rest face to face with her mother's mangled body. Like a mother watching her daughter sleeping soundly, Nomsa's expression was frozen in an unearthly stare. A dark halo of blood began to grow from beneath Nomsa's head, oozing out in a dark circle.

Now moving at no more than a jog, Blake turned the sharp corner in the road. What he saw lying at his feet made him stop in his tracks. It was Sarah's cap. He couldn't move forward. Then his gaze extended further up along the road. A sudden shock of terror pulled at his insides when he saw the two lifeless bodies lying on the tarmac.

CHAPTER 8

3 months later: Wednesday 18 March

A black cat stared intently at the robin pecking at invisible traces of food. The cat sat almost motionless except for the small sideways movement of its ribcage as it breathed and waited patiently for the right moment to strike. Unaware of the other animal's presence, the bird hopped frenetically from foot to foot up the gravel path, continually reorienting its body towards the next morsel. Slowly, the cat arched its back and tightened the muscles around its shoulders in preparation. It edged forward, its shoulder blades moving up and down like the pistons of an engine as it closed in. The animal exploded into a committed sprint across the graveyard towards the bird.

Blake's fingertips followed the letters of Nomsa's name. Her headstone was a simple affair: pink granite with three lines of lettering carved into it: her name, a series of dates, and a simple dedication.

The light that brought me here has taken me home.

It was the same inscription on her mother's gravestone in Harare. He took a step back and saw flecks of mica in the pale granite sparkle in the early spring sunshine. Blake's breathing faltered momentarily, and tears filled his eyes. His hand plunged into his coat pocket and tightened around something soft. He squeezed it tightly. It was Sarah's glove.

Slowly Blake became aware of the sound of feet moving on the gravel behind him. He turned around.

'I don't mean to intrude. I just wondered if you were okay?'

The voice belonged to a vicar. A large man in his sixties dressed in a black suit, well-worn brown brogues and a dog collar around a thick neck. Blake tried to compose himself and wiped his eyes with the arm of his coat.

'Yes, yes, I'm okay, thank you.'

'I didn't mean to disturb,' said the clergyman.

As Blake studied the man, he noticed he was trying to conceal a lit cigarette behind his back.

'Terrible habit, I know,' said the vicar, realising he had been clocked. 'Throwback to my army days, I'm afraid. Tried to give it up for Lent. Do you partake?' the vicar asked, offering Blake a cigarette from a packet he had quickly produced from his jacket.

'No, thank you. I gave up years ago,' said Blake.

'Good for you. Good for you.'

The vicar took a drag and returned the cigarette to a position behind his back.

'Do you mind me asking if the deceased was family?'

'My wife,' said Blake.

'Oh, I'm so sorry.'

For an awkward moment, the two men stared at Nomsa's gravestone in silence. Finally, the vicar cleared his throat.

'I'm sorry, I don't recognise you. I've just joined the parish. Are you a member of the congregation here?'

Blake shook his head, trying not to look at the clergyman's face.

'No, I'm afraid my church-going days are over.'

'I see. But you are welcome. Our doors are always open.'

Blake nodded and then said, 'Would you mind if I ask you a question?'

'Fire away,' said the pastor, staring down his nose.

'You said you were in the army?'

'Thirty-two years all told. Twenty-two as a Royal Marine and ten as a military chaplain.'

'You saw action?'

'Oh yes,' said the vicar.

Blake's eyes beckoned him to continue.

'Bosnia, Kosovo, Sierra Leone and Iraq. All the hot spots.'

'You were a chaplain on the front line?' said Blake quizzically. 'You carried a gun?'

The vicar retrieved the cigarette from behind his back and gave it a long drag.

'Oh no, chaplains aren't permitted to carry weapons.'

'But you were on the front line?'

'Yes, my friend. When soldiers see a churchman willing to risk his life and go into battle with them, side by side in the trenches, then they see that God hasn't abandoned them. Anyway, it's nothing new. The Israelites brought their priests into battle too, thousands of years ago.'

'But you think force can be justified for the right reason?' asked Blake.

'It's not an easy question. Depends on the reason,' replied the clergyman, flicking ash onto the gravel path. 'The thing I know for sure is that there is evil in the world, and it needs to be confronted.'

'I think you're right,' Blake said slowly. 'If you don't mind, I'll take that cigarette now.'

'Don't want to be a bad influence,' said the vicar through a lopsided smile. He offered Blake the packet of cigarettes. Blake took one and leaned forward for the clergyman to light it.

As Blake drew the smoke deep into his lungs, he noticed the cat sitting proudly further up the gravel path, the body of a dead bird in its paws.

CHAPTER 9

Thursday 19 March

The Snakeheads arrived on the main stage of the Koko Club in complete darkness, although small red lights shone out from the Marshall speaker stacks. The audience sensed the band's arrival and surged forward like an ocean swell. The band's frontman looked out into the swirling blackness. With the toe of his combat boot, he tapped a switch on his guitar's overdrive foot pedal and waited. From high on the balcony, a single spotlight cut through the darkness, bleaching the singer's white skin in its beam.

'You fuckers ready to rock and roll?' the frontman snarled into the void.

A riff blasted from his guitar, and the crowd convulsed as though being jacked into the electrical mains. Still in darkness, the Snakeheads' drummer counted in the rest of the band with his drumsticks raised high above his head. On the four count, he brought the sticks down hard onto the edge of the high hat and started spitting out a ferocious beat like a machine gun. The crowd shook with the urgency of the rhythm, while the stage lights pulsed on and off in rapid succession. The strobing light caught a plastic beer cup stuttering along its trajectory towards the stage. After landing just in front of the singer's microphone, it detonated in an eruption of froth. Without interrupting his frenzied strumming, the singer kicked the empty plastic cup back into the audience to a roar of approval. His eyes were alight with menace. He screamed the opening words of the song, looking like a crazed animal ready to attack.

The sizeable doorman at Camden's Koko Club didn't know what to make of the man standing in front of him. He didn't look like the usual punter at a Snakeheads gig. Instead of the standard black leather and battered denim, this man was wearing a suit, and he was leaning on a soaked umbrella. With an eyebrow raised, the doorman looked him up and down.

'Hand,' the doorman grunted, slightly annoyed that someone would be arriving so late to the gig and distracting him from his crossword puzzle.

'Pardon?' said Blake.

'Hand stamp. You ain't getting in without a hand stamp.' The doorman was now on his feet, a layer of thick stomach fat wobbling in mid-air behind a straining Rolling Stones t-shirt. With a slightly miffed expression, he nodded over to the ticket counter at one end of the foyer.

'Right,' conceded Blake, who walked past the tables of Snakeheads merchandise towards the ticket counter.

After reassembling the pages of his newspaper fluttering in the arc of the fan next to his seat, the doorman returned his attention to the crossword puzzle: *Four across. 7 letters. Caesar's crossing caused certain war?*

Blake pushed his way through the sea of black leather. He strained his eyes upwards. Eight Ball's office was directly above the stage, set off a long corridor leading from the venue's large balcony. Blake knew where the staircase was. He had been to the Koko before, but always in daylight. Now the light was harsh and pulsing in time to a deafening drumbeat. Towards the side of the stage the crowd thinned out, and within minutes, he was standing face-to-face with the door to Eight Ball's office.

The door was a custom job. It had to be, as it served multiple purposes. First there was the sound-proofing. The typical concert downstairs would peak at 120 decibels, close to the threshold that caused pain to the human ear. The core of the door, a multi-layered sandwich of dense hardwood bordered with rubber acoustic seals, muffled sound from either direction.

Its second job was security. At a weekend, the office safe could hold bar takings in excess of five figures. The door needed to be secure enough to withstand a sustained attack by a couple of determined hard cases. The five millimetres of galvanised steel plate that encased the door and its frame did the job.

The whole design was very heavy at just shy of 160 kilos. It was hung on five enclosed specialist hinges and would only open if the twelve-point locking mechanism was released from the doorframe.

The door design also served well for Eight Ball's other lines of business, the main one being drugs. Initially Jamaican skunk, then speed imported from the south-west of Mexico, and finally Colombian cocaine. The margins were good, but managing a distribution network could present challenges. Things could get very unpredictable indeed. And an unpredictable supply chain was bad for business. More to the point, it was bad for Eight Ball's health. The missing thumb on his left hand was testament to that.

Slowly, he realised that his business model was flawed. Eight Ball was a student of the capitalist economics of supply and demand. Selling product was old economics. He needed to embrace the new economic reality of the service industry. He knew a lot of people. People who needed things and people who could supply those things. He became a facilitator, bringing buyers and sellers together. He didn't touch the product but merely opened doors.

Some jobs were difficult, but he always found a way: gun importers, fences, getaway drivers, bent locksmiths, underground importers, plastic surgeons who left no records, military equipment suppliers, lawyers with questionable moral codes, airport luggage handlers, CCTV camera operators, forgers of all types, GPs with open prescription pads, accountants, working girls providing exotic services, prison guards who could keep quiet. All could be suppliers of his services; all could be consumers of his services. That was the beauty of the new business model; a kind of self-sustaining perpetual motion machine. Introduction fees were paid upfront and were non-refundable. He only dealt with professionals who knew their trade. Eight Ball's introductions came with his personal seal of approval.

Blake's fist banged loudly on the steel door. He waited and looked down at his feet. His shoes were filthy, the toes worn down to the leather. He banged again. No answer. This time he started kicking at the base of the door.

'Okay, okay.' A muffled voice became audible from behind the sheet of metal.

Finally, there were the sounds of bolts being drawn, and the door opened inwards by a few inches. Eight Ball stood in the gap, eyes scanning up and down. Even through the small opening, Blake could see his expression drop.

The door closed swiftly, but instead of locking in place it flew open again. Quickly, Eight Ball grabbed out for the handle but instead found empty air, the edge of the door missing his head by an inch. It slammed into the inside wall and secured itself onto a magnetic fire-door holder fixed to the skirting board. At the same time, Blake's umbrella fell to the floor with a clatter, its once-straight body now a contorted 'V' shape forged by the impact of the door. Blake's reactions had been sharp, but his umbrella was dead.

Eight Ball stood in the doorway, his grim expression revealing his anger at Blake's unexpected visit. He ran his fingers through his tangled dreadlocks and moved from side to side, as if performing some kind of rain dance.

'You got some balls turning up here. I guess you haven't come to see the Snakeheads?' Eight Ball said sarcastically.

Blake shook his head and clocked the cluster of small dark needle marks running up the man's forearm.

'What the hell do you want?'

Without acknowledging the comment, Blake stepped through the doorway into the office. Eight Ball unclipped the door from the fire holder and followed Blake inside, his face tightening with every step. The heavy steel door clicked shut behind him.

The decor of Eight Ball's shabby office had an over-the-top Asian influence. Lots of cheap wood and rickety bamboo furniture held together with fraying rope. Two large colourful plastic plants stood on either side of the large rattan desk. One was elevated off the ground by a squat bar stool; the other was a foot higher on top of a mid-sized safe.

'I need some information,' said Blake.

Before Eight Ball fell into the leather chair, Blake had tossed a photograph onto the desk of a police mug shot.

'Tarek Vinka. You know him?'

A dark expression fell over Eight Ball's face. He scratched at the thick stubble under his chin and looked at Blake.

'You know him?' Blake repeated.

Eight Ball shrugged.

'He's dead,' said Blake. 'Assassinated in a crowded restaurant in Soho. Shot through the head with a sniper's rifle.' He raised his arm showing Eight Ball the freshly applied inky door stamp on the back of his hand. 'When he was shot, Vinka had a Koko Club door stamp on his wrist. I don't believe he came to the club to listen to the music. I think he came to the club to see you.' Blake's icy stare drilled into Eight Ball's head.

'Look, I've told DCI Milton everything.' Eight Ball took a handful of matted locks from the back of his head, squeezed them and then let them fall once again around his shoulders.

'Why did Vinka come to see you? What did he want?'

'You're wasting your time.'

Blake's jaw line tightened, 'What did he want?'

'Fuck you!'

Blake's foot kicked out at the desk, sending a half-empty bottle of Jack Daniels crashing to the floor.

'What the hell—' Eight Ball's brooding eyes narrowed at his uninvited guest. 'Look, you gotta calm down and show some respect or you gonna regret it.'

'Calm down?' Blake bit down on his lip. 'My wife is dead and my daughter can't breathe without a machine.' Blake checked himself for a moment and then continued. 'And all because of the book that Vinka was carrying that night.' His face was now black as a storm cloud.

'Book? I don't know about any book.'

'But you know about Vinka, don't you? Who was he working for?'

'I tell you, you got some damn nerve turning up here unannounced,' said Eight Ball, shaking his head.

Again Blake's foot kicked out. This time the whole desk moved a couple of inches backwards and jabbed its edge into Eight Ball's stomach.

'Look, you piece of shit, you need to start showing some manners,' sneered the club manager. Before he finished speaking, he had opened the desk drawer with his right hand and grabbed hold of the heavy and angular object lying inside. He stood up, kicked his chair to one side, and pointed the clawed end of a hammer in Blake's direction.

'You piece of shit, get out of my office before I rip you up!'

Eight Ball launched forward, the head of the hammer poking Blake hard in the chest. Blake stumbled backwards. A second later Eight Ball had him pinned to the wall, a hand around his throat and the claw of the hammer grinding into the flesh of his cheek. He could feel Eight Ball snorting against his skin like a rabid dog. Blake's cheek was leaking blood.

'Get the fuck out of here! If I see you in this club again, you're going to end up the same way as your wife.'

What the hell did he say? Blake gasped. A white-hot rage blazed across his brain. His knee powered upwards. Contact was instant, and so was the effect. A gut-wrenching ache detonated around Eight Ball's crotch, sending searing lines of pain to every corner of his body. His chest seized hard and he fell to his knees. The hammer dropped to the floor with a thud. Blake staggered crab-like for a few steps against the wall until he could pick it up.

'My wife? What do you know about my wife?' His face was wild.

Eight Ball moaned with pain.

Now standing over Eight Ball, Blake reached down, grabbed his attacker's right wrist and yanked him closer to the desk. Then he slammed Eight Ball's hand flat down on the desk, his full body weight bearing down.

Blake raised the hammer. 'Four fingers, one thumb. If you don't tell me, you're going to lose them all.'

'Fuck you!' spat Eight Ball. 'You ... you have no idea. No idea ... who you are dealing with.'

'Last chance.' Blake's arm extended to full reach, the hammer just missing the ceiling's strip lighting. 'Vinka, who is he?'

Eight Ball's hand was shaking. Seconds later, so was his whole body.

'Okay, okay, He's a heavyweight ... Serbian or Croatian ... something like that.'

'What else?'

Blake relaxed his arm, bringing the head of the hammer onto the back of Eight Ball's hand. He twisted it hard.

'Ahhh, fuck, okay, okay!' Eight Ball gasped for breath. 'Ex-army. They're all ex-army, okay.'

'What do you mean? How many?'

'There were three of them,' he panted. 'I only met Vinka. He was the equipment man.'

'Want did he want?'

'A passport. He wanted a French passport.' Eight Ball struggled to catch his breath. 'I know a woman who can steal them from foreign students,' he gasped.

'What was the name on the passport?' shouted Blake.

Blake twisted the hammer again, and the claw tore at the back of the man's hand. 'Pineau. François Pineau, that was the name,' squealed Eight Ball.

'Who was Vinka working for?'

Eight Ball's face grimaced as Blake twisted the hammer again.

'The Drak ...'

'What did you say?'

'The Drakon. The Drakon.' Eight Ball clenched his eyes shut.

'Who?'

He shook his head. 'No one knows who the Drakon is. Vinka never knew, I'm sure of that. Just rumours.'

Eight Ball spat a large ball of phlegm onto the carpet.

'They work through dead drops. There's always a middleman. No one deals directly with the Drakon. They're always one person removed.' He paused. In a flash, his free arm punched sideways under the desk. His outstretched fingers just reached the alarm button taped to the underside before Blake hauled him back.

'Now, you're fucked!' A strained smile flashed across Eight Ball's face. 'I've just triggered the alarm. You've got seconds, then security will be all over this place. You're well and truly fucked.'

Blake's eyes travelled fast around Eight Ball's face.

The Snakeheads' bass player strutted across the stage like a defiant matador, his fingers dancing effortlessly across the fretboard. Aiming the neck of his bass directly towards the centre of the crowd, he pretended to spray bullets into the heaving mob. Abruptly, he changed direction and began to jump from side to side. After a blistering drum solo, the stage was once more plunged into complete darkness.

Blake made quickly for the exit at the rear of the concert venue. Half-running, half-walking, he passed the vacant seat that had been occupied minutes before by the doorman. He stepped over the pages of an abandoned newspaper fluttering in the sweep of an electric fan. The pages turned by themselves as the fan moved through its arc and then stopped to reveal the crossword puzzle page. The answer to four across—'*7 letters. Caesar's crossing caused certain war?*'—had been neatly completed in blue ink.

'Rubicon.'

CHAPTER 10

Friday 20 March

Blake's hands had stopped shaking, but he still struggled to open the door of his bedside cabinet. It was stiff, and he strained to muster the power to tug the door free from its wooden frame. Once inside, his hands scrabbled to locate something. Finally, he flung himself back on the bed while holding a transparent zip-lock bag close to his chest. Blake held it up to the light and studied the five blue tablets huddled in one corner of the bag.

His doctor had prescribed him diazepam after the accident. Now he needed it to stop the questions echoing in his head. *Who was the Drakon? What had Newton coded in his notebook? Why was it so important? So important that the Drakon would kill for it?* It made no sense. Blake swigged down two of the blue pills with a slug of whisky from the bottle next to his bed. The liquid tugged the hard tablets down into his stomach. His fingers tentatively touched his cheek. It stung like hell.

Blake rolled over onto his side and felt the sharp edge of his mobile phone in his pocket dig into his hip. He rolled onto his back and with several large tugs liberated the phone from the vice-like grip of his pocket. All of a sudden, the phone started to feel heavy in his hand. Half-heartedly, he attempted to place the mobile onto the bedside cabinet, but it fell from his fading grip and lodged itself between the wall and the back of the cupboard. He gave in to the increasing feeling of tiredness. As he closed his eyes, he thought of Nomsa, Sarah and the life he used to have.

When he awoke, he experienced the most curious feeling of falling backwards and threw his arms out to stop his imagined descent. As his palms slapped the mattress, his senses re-entered the world. Only a small part of his mind felt relieved with the realisation of where he was. The digital display of his Casio watch said the time was 7.21, but he had no idea whether it was a.m. or p.m.

He felt hot and kicked the duvet onto the floor, but this seemed to have no discernible effect on lowering his temperature. Realising he was still fully dressed, Blake started to strip off his clothes. He fought with his shoes to release enough of the lace to enable his feet to wriggle free. As he kicked them off, sweat started to form on his brow. Once his feet were released from their constraints, Blake dragged them through the legs of his suit trousers, which he threw into a crumpled mess in the middle of the room. Next came his jacket, and then finally, his shirt. It was covered in blood. A series of unsettling thoughts tumbled into his mind one after another: *Eight Ball; Vinka; the Drakon; the hammer!* He collapsed back onto his bed panting.

The sound of his breath was joined by the incessant ringing of his mobile phone from somewhere over his shoulder. He waited for the next ring. The sound echoed close to the floor. He saw the handset lodged behind the back of the pine cabinet, its display flashing. Before putting the phone to his ear, he checked the caller display to see the incoming call from Milton along with six voicemail alerts.

'Vincent, is that you?'

'Lukas?'

'Did you get any of my messages?' The detective was seriously pissed off.

'No, I've been asleep.'

There was a moment of silence before Milton came at him like a torrent.

'What the hell, man? You can't go around intimidating people, even scumbags like Eight Ball. He's lodged a complaint. You're lucky you haven't been charged.'

Blake sat bolt upright. The side of his face throbbed with pain.

'You there? I mean, what were you thinking of? With your history with him, you could have got yourself killed.'

Blake's hand gripped the edge of the bed.

'It's bullshit, Lukas. He came at me with a bloody hammer.'

A moment of silence. Then finally, 'You okay?'

'I'm still alive,' said Blake. 'Listen, Lukas, there were three of them doing the robberies. Vinka went to see Eight Ball to buy a stolen French passport. The passport belonged to a foreign student, a François Pineau.'

'Give me that name again,' said Milton.

Blake spelled it out.

'With Vinka out of the picture, there are two of them left.'

'How do you know that?'

'Eight Ball was very talkative ... eventually,' said Blake. 'And there's something else. They are working for someone called the Drakon.'

'Say that again?'

'The Drakon. It's Greek mythology.'

'What?'

'The Drakon was a huge dragon that terrorised the land of Anatolia. Anyway, the other two are working to commission for someone called the Drakon, Eight Ball says Vinka never dealt with him direct, always anonymously through secure phones or dead drops. They are stealing to furnish the Drakon's private collection, I'm sure of it. If only I could—'

The detective cut him off.

'Vincent, Vincent listen to me,' he said, each word getting louder. 'The Chief is at my throat over this.'

Blake could hear Milton take a deep breath down the other end of the line.

'I can't imagine the shit you're going through with Nomsa and Sarah and everything, but I'm sorry I've got no choice. I can't have you going rogue on me, and I can't have another dead body on my hands.'

Blake braced himself for what was coming.

'I'm sorry, I've got to pull you off the case. You're too close. You've lost your objectivity.'

'You can't do that, Lukas. The Newton robberies, Vinka, Nomsa's murder ... they're all linked somehow.'

'I'm sorry, I have no choice. I'll check out the names and keep you updated where I can, but as of now you're off the case.'

The line went dead.

Blake looked up at the ceiling and screamed.

CHAPTER 11

7 Months Later: Saturday 31 October

The problem was just as big today as it was in 1936, when the documents were first acquired for the Vatican's collection. The great resources of the Holy Roman Church could be summoned easily to purchase documents of special theological or historical interest, but the difficulty lay in how fast the Church's academic staff could *process* them. The pool of suitably qualified and sympathetic researchers able to sift through the mountains of acquired material, and understand their significance to the Catholic Church, had always been highly limited. As a result, important documents, once secured for the Church, often lay uncatalogued for decades in the Vatican's massive underground repositories.

Recently, a German magazine had proposed an alternative theory, suggesting that the Vatican was actively pursuing a policy of purchasing non-canonical writings dating back to the foundations of the Early Church to hide them from public scrutiny. So the theory went, the heretical works would be hidden in the miles of catacombs running under the Vatican complex and far away from the prying eyes of the academic community.

Brother Nathan Vittori liked to work on Saturdays. The library was always empty, and he was seldom disturbed. He surveyed the physical condition of the cardboard box sitting on his office desk. The flaps of the box had been taped shut with a label that had once been white but was now a pale yellow. Its surface bore three neat lines of faded Italian copperplate writing: *'Isaac Newton: Miscellaneous Papers. Acquired Sotheby's sale, 15 July. Lot 249.'* As Brother Nathan scrapped off decades of accumulated dust from the wax seal, the familiar crossed-keys emblem of the Vatican emerged. He opened the central drawer of his desk and located his letter knife. After several saw-like motions, he sliced through the seal and the paper label underneath.

Brother Nathan was a tall, plump man in his late sixties. He had refused to wear a clerical collar for many years and so wasn't easily identifiable as a priest—a constant source of contention with his superiors. He had always argued that, although the *collarina romana* dated back to the seventeenth century, canon law actually did not require the dog collar to be worn, and so he didn't.

Brother Nathan, Chief Librarian at the Vatican Observatory, often thought that God Himself had handpicked him for the job. A former chief researcher at the Vatican Advanced Technology Telescope (VATT) in Arizona, he possessed a passion for the history of science that was matched only by his love of Christ. His first stay at the Vatican Observatory, one of the oldest astronomical research institutions in the world, should have lasted just two weeks, but almost seven years later, he was still there. At the time, he had been recuperating from a bout of nervous exhaustion, and his doctor had ordered him to take a complete break from his scientific research work or face the consequences.

His mentor, Cardinal Antonio, had organised a room for Brother Nathan at the Observatory perched high above the sapphire waters of Lake Albano, thirty kilometres south-east of Rome. There he slept, painted watercolours of the lake, prayed under the warm sun and slowly regained his strength. As the days passed quietly, he learned about the history of the Observatory. Its roots could be traced back to 1582, when Pope Gregory XIII had set out to reform the calendar to fix the official date for Easter, a date which had varied widely across Christendom at the time.

After morning prayers, Brother Nathan would head for the remarkable library attached to the Observatory. There, surrounded by the astonishing collection of rare antique books, including works by Copernicus, Galileo, Newton and Kepler, he found solace and gradually found his spirits rising again. When its administrator was called away to tend to family affairs in Prague, Brother Nathan offered his services to stand in. Seven years later, he was still running the library, and he relished the vocation.

After hearing of the original auction records in the Vatican archives, Brother Nathan had made the request to examine the contents of the box to the Vatican's Director of Historical Records in Rome. A large quantity of notes penned in Newton's own hand would be a prized addition to the library's collection. To his great surprise, his request was answered promptly, and the box had arrived at the Observatory the following week.

His dear friend Dr Carla Sabatini had been overjoyed by his find. Sabatini was more like a daughter than a former research student. Now a director at the Pontifical Academy of Sciences, Sabatini spent her time studying the epistemological problems that could result from the latest international scientific research. She saw no conflict in her role. As far as Sabatini was concerned, both science and religion sought out the truth in God's design, and things had changed since the Church's persecution of Galileo. She held postgraduate qualifications in both theology and astronomy and enjoyed the rare distinction of being respected as an expert in both fields. The Vatican allowed her great freedom in performing her duties, and she split her time between offices in Rome and Madrid. She shared her old mentor's passion for all things scientific, and was now regarded as a world authority on the history of European science. The directors of the Observatory often called upon her expertise, and she always relished the opportunity to spend time with her old mentor.

Several days ago, Brother Nathan and Sabatini chatted on the phone for hours about the discovery of the box and its potential contents. A new cache of handwritten notes, penned by the great scientist himself, was just too good to be true. She would fly in from London to visit Brother Nathan as soon as he had catalogued the box's contents.

Before lifting the cardboard flaps, Brother Nathan dragged the box closer to his chest. Though the box measured only some ten inches across, its comparatively small dimensions belied its surprising weight.

He wondered if there might be some heavy object such as a sculpture contained within, but as he arranged the contents carefully on his desk, he realised that the box's weight came solely from the bundles of paper packed inside. The jumbled collection of several hundred sheets included some bound together to form complete essays, while others appeared to be scraps of larger existing works. All were written in Newton's distinctive close and unfussy handwriting. Brother Nathan scanned each page, one after another, and then quickly allocated the sheet to one of a growing number of piles on his desk.

Brother Nathan leant back in his chair and marvelled at the breadth of research represented by the stacks of paper arranged in front of him. As he lifted the final few sheets from the bottom of the box, he uncovered something that made him jump back in his seat.

For an instant, his mind associated the bright crimson colour that had just been revealed with the colour of the red leatherback lizard, the small aggressive reptile that sometimes sunbathed on the library walls at the height of the summer. Chiding himself for his overreaction, Brother Nathan repositioned himself in his chair and looked at the small red book, no bigger than a thin paperback, that lay at the bottom of the box. He picked it up, and with the book now in his hands, realised that its cover was made of a thick red velvet material. The gold-leaf-embossed design on the front cover held Brother Nathan's attention for some time. The motif was a large hexagram of two interlocking equilateral triangles. In each of the six smaller triangular compartments that formed the outer wings of the star was stamped a single golden symbol. He had seen similar designs in medieval books of spells and incantations in the Vatican's manuscript collections relating to the Inquisition. His sense of unease started to build.

For a moment, his fingers hovered over the elaborate border of gold leaf that ran around the book's perimeter, and then with a sharp intake of breath he opened it and started to flick through its pages. Each facing page was illuminated in elaborate gilt lettering. After acclimatising his eyes to the form of the calligraphy, Brother Nathan realised that the language of the writing was a form of medieval French. On the opposite pages to the original French text was written a narration in small copperplate lettering, obviously added at a later date. He recognised the handwriting immediately; it was the same handwriting that appeared on each of the papers now organised into piles on his desk.

He quickly located the title page. Its illuminated writing declared grandly that the volume represented the writings of one Gérard de Ridefort. Brother Nathan leant back in his chair and started reading Newton's handwritten narrative on the opposite side of the page.

I feel that the time is approaching, when Almighty God will call me from this transitory life. In these, my last days, I have searched after knowledge in the prophetic scriptures, and thought myself bound to communicate it for the benefit of the few scattered persons whom God hath chosen, and set sincerely to inherit the yoke from me. With these words, I shoot an arrow into the darkness, praying that Almighty God will guide its flight to a righteous man, for I impart something of extraordinary importance. Without correct instruction and warning, a calamity not seen since the Great Flood could be unleashed upon the world, such is the power of the relic and its author, our Lord in Heaven. Reader take great heed; I have been set against a formidable enemy, one that is armed with terrors that few men are sufficiently fortified to resist.

In the year of our Lord, 1666, Almighty God set the City of London upon His anvil. Like Job's messengers, first plague and then the Great Fire cleansed the land of its profanity. London lay exceedingly ragged and ruinous. The city lay dark and unfrequented, and the great Cathedral of St Paul's lay badly damaged with vast stones split asunder. Dr Christopher Wren, Architect of His Majesty's buildings, a man of assured and undaunted spirit, was instructed by His Majesty to take charge of the great rebuilding.

I am compelled to recount the particular incidents of the night when I was summoned urgently to the Royal Society by Dr Wren. He was sadly troubled by knowledge that had taken such a deep root in his mind, he could bear it no longer. Without pausing for pleasantries, he solemnly implored God for protection, and then disburdened himself of the matter to me. With terrible apprehension, the Architect recounted the tragic events that had occurred the previous morning.

Following the calamity of the great conflagration, the work of dismantling St Paul's down to its crypt had only just begun some two months previous. The Architect himself had taken personal supervision of the demolition and was suddenly called from his duties by a labourer who had caused disturbance to an underground vault with his pickaxe. On inspection, the Architect made instruction for the chamber to be opened further, and after great and troublesome labour, a hole of about three feet was dug through the end wall of the vault. The place had lain undisturbed for a great age. Of natural inquisitive temper, the workman thought to proceed into the subterranean chamber without charge, and took to himself to disappear into its darkness.

The humble labourer was gone from his station for no more than a trifle when a terrible cry came out from deep within the vault; a cry of such frightful manner that it was enough to place horror upon the stoutest heart. As he recounted these events to me, tears ran plentifully down the Architect's face. With piteous lamentation, he continued to discourse how he had rushed to the scene, filled with the greatest of disquiet, and entered the chamber with a burning lantern held aloft. The sight that met him was of such dreadful consequence that for a long while he couldn't will himself to move forward. For the young labourer was now a dead corpse and, where his eyeballs had once been, were now steaming blackened pits of flesh, as if an angel of death had branded them closed. Fearing the utmost peril, the Architect moved closer to the wretched body and, in the shifting light of his lantern, saw that some object was clasped to his chest.

Before I could enquire as to the nature of this curio, the Architect had produced a wrapped bundle from beneath his coat and placed it on the table. With the greatest of attention he unwrapped it and laid the thing before my sight, but not before warning me with grave solemnity not to touch it with my flesh. Such an odd thing I had never seen before ...

CHAPTER 12

Brother Nathan switched on the lamp stationed at the corner of his desk. The rich gilded lettering of the pages seemed to glow in response to the sudden illumination. The priest adjusted the half-moon glasses balanced on the end of his nose and read on.

The Architect's discourse had shocked me and I stood wavering for a while, staring at the strange object that he had presented to my person that December evening. It had the appearance of a wooden staff, with proportions of some two feet in length and some one inch in bore, its axis being tightly coiled, as if the tree from which it had originated had been firmly twisted during its growth. But the most curious of all was the inscription that ran down its length, carved in Hebrew characters and inlaid with gemstones, which, on cursory inspection, took the nature of blue sapphires. I am obliged to acknowledge that I was oddly drawn to this strange object, but seeing my disposition, my learned friend again admonished me of my close proximity to it, and recounted the tragic fate of Uzzah in the scriptures who, against Divine Law, steadied the Holy Arc with his hand and was killed instantly by the vengeance of God. But of this I shall speak again presently.

Knowing of my reading of ancient languages and antiquities and granting me to be more conversant with those things than he, the Architect beseeched me for an interpretation of the characters. For a long while I cast myself entirely upon the translation and not a word of discourse passed our lips. The inscription took the form of two intertwined lines. The first contained a chain of ten Hebrew symbols, באחב עדש דצכ, the meaning of which vexed me till some time later. The second line was a trifle to decipher from the carved Hebrew letters: 'To the extent of God, let these come to pass.' Contrary to easing his distress, my meagre translation seemed to increase his deep concern. I ventured to ask what he made of the curiosity in our midst and his answer gave me much disquiet. I have mentioned the high regard I have for my friend the Architect. He is a man who possesses extraordinary genius and proficiency in rational things, but that winter's evening, he was seized only by the thoughts of the supernatural.

We conversed at great length until the first light of morning had broken over Gresham College. I resolved with the gentleman Architect to meet again when the Royal Society reconvened two weeks hence. In the meantime, I would take the staff to Cambridge for safe keeping and to complete my studies upon it. We determined not so much as to speak with anyone about this matter and to use great caution in our ordinary conduct, for we both feared for our person, being in knowledge of such a relic. That very morning, with the staff hidden in my baggage, I made for Cambridge.

The following days, I shunned all trivial discourse concerning my duties at the University and locked myself in my quarters to study, not coming out for fresh air or sustenance. Deciphering the inscription became my duty of the first moment and so, on the fifth day, I sent coded word to London to meet with a man whom I shall call Mr F. He had come to my acquaintance through secret study of Kabbalist alchemy, and I knew him to be adept in many arcane practices. A scholar of the Early Church, he read and perfectly understood Hebrew, Greek, Latin and Syriac, and debated in divinity, astrology and in history, both ecclesiastic and profane. Through his travels to the East, he was trusted with many great secrets and was curious of knowing everything to some excess.

As not to draw attention to our meeting, we convened 'twixt the hours of ten and eleven at night, at a place named Whalebone, east of the city; a place so called because a rib bone of a great whale was taken there from the Thames some years past. We rode on to his residence at Devil's Ditch through a prodigious and dangerous mist, which, I later realised, gave some portent to future happenings. His rooms were large and furnished with curiosities of all kinds: atlases, maps, hieroglyphical charts, magical charms, talismans, medals, a skull carved out of wood, and books of all sizes, some embossed with gold and silver, all topsy-turvy. Several shelves displayed many curious clocks, watches and pendules of exquisite work, which would not look out of place in the newly established Observatory in Greenwich Park.

Without trifle or pleasantry, I recounted the events of the previous days, for I knew him to be an incorrupt gentleman, sober and discreet in his discourse, and a safe custodian of the alchemist's intent. As Mr F sat and listened silently, his face became ever more burdened by a tremendous worry. On showing him the copy I had made of the rod's inscription in my notebook, he stood up and, with much diligence, consulted a book covered in crimson velvet and richly embossed with a hexagram design of golden-leaf gilt.

Brother Nathan's eyes widened. He quickly turned to the front cover of the volume. With his gaze fixed upon the star-shaped design embossed onto its red fabric, he traced a slow path with his index finger along the gilded edge of the symbol. He swallowed loudly and then returned to his place in Newton's handwritten commentary.

Mr F lost little time finding the pages of his enquiry and from the angle of my sitting was able to glance upon Hebrew characters so exquisitely written, as no printed letter comes close to them. As if taken by a sudden ague, he became mightily afflicted and could not fetch his breath for a short while. After sitting and not speaking for several minutes, he inspected the bolt across the door and found it to be secure and we started a solemn discourse. At first, Mr F was apprehensive of my intentions, but on pressing, he consented to divulge his true opinion regarding the matter. I speak this not as my own sense, but what was the true dissertation of this learned traveller on that night. I set the particulars of his dreadful estimation down before you and pray that God will have mercy on your soul.

In the year of our Lord 1185, the holy city of Jerusalem was under great peril from the Muslim armies of Saladin. Many knights from the Orders of Templar and St John Hospitallers saw the holy city of David and Solomon on the brink of a great calamity. In the last resort, Baldwin IV, the King of Jerusalem, gave blessing for a delegation of the highest urgency to set passage for England, imploring King Henry II to send a Crusade to rescue the Holy Land from heathen powers. After making the perilous journey across the lands of Europe, Heraclius, the Patriarch of Jerusalem, and Lord Roger des Moulins, Grand Master of the Knights Hospitallers, met with the King at Reading Abbey in March. With them they carried a golden reliquary which they laid before the King, and solemnly petitioned his support to banish Saladin's army from the Holy Land. It was of the greatest imperative not to let the tomb of Christ fall into the hands of infidels.

Yet the true intent of the knights' mission in Jerusalem was hidden from good King Henry. The Pope's Crusade to the Holy Land had a secret mission, now obscured by the flying sands of time. Their authentic purpose was to search out the holy relics of the city, and to secure them for the Kingdom of Rome. The Templars set up barracks and a military arsenal on Temple Mount, the site of Solomon's ancient temple. On the south side of the Mount, they found underground cellars dating back from the times of King Herod, which they later used to stable their horses. Below these chambers they found the entrance to an aqueduct that travelled a great distance under the holy city.

Mr F took leave to the kitchen and returned quickly with a sack over his shoulder. He took a handful of the contents, which I discerned to be flour, and threw it over the table, like a farmer sowing seed. In a trifle, the white dust had settled, leaving a surface of virgin powder on the table. Now almost whispering, the curious traveller continued his discourse. I strained to catch his every word. With the tip of his finger, he traced out a large triangle in the white dust, each corner being pronounced with a circling of his thumb. He tapped the lower right corner of the triangular design with his finger; this is the Temple Mount, the very place where Abraham offered his son Isaac to Almighty God for sacrifice. Mr F instructed me that the underground aqueduct followed the shape of the triangle and first travelled south-west under the old city. He traced its path with a straight line along the furrow of flour, until his finger reached the next terminus. Directly above this point, he explained, were set the foundations of a church long since decayed, which marked where James the Apostle and James the brother of Christ were both put to death. Years later, on realising the great significance of the place, the Knights built a glorious cathedral there in honour of the hallowed ground.

I lost little time in enquiring as to the location of the apex of the triangle set in white powder on the table. I faithfully recount what he imparted to me next.

In a voice as smooth as quicksilver, he stated: 'It is the Church of the Holy Sepulchre; the place of Christ's crucifixion, burial and resurrection.' He beckoned me closer and in the flickering candlelight told me of the treasure that was found under the foundations of that great and magnificent church. Not a treasure of gilt metal, but a remarkable relic of antiquity. For the aqueduct led to a sealed chamber containing a fine wooden chest of shittim wood, engraved on all sides with Hebrew characters. Before I had the opportunity for deliberation, Mr F handed me the crimson book that he had consulted previously. The volume was opened at a page splendid in design, with intricate Hebrew letters dense and interlaced in golden leaf. As my esteemed teacher disclosed to me that these markings had been transcribed by one of the three knights that had made the discovery, I realised that they matched in entirety the inscription that ran down the shaft of the relic in my possession. Feeling I was on the brink of a dreadful truth and with my guts in my throat, I enquired as to the contents of the chest. Little did I fathom that his answer would alter the course of my life.

Brother Nathan's attention was diverted from the book by the sound of footsteps travelling quickly on the gravel path outside. He strained his senses to determine their direction of travel. Abruptly, the priest rose to his feet and, with his eyes fixed upon the library entrance, he slipped the small crimson volume into his jacket pocket. In no time, he disappeared behind the large velvet curtain leading to the covered walkway to the accommodation building.

CHAPTER 13

Why were these places always so bloody hot? Vincent Blake loosened his tie. Dragging the knot downwards to his chest, he pulled the narrow loop of material over his shirt collar and threw it like a lasso onto the back of the chair at the foot of Sarah's hospital bed. The private room on the fourth floor of the London Bridge Hospital was large and bright. It contained a single bed, two armchairs and a bank of medical equipment lining one wall. Blake stared at Sarah's thin fragile body lying in the oversized hospital bed. Since the accident, Sarah's once-dark complexion had faded into ashen white. The bright hospital lights made it worse, draining all colour from her body.

Radiating from his daughter's body were wires and tubes of all sizes and colours. Solemnly, Blake counted them as if he were taking an inventory: an intravenous line in her forearm to deliver fluids and medicines; an arterial line to measure blood pressure; a PEG feeding tube in her abdomen; and a white plastic tube connecting her windpipe to the ventilator at the side of her bed. Sarah's arms were thin and almost devoid of muscle mass. The room was filled with the constant sounds of the medical apparatus regulating Sarah's breathing and the electronic beep of the heart monitor. The artificial noise jarred against Blake's mind.

The door to the hospital room opened and in walked two nurses. Blake didn't recognise them. Pausing only momentarily to introduce themselves, the two women began their well-rehearsed routine of checking charts and preparing medications. Feeling awkward and useless, Blake retreated to a corner of the room.

One of the nurses was a stocky lady with large hands and big shoulders. Her greying hair was tied in a ponytail pulled tightly back from her wide forehead. Contrary to her size, she was surprisingly dainty on her feet, as if she had spent her childhood studying ballet.

Her feet were small, and her shoes squeaked on the grey plastic flooring every time she moved. She said something to Blake in a thick Eastern European accent and smiled a reassuring look in his direction. He nodded dutifully, but he hadn't understood a word.

The other nurse was of a completely opposite stature. *Asian, maybe Filipina*, he thought. She was barely five feet tall, slim and dark-skinned. Blake put her age at forty, but he could have been wrong by ten years either way. She wore a tiny silver crucifix around her neck and, according to her name badge, her name was Anje. He tried to think of something to say to the nurses, but nothing came out. Nomsa would have known what to say. She had always been good with strangers and awkward situations; she put everyone at ease. He blinked and his view became gauzy. He stood there, his eyes fixed upon a point on the wall. He was teetering on the brink, like he had been so many times since the accident and Nomsa's funeral. His heart called out to his wife. Nothing came back but the incessant bleep of the heart monitor.

Blake moved to the window and studied the reflection of the two nurses standing on either side of Sarah's bed. The reflection was clear like a mirror. He watched the two ladies temporarily disconnect the intravenous line and heart-monitoring equipment in preparation for the well-rehearsed manoeuvre. Moving coma patients from side to side every two or three hours was an essential part of their treatment protocol. The most common cause of death for patients who lay still for extended periods was secondary infection, and regularly changing the position of the patient helped prevent life-threatening conditions, such as bedsores and pneumonia. Forlornly, Blake watched the reflection of his daughter being rolled from one side of the bed to another, her thin limbs twisting awkwardly beneath her.

Lengthening his focal point, he stared out over the London skyline. Heavy rain clouds hung above the River Thames like a dark shadow stretching across the horizon. He followed the river's course eastwards, past the grey outline of the permanently moored World War II warship, *HMS Belfast,* and beyond to the familiar sight of London Bridge itself.

His focus then snapped back to his own reflection staring back at him. What he saw startled him and made him take a quick intake of breath. He rubbed his fatigue-bruised eyes, but it made no difference. He looked a mess, shattered, barely alive. The pits of his cheeks were filled with dark shadows.

Instinctively, he raised his hand to drag it through his hair, but his fingers were met by the raised bristles of his recently shaven head. Blake had first taken a razor to his head the same day the nurse had shaved Sarah's before the surgery to remove the blood clot on her brain. Somehow the act of sharing the experience had made him feel closer to her. Once again, Blake adjusted his gaze and followed a fat droplet of condensation making its erratic journey down the inside of the windowpane.

After checking the watch pinned to her pressed blue uniform, the larger of the two nurses clicked down on the top of her pen and signalled to her colleague that it was time to leave.

'Mr Blake, the consultant has just finished her ward round downstairs and will be with you any minute,' said the Asian nurse squaring up a light brown Gideon Bible with the edge of the small bedside cabinet. 'Goodbye, Mr Blake, God bless. I hope you have a good day,' she smiled politely. Blake nodded, gazed into the middle distance and wondered whether he would ever have a good day again.

The nurses' exit through the door was slowed by the arrival of the consultant coming the other way. She was a tall woman in her mid-forties. Her close-fitting, tailored blue dress gave her the demeanour of a successful business woman rather than a hospital medic. Effortlessly, she rearranged the features of her face into an expression of concern. She gestured Blake to sit down and pulled up a chair next to his.

'Mr Blake, whilst Sarah's condition is stable, she is unfortunately showing no signs of improvement.' The consultant's voice was quiet but direct. 'She has been in a deep coma for over ten months now. The length of a coma cannot be accurately predicted, but the chances of making a full recovery are now becoming very slim.' As the woman spoke, she moved closer to the edge of the seat and turned to sling one leg over the other. 'Mr Blake, I was going to call you, but now that you are here, I need to talk to you about Sarah's care.'

'Sarah's care?' said Blake.

'At London Bridge Hospital, we provide the best possible care for coma patients. We always have our patients' well-being as our first priority.' The consultant shuffled on the edge of her chair. 'I am sorry to bring it up, but we have been notified by your insurance company that their financial contribution to Sarah's treatment came to an end several months ago, which means we will need to discuss your financial arrangements and Sarah's care plan going forward. The accounts department tell me that there are invoices still unpaid.' The consultant's comment calcified in mid-air.

Blake's face blanched. After an uncomfortable pause he spoke, his words deliberate and weighty. 'Doctor, don't worry about the money. I will make sure all of your bills are paid. I have sold my house. You just make sure that she gets the best care. The best care available anywhere. Do you understand?'

Tilting her head slightly, the consultant placed her hands on her knees and her feet squarely on the floor. 'I know the last year has been quite terrible for you, with the passing of your wife and Sarah's condition. I can only imagine the worry you have been through. Mr Blake, how have *you* been coping?'

Blake was momentarily disorientated by the question. The doctor's concerned stare seemed to pin Blake to the spot. After a pronounced silence, he spoke up.

'Me? I'm okay. Just look after Sarah. Promise me that,' said Blake.

The consultant surveyed the dishevelled appearance of the man sitting in front of her: his jacket, crumpled white shirt, and jeans were all stained to differing degrees, and his scuffed boots were laced so loosely they were almost falling off his feet. She had admitted healthier-looking people as patients to the hospital.

'Of course we will, Mr Blake. Don't you worry.'

Blake's red-rimmed eyes followed the consultant and her perfectly tailored dress out of the door. Before the door clicked shut, Blake was on his feet. He walked over to the head of Sarah's bed, opened the drawer to her bedside cabinet, picked up the Gideon Bible and dropped it into the drawer, which he pushed shut with a little more force than necessary.

CHAPTER 14

Brother Nathan quickly gathered up the assorted papers on the simple wooden writing desk and threw them onto his bed. After closing the window shutters, he sat down and found the page in the crimson notebook. The thumping of his heart sounded in his ears.

I stared at the pictogram marked out in base flour on the table before me and started to tremble, the passions of hope and fear so strong in my heart. It was as if the motions of the heavens had stopped, waiting for Mr F to answer my question. What did the knights discover to be in the chest buried so deep beneath the foundations of the Church of the Holy Sepulchre? Before Mr F could answer, the front door of the house rattled remarkably with a bluster of wind, which gave myself and the learned gentleman a dreadful fright.

After a long silence, he held up the crimson book and explained that it was the journal of Gérard de Ridefort, Grand Master of the Knights Templar. According to the words contained within, so exactly published in illuminated French and Hebrew script, the wooden chest contained a religious relic of such importance that the fate of Christendom itself lay in its safe keeping. This most virtuous and religious knight had no doubt the relic was none other than the rod of Aaron, an object hewn by Almighty God himself that had journeyed with the prophets and kings of Israel across the millennia. An object so endowed with the miraculous power of God that it will be given as a sceptre to the Christ on his second coming, in token of his authority over the heathen.

I hung on his every word. His answer seemed not the rash conjecture of a fanciful man but the considered conclusion of an incorrupt seeker of truth. He returned to the crimson book and read aloud from it; the French tongue I understood well. From its account I heard again how the holy relic had voyaged with Heraclius, the Patriarch of Jerusalem, and

Lord Roger des Moulins, Grand Master of the Knights Hospitallers, to the shores of England some sixty years after its discovery in Jerusalem. Their undisclosed undertaking was to secretly intern it at some sanctified place in England until the danger from Saladin and his hoards was past, or the arrival of Christ Himself from the heavens.

Though a man of some seventy years, Mr F was brisk and vigorous and circled the table quickly. With his finger, he added to the outline of the drawing set out in powder on the surface of the table. I leant forward to have some better view of his design. Compounding another perfect triangle with the one he had earlier made, my learned friend had created the form of a hexagram, a symbol with which I was well accustomed from my alchemic studies to mean transmutation, the upward triangle symbolising fire and the downward water. But I realised that the cryptogram laid out before me had an altogether different significance.

Praying I would retain every particular to give a full account of things later, I begged him to continue. He told me thus: According to Gérard de Ridefort's journal, the month before their meeting at Reading Abbey, the Patriarch and the Grand Master had already met the King and consecrated two new churches in London. Commissioned by the Knights Templar and the Knights of the Hospital of St John, the foundations of the Temple Church and the Priory of St John were placed in a holy geometry with the great Cathedral of St Paul's. Taking three nutmegs from a pot near the fireplace, he placed one at each corner of the newest triangle—St John's to the north, the Temple Church to the west and St Paul's to the east—, their foundations forming a perfect triangle. With an earnest countenance, he then imparted that a pledge of the utmost secrecy was then sealed between the parties to hide the blessed relic within the territory of these three London churches. The exact location of its internment had been coded in a map on the last page of Gérard de Ridefort's journal. Like a bolt of lightning, Mr F snapped the book shut, giving me stern warning not to betray its whereabouts.

The first bell for evening prayers sounded down the corridor outside Brother Nathan's room. The noise momentarily shook the priest from his intense concentration. Ignoring the bell's call, Brother Nathan inhaled deeply and continued reading. The pages that followed turned his face white with shock.

CHAPTER 15

Mary always kept the needle in her shoe. After unpicking it from the sheet of cardboard that formed the insole, Mary placed it between her lips. It felt cold and sharp against her tongue, but soon it would feel like fire. Her other materials were laid out on the step in front of her: a reel of sewing thread, a metal teaspoon, a box of matches, a bottle of writing ink, and a half-bottle of Captain Morgan's spiced rum. Mary sat alone in the doorway, although a black dog paced along the pavement in front of her. She would have to work fast. Before long, her hands would be too cold to hold the needle. On the third attempt, she managed to light a match and began to move the needle back and forth across the sterilising flame, its burnished surface becoming blackened by soot. Before the match was consumed fully by the flame, she extinguished it with a puff from her mouth. She then unwound a length of the white thread from the reel and snapped it off with a sharp tug. Shifting her body so that her hands were in the direct light of the street lamp above, she began to wind the cotton thread tightly around the needle. After every circumference, she pulled it taut. Within a few minutes, she had created a densely packed sheath of thread along its length some five layers thick, only the last millimetres of the sharp point left exposed.

On seeing Mary rock herself onto her feet, the dog stopped its pacing and stared at the thin dishevelled woman moving restlessly in the doorway, her shoulders wrapped in an old blanket. She bent down and picked up the unopened bottle of rum that stood upright by her feet. The weight of the bottle felt good in her hand, but she would need every drop to finish what she had just started. She broke the seal and took four long swigs of the tawny liquid. It burned as it travelled down. She crouched, almost tottering over as she did so, and placed the bottle of ink and the teaspoon next to each other on the ledge beside the fire-exit door. With trembling hands, she poured a small quantity of the black ink onto the spoon; large drops of the dark pigment coalesced at the bottom. It was time.

As Mary turned to face the deserted back street, she let the thick blanket around her shoulders drop to the ground. She tugged at the layers of clothing surrounding her right arm leaving her forearm exposed to the orange glow of the street light. A series of black marks criss-crossed her pale skin. Squinting, she located the most prominent mark, a fresh scab forming the outline of the letter 'M' gouged into the surface. She picked up the needle in her left hand, leant over to the ledge supporting the spoon and dipped the tip into the ink. The black pigment was quickly drawn up through the loops of cotton thread to form a reservoir of ink behind the sharp point of the needle. Holding it between her thumb and index finger, she measured a finger width from the scab and then pricked deep into the white skin. She gasped as the cold jolt of pain shot down her arm. She did it again and again, only pausing to recharge the needle with more ink. When it was over, she poured rum over the tracts of the wound and fell to the ground exhausted. The word was complete: 'MASTEMA'.

The black dog emerged from the shadows and climbed the steps to the doorway. He lay down next to Mary's shaking body and for a brief moment they stared at each other. Then she wrapped the heavy blanket around herself and the dog.

CHAPTER 16

A single shaft of light streamed through the gap in the window shutters of Brother Nathan's bedroom. Even though the bare uninsulated walls of the priest's sleeping quarters were thoroughly chilled by the cool night air, Brother Nathan's forehead was bathed in sweat. The priest double-checked the position of the chair wedged against the handle of his bedroom door and returned to the small crimson book lying on his desk. Trembling, he turned the page.

Sighing grievously, Mr F then spoke of the old religion and the many names and forms, both male and female, that the dark angel was known by. He talked at great length of the folly of common interpreters of history, who are blind to the concealed truth of events and understand them no more than do ass or monkey. Since its arrival onto the shores of this land, the agents of the enemy have been close behind in search of the holy relic and have left little unsearched.

The learned gentleman recounted the events of the Great Rising of the year 1381, events some now call the Peasants' Revolt. This is what he imparted to me: It was true that the taxes for the common folk of England at that time were grievous and intolerable, leaving little for bodily sustenance or rent, but the truth of the direction of the ensuing riots across London was part of a concealed devilish plot to uncover the holy relic. Christendom was never in so much danger as when these peoples rose against the will of God.

Vast mobs with swords, staves, forks and stones stormed the properties of the Knights. On the day of the tenth of June, a furious and zealous horde sacked and burned the Hospitaller Commandery of Cressing Temple. Two days later, they were moving through the city like an avenging cloud, looting and destroying all Hospitaller property. The Temple Church was ransacked. The rolls and records of the church were burned in the streets.

Those valiant Knights who conducted themselves so bravely on that day were barbarously run through by sword and murdered in cold blood. All places of holy sanctity were violated by the fury of the sacrilegious mob. The miserable spectacle moved to the Grand Priory of St John at Clerkenwell, where pillaging erupted with a devilish passion. They went with axes and hammers and shut themselves in. Then they tore the floor, not sparing the monuments of the dead, so hellish an avarice possessed them. After the underground crypt had been searched for a long while, that most venerable church was razed to the ground.

Walter the Tyler, the leader of the rebellion, accompanied by a small band of henchmen, commanded that the drawbridge of the Tower of London be put down. Inside they found Sir Robert Hales, the Prior of the Order of the Knights Hospitaller, who was at solemn prayer. It is written in the chronicles that fearing some great jeopardy to the Prior's life, the priest held the consecrated host in front of the horde, trying to repel them back, a custom known to drive out demonic forces. But alas, the resistance proved useless, and the virtuous knight was dragged outside, his head struck off with a hatchet and mounted on a spike on London Bridge.

After such a horrid act of murder, the Tyler's deputy in arms, one Jack Strawe, accompanied by a band of rebels, then marched north to the Hospitaller Manor of Highbury and destroyed it utterly. Plans were then devised to search the crypt of the mighty St Paul's Cathedral and were only foiled by the timely death of the Tyler on Smithfield at the blade of the Lord Mayor. Seeing their leader mortally wounded, the rebel advance was stalled, and the King's nobleman quickly regained control of the city. During those fateful days in the summer of 1381, the holy staff was in great peril of discovery, such that the whole of Christendom was teetering on the brink of a fiery pit. My learned friend imparted that he had no knowledge of whether the sanctity of the three churches had been broken and the relic lost forever, until that very evening when I recounted the events of the past days.

Not fully comprehending the terrible apprehension in his warnings, I returned to the subject of the holy relic and the interpretation of its finding within the scriptures. With a voice and countenance full of solemn portent, he recalled the clear prophecies concerning the things to be done to herald in Christ's second coming and the re-establishment of his kingdom where all righteousness dwells. These were the three signs concerning the end of times.

Like a clergyman preaching from the pulpit, he named the first two signs. First, the nation of Israel will be rebuilt, ruins restored, and places built to honour the Holy One of Israel. With his face consumed with zeal, he delivered the second sign: the return of the Jewish people to the Promised Land. To mark the foretelling, he quoted from the prophet Ezekiel: 'I will save my people from the countries of the East and the West. I will bring them back to live in Jerusalem; they will be my people, and I will be faithful and righteous to them as their God.' He panted for breath and for a moment fell silent. I pressed him to reveal the third sign to me, my mind resolute that I must know. Gravely, he gave account of the last sign: the rebuilding of the third Temple in Jerusalem from which Christ Himself will rule during the end times. 'He shall build the temple of the Lord; and he shall bear the glory, and shall sit and rule upon his throne; and he shall be a priest upon his throne.' With his eyes fixed upon me like daggers, Mr F made clear that the discovery of the hidden rod was the signal for the start of the rebuilding. Without it, the third sign could not come to pass. He recounted what was written in the sacred scriptures on this matter: 'When the Messiah comes it will be given to him a sceptre in token of His authority and He will rule them with a sceptre'.

With that, he drew a great breath into his lungs and blew as hard as he could across the hexagram, creating a cloud of flour like a snowstorm in the air and erasing its form from the table. His last words filled my heart with terror. The rod, he solemnly imparted, was the key to the unsealing of the Revelation of St. John the Divine. The return of the rod to Jerusalem would herald the rebuilding of the Temple and the beginning of the end of days. Grabbing my arm, and greatly agitated in his mind, my learned teacher declared to me that now was the time for God's anger, and dreadful judgements were approaching, such that all but a few would soon perish in the flames of Armageddon. Now fighting to catch his breath, he slumped into his chair. Shaking his head with most disquiet, he uncovered a small golden amulet that was tied around his neck and kissed it. Later, I saw that the talisman was also fashioned into the shape of a hexagram. After imparting such a terrible warning, Mr F compelled me to leave and we agreed to meet again the following morning.

Newton's handwriting was then interrupted by a curious diagram. Brother Nathan moved the book closer to the light. Though only two inches or so in height, the drawing had been expertly executed in fine black ink. The design was of a circle divided into twelve equal quadrants, like the hours of a clock or the quadrants of a compass. At the centre of the circle was written a single word: *Clavis*.

CHAPTER 17

Tuesday 10 November

Brother Nathan was expecting his friend to arrive at the Observatory's library reception area at eleven o'clock in the morning, but she was fifteen minutes early. He watched the arrival of the Mercedes taxi from his office window and waited for her to emerge from the back of the vehicle. The dark burden he had inherited from the pages of Gérard de Ridefort's book was etched deeply on his face.

Sabatini closed the door of the taxi and paid the driver. The traffic from Fiumicino Airport had been unexpectedly light, and she had made good time. She was an attractive Italian woman in her mid-thirties, with striking dark eyes. Though she was tall, her shoulders barely reached the top of the ornamental stone vases that lined the driveway to the library. Swinging her large leather suitcase in time with the crunching sound of the gravel under her feet, she quickly covered the short distance to the library entrance.

'Ciao, Brother Hummingbird,' she shouted across the courtyard, her arms waving excitedly. Hummingbird was the pet name she had given him when she had been his research student in the States. It was a name that just seemed to fit with his boundless vigour and love for alcoholic nectar. The friendly dig at his ever-expanding waistline compared to the tiny weight of a hummingbird also added to the name's attraction.

'Ciao, Carla.' The two friends moved closer to embrace, but almost instantly Sabatini detected a heaviness in her old mentor's demeanour.

'Nathan, is anything wrong? You look very serious.'

The priest returned a strained smile.

'I guess I have been feeling the cold more than usual. Let's get indoors. I'm sure I will feel better with some coffee inside me.'

Brother Nathan took Sabatini by the arm and led her through the main doors of the library. A small table with a steaming pot of coffee and a collection of assorted pastries had been set up at one side of the foyer. The priest poured the coffee into two small white china cups. The delicious aroma of Colombian coffee quickly lifted Brother Nathan's spirits. He handed one of the china cups to Sabatini and warmed his hands on the coffee pot. The warmth seemed to melt away the frown from his ruddy round face.

'My dear Carla, tell me more about the Sotheby's auction.'

Sabatini nodded and took a welcome sip of the strong black coffee.

'Since his death in 1727, Newton's personal papers and effects were kept hidden from public view at Hurstbourne Park, the family home of the Earls of Portsmouth. The collection was concealed from academic scrutiny until 1936, when Viscount Lymington instructed Sotheby's to auction the papers in an open sale to clear substantial death duties.

'The papers were organised into 331 separate sales lots, and up until your phone call, I believed that Lot 249 had been lost to a private collector. Now I know that the papers were acquired on behalf of the Vatican, who at that time had become very interested in Newton's writings on the Early Church.'

Excitedly, Sabatini returned her cup to the table. 'Nathan, can I see the papers?'

Brother Nathan smiled at his ex-student. She was as impatient as ever.

'Very well, very well. I have taken the liberty of laying them out on a table in the reading room. The room has been reserved for your private use for the day, so you won't be disturbed.'

Unlike the rest of the library, which reflected the relative age of the original building, the reading room was of a thoroughly modern design. Measuring some twenty metres square, the light open-plan workspace looked like the sleek offices of an advertising company. A small plaque positioned over the large glass doors leading to the room detailed that the facility had opened the previous year and that its construction was funded by the donations of a syndicate of wealthy sponsors.

On seeing the large table in the centre of the room, Sabatini let out an excited gasp. The surface of the table was covered by a patchwork of paper. Essays of many pages were laid out next to single sheets of numerous different sizes and conditions.

'Nathan, this is wonderful, truly wonderful. Wait, I almost forgot. I've got something to show you.'

From the inside pocket of her jacket, Sabatini produced a small blue paper pamphlet, which she unfolded carefully and handed to her host.

'This is a copy of the original auction catalogue.'

Brother Nathan looked down at the pale blue cover page of the guide.

Sotheby's & Co.
34 & 35 New Bond Street, London, W(1)
CATALOGUE OF THE NEWTON PAPERS
Sold by Order of the Viscount Lymington
Days of Sale
First Day. Monday 14 July. Lots 1 to 174
Second Day. Tuesday 15 July. Lots 175 to 331
1936
Illustrated Copy: Seven shillings and sixpence

'If you go to page 27, there's a brief description of Lot 249.' Brother Nathan followed his friend's instructions and read the entry out loud.

'Lot 249. Subject Area: Religion: Miscellaneous unpublished papers, including a large collection of drafts and fair copies of various sections, considerable portions, being more or less complete in themselves. Also including a large number of loose un-numbered sheets and notes on scraps.
Topics include:

- *The Theology of the Heathens, Cabbalists and Ancient Hereticks*
- *The Abomination of Desolation*
- *Of the Christian Religion and its Corruption in its Morals*

- *Of the Rise and Dominion of the Roman Catholick Church*
- *Of the Revelation of the Man of Sin*

Lot also includes an illuminated volume of the works of Gérard de Ridefort, Grand Master of the Knights Templar. Part of Newton's personal library, Medieval French.'

CHAPTER 18

Brother Nathan had left his old friend alone in the reading room for several hours, when he reappeared with a tray of sandwiches, a small carafe of red wine, and a jug of iced water. Sabatini wore a wide smile.

'Nathan, this is a wonderful discovery.'

She beckoned Brother Nathan over to the table and gestured to the single sheet of paper stationed on the table in front of her. She handed the priest a large magnifying glass and moved her seat slightly to one side to allow him to examine the yellowing folio.

'See the forward tilt in the loop of the letters, the execution of the number four? It's Newton's handwriting for sure.'

Sabatini rose from her seat in obvious satisfaction and headed for the food. Once she was a safe distance from the table, she took a large bite from a ham and cheese sandwich.

'Nathan, if you don't mind, I would like to make a proper study of this material in the New Year. There may be something here of great academic interest.' She took another bite. 'There is one thing that has confused me.'

'What's that, my child?' The priest began to pour the wine.

'The auction catalogue is an exact match to the papers on the table, except for the Gérard de Ridefort volume. I can't see anything that fits that description here. Is it somewhere else in the library?'

Brother Nathan felt a cold shudder and slowly shook his head. His right hand started to tremble slightly.

'I'm sorry, Carla, but these are the complete contents of the box that was transported here from the Vatican's manuscript storage facility in Rome. I guess the book could still be there. I can contact Cardinal Dradi at the Vatican archives. Perhaps he might be able to track it down.'

'Not to worry, Nathan. I was just curious.'

A pause followed as the two friends helped themselves to the simple meal.

Brother Nathan toyed with the sandwich balanced at the side of his plate, trying to sense the right moment to deliver the question that had been churning over and over in his head ever since he had read Gérard de Ridefort's crimson book.

'Carla, it's a silly thing, but let me show you something.'

The priest reached up high to the bookshelf that ran the entire length of the reading room and quickly selected a contemporary looking volume from the hundreds of carefully catalogued books lining the shelves. As he brought the book down from case, he grimaced visibly at the effort of the movement. He rested for a moment, touching his chest lightly with his right hand. Sabatini winced in sympathy for her old friend. All of a sudden he looked tired and worn-out. Perhaps his angina was giving him trouble, she thought.

'I'm okay.'

Brother Nathan found the relevant page and opened it up on the table next to the half-empty tray of sandwiches.

Sabatini recognised the page instantly. It was a modern facsimile of Newton's *Principia Mathematica*. Often described as the most important science book ever written, it described for the first time the mathematical laws surrounding the force of gravity. The selected page displayed a neatly tabulated grid of results describing the recorded flight times of a weighted object dropped from varying distances above the ground.

Sabatini stared at her friend quizzically.

Brother Nathan pointed to the top row of the table.

'Look at the timings. They are measured to a tenth of a second.'

Sabatini shrugged her shoulders, still not following her friend's train of thought.

'It's amazing to think that clocks and watches were in their infancy when Newton recorded these results, and yet he was measuring timings to a tenth of a second. Truly remarkable.'

Not looking up from the book, he asked his question.

'To produce this level of accuracy, Newton must have possessed a particularly fine timepiece. I am curious. Do you know anything about it?' Brother Nathan could feel sweat forming on his top lip. He wiped it away with his finger.

Laughing, Sabatini returned her wine glass to the table and picked up the pale blue Sotheby's auction pamphlet that she had brought from London.

'Nathan, I can do much better than that. Look at Lot 22, which ended up in Trinity College, Cambridge.'

Peering through his glasses, the priest quickly found the entry and read it aloud.

'Lot 22'

'Subject Area: Natural Philosophy (Physics)'

'Contents of the lot include: Newton's personal copy of the Principia (volume includes numerous notes in Newton's own handwriting), several notebooks, and correspondence to Robert Hooke regarding the orbital movement of objects around the earth.'

'Lot also contains several items of personal property. Items inherited by Catherine Conduitt, Viscountess Lymington, Grand Niece of Sir Isaac Newton, including his walking stick, a lock of hair and pocket watch (still in good working order).'

The priest stared at the last entry and felt a shot of adrenalin surge through his bloodstream. The words seemed locked in position on the page, whilst those surrounding it appeared to fall out of focus. Suddenly he became aware that his friend was staring directly at him. By her concerned facial expression, he guessed that she must have had said something to him and was now expecting a response.

'Nathan, you're bleeding!'

'Bleeding?'

Nathan looked down at his white shirt. A small crimson arrowhead of blood several centimetres in length had appeared above the breast pocket. He quickly grabbed the gingham napkin from his plate and placed it over the bloodstain. The priest began to feel breathless, as if a dark weight were pressing against his lungs.

'Nathan, are you alright?'

'I'm fine. Honestly, I'm fine. I had a fall yesterday by the lake, and cut myself on a branch. Tell me again about the pocket watch. It's in Trinity College you say?'

She nodded.

The priest took Sabatini's hand.

'Carla, I need you to arrange for us to go and see it.'

CHAPTER 19

Monday 23 November

The immigration officer took the French passport and scanned it mechanically through the electronic reader. The ball of his foot bounced impatiently for the result. The system had been slow for most of the day. It wasn't unusual for the cross-referencing of a passport against the UK Border Agency's 'watcher' databases to take several seconds. The final boat for the day had just disembarked at Dover Ferry Port, and from the size of the queue zigzagging its way across the arrivals hall, it would be another twenty minutes before the line of passengers would be fully processed.

The immigration officer quickly clocked the small red rectangle flashing in the top left-hand corner of his screen. Just below the triangle was a small alphanumeric string of characters indicating the nature of the alert. His heart sank. Alert code thirty-two signified a passport that had been reported stolen. The immigration official let out an inaudible sigh. This was the fifth code-thirty-two alert he had been presented with today, and being so close to the end of his shift meant he would inevitably be late getting home ... again.

Since its launch several months earlier, the linking of European stolen passport databases had been nothing but trouble. The problem lay not in its ambition but in its execution. The concept was simple: Each participating country would send twice-daily updates of passports reported stolen across the European Union to a secure server based in Ghent, Belgium. Immigration officers at national points of entry would cross-reference against this master file to ensure that passengers were travelling on legitimate documentation. However, before long, a hitch to the plan became apparent whenever a passport previously reported as stolen was subsequently found again. The data concerning the found passport was seldom updated on the master file. This situation occurred more frequently than the architects of the system had ever expected. As a result, there was only a limited chance that a code thirty-two alert was legitimate. The previous alerts that day had been a waste of time, but protocol was protocol.

The immigration officer looked up at the passenger staring back at him. He was tall and had the physique of an Olympic rower, his wide shoulders stretching taut the fine merino wool of his suit jacket.

'Sir, are you travelling alone?'

The passenger stood impassively, his head bent forward, his eyes slightly raised to meet the gaze of the immigration official. After a drawn-out second, he nodded.

'Calais was your port of embarkation?'

Another nod.

'Can you please tell me the purpose of your visit?'

'Business.' The accent sounded Eastern European or Russian.

By the time the immigration officer had finished asking his next question, his foot had activated the concealed security button in the floor of his control booth. Protocol was protocol, after all. Almost immediately, a member of the staff security team appeared behind the booth, ready to do his job.

'What is the nature of your business?'

A pause. The immigration officer thought he could detect an almost imperceptible tightening in the passenger's face.

'A sales conference.'

'In London?'

Another pause.

'Sir, I will have to ask you to answer a few questions. Would you please follow me?'

The immigration officer rose to his feet, and as he did so the security officer took several steps forward to make sure the passenger was aware of his physical presence.

Detective Milton looked up from his workstation, obviously annoyed by the interruption.

'Boss, just got an alert from Passport Control at Dover. A man using a passport belonging to François Pineau triggered a code-thirty-two alert ten minutes ago.' The uniformed police officer tried to catch his breath. 'I've just come off the phone to them. They've got him in an interview room!'

'Who?' Detective Milton shrugged his shoulders, his brain struggling to make a connection.

'Pineau! The name Dr Blake gave us regarding the Newton case.'

'I don't follow,' said Milton, pinching the bridge of his nose where his glasses sat.

The uniformed police officer gulped down breaths.

'Sir, it's the name on the passport Eight Ball sold to Vinka.'

The penny dropped. Milton was now on the edge of his seat.

'So, who the hell is travelling on the passport? And who the hell is in an interview room in Dover?' Detective Milton was already on his feet, his hands frantically searching for his car keys in his pocket.

'Get on the phone.' Milton was now roaring commands. 'Tell them on no circumstances to let that guy go. He's dangerous, extremely dangerous. You understand me?' His voice reverberated around the open office. 'We've got one of the bastards at last!'

'You think it might be the Drakon?'

'Who knows, but we're going to nail him. Get your coat. Tell the passport boys we'll be in Dover in two hours.'

CHAPTER 20

Denic sat perfectly still in the interview room, his head bowed to minimise his exposure to the CCTV camera secured high on the wall. The security guard by the door looked out of shape, and his ill-fitting uniform seemed two sizes too small. Denic could see that his left shoelace had come undone.

The handle of the door jolted downwards and in stepped the immigration officer who had just escorted him from the passport hall. The officer pushed the door shut with the edge of his clipboard. Without acknowledging the presence of the security guard, he quickly delivered the piping hot cup of coffee onto the table at the centre of the room and took a seat.

He checked the time on his watch and made a couple of attempts to record it on the interview sheet, but the ink in his pen stubbornly refused to flow. After scribbling unsuccessfully on the top corner of the paper, he abandoned the pen next to the coffee cup and searched for a substitute amongst the others standing to attention in the breast pocket of his shirt. He looked up at the detainee and started the usual interview procedure that he had carried out hundreds of times before.

'Mr Pineau, I need to verify some details on your passport with you. Can you please tell me your date of birth?'

The detainee sat motionless.

He tried again. 'Date of birth?'

Still no response.

'You speak English?' said the immigration officer. He stared at the man, whose head was bowed as if in prayer.

'Sir, I'm asking you to cooperate. What is your date of birth?'

Nothing.

'Okay then. What is your address? Sir, I must warn you, if you do not answer my questions satisfactorily, I will have to hand you over to the police.'

Denic's body appeared motionless to his captors, but his brain was working overtime. Thoughts ricocheted around his mind to assess his options. Then, without warning, he exploded forwards from his seat.

In a single orchestrated movement, Denic's left hand launched the scalding contents of the coffee cup into the face of the immigration officer, whilst his right grabbed the abandoned pen from the table in his fist. The officer, now debilitated by searing pain from the burning liquid, sat bolt upright and began to scream.

After throwing the table aside, Denic rushed forward and with a massive force slammed the barrel of the pen through the sinews of the man's neck. Denic's forward motion was only temporarily curtailed by a sharp tug of the pen as he pulled it free from its target. A geyser of blood erupted from the pen's exit wound.

Denic continued his charge, accelerating in the direction of the security guard, who was now fumbling for the door handle. In a fraction of a second, Denic's hand was around the guard's throat, driving his body backwards. The guard's head slammed against the wall. Dazed, he tried to push back against his attacker, but his body was driven upwards against the wall by an unrelenting force. As Denic pressed his fingers hard into the guard's voice box, he quickly pulled back his fist and drove the pen upwards through the guard's trousers. The steel tip skewered the guard's left testicle and passed through his rectum, only coming to rest as it was met by the hard bone of the man's pelvis.

The man's body convulsed in Denic's grip, as if it were shocked by a massive electric current, and then it slumped forward. Denic released his hold, and the guard's limp body dropped to the floor. The frozen eyes stared back in an expression of sheer terror, and an ever-increasing pool of blood oozed from the body's backside.

Pausing only to remove the security badge from the guard's uniform, Denic opened the door to the interview room and stepped quickly into the empty corridor.

'Hold on, I can't hear myself think in here.' Detective Milton looked at the driver of the squad car with obvious frustration.

'Can you please turn that bloody radio off!'

The driver pressed a control on the steering wheel and the music station was silenced, leaving only the sound of the sirens above. The detective returned his mobile phone to his ear.

'Say again.'

Milton closed his eyes and processed the information being relayed to him by the port police sergeant. Without acknowledging the end of the conversation, and with the sergeant still talking on the other end of the line, he dropped the phone into his lap and looked out at the lights of the speeding motorway traffic outside. His fist lashed out at the glove compartment.

'Fuck, fuck, fuck!' each expletive more intense than the last.

The DCI slumped back in the passenger's seat.

'Two men dead, and he's fucking got away!'

As the police squad car sped its way southwards on the M20, it hurtled passed a registered Dover Port Authority taxi on the other side of the carriageway. The taxi was carrying a single passenger. The cab driver repeated his question to the dark silhouetted figure reflected in his mirror.

'So where exactly do you want go, mate?'

This time the driver heard the reply over the receding police sirens.

'Cambridge.'

CHAPTER 21

Tuesday 24 November

Max Crossland had done the calculation. With another 100,000 euros tucked away in an offshore account, he could disappear for a very long time. If he was disciplined and didn't throw too much of it away on cards and women, then this might even be his final job. He took a large mouthful of Guinness and felt the bittersweet liquid quench his parched throat. He sat with his back to the wall and watched the landlord deliver his standard Cambridge history spiel to the overfamiliar American couple who had just ordered fish and chips and pints of gassy Danish beer.

His focus abruptly shifted to the figure that just entered the bar. He recognised the tall and powerful outline immediately. The recognition was mutual, and the figure quickly passed the American couple and stopped at Crossland's table.

'Good to see you, Sergeant.' Crossland slapped the new arrival on the shoulder. 'So it looks like the team is back for another job.'

'It very nearly didn't happen. I got delayed at Dover, by an immigration officer.'

Crossland's face turned serious.

'What you mean?'

Denic lowered his voice and checked that the American couple at the bar were still engrossed in the landlord's history lecture.

'It was a real fuck-up. I was travelling on the passport Vinka got hold of from that Haitian cockroach. As soon as the passport guy swiped it, I was blown.'

Crossland hit the edge of the table in frustration.

'That bastard! He can't be trusted.' His face tightened even further. 'So, what happened?'

Denic leant over the table, picked up Crossland's drink and drained the remaining Guinness from it. An inch of creamy white froth slowly collapsed at the bottom of the pint glass.

'I was resourceful,' Denic said.

The two men looked at each other earnestly for a second and then broke into laughter.

Denic gave his old corporal the once-over in the faded light of the pub alcove. He looked fit and battle-ready. He was wearing jeans, Converse boots, and a scratched black leather jacket that looked like it had a long and exotic history. His neck was as thick as a tree trunk, the result of obsessive gym work. His trademark long moustache, which reminded Denic of old Fu Manchu films, was framed by Crossland's characteristic two long sideburns that ran into a continuum with his closely shorn scalp.

Denic's expression turned rigid as the distinctive double bleep of his secure satellite phone was clearly audible above the background noise of the bar. He removed the device from his pocket, carefully studied the decrypted message, and then reread it twice. Crossland waited patiently, his concerned expression mirroring that of his comrade. At last Denic slumped back in his chair.

'It's the Drakon, with final arrangements for the equipment pick up.'

'And?'

'The container arrived yesterday and is being trucked up to Cambridge tonight.'

It was obvious from Denic's expression that there was more.

'And?'

A long pause followed.

Denic's eyes lowered.

'The Drakon knows about my fuck-up at Dover.'

'Shit!' Crossland's enormous hand hit down hard onto the table.

The two men looked at each other.

'We can't screw up on this one, Max. There'll be repercussions. Serious repercussions.'

'You mean like Vinka?' said Crossland.

'Vinka ended up with a bullet in his head because he got sloppy. Remember? He dropped his phone during the job in Cannes. The police found it, and they were there waiting for him at the drop. He fucked up all right. Mark my words, he would have squealed to the cops. Just get the job done and we'll be able to walk away from this okay.'

'You've worked for the Drakon for years,' said Crossland.

Denic nodded.

'What the hell do you actually know about him?'

Denic shrugged his shoulders.

'No one has ever seen him. He always communicates through intermediaries, secure lines, messages routed through multiple servers. You know the stuff.' He paused, pushing his satellite phone into the centre of the table. 'The word is that he's rich, very rich, but make no mistake: he's a serious piece of work, a real evil fucker. The only thing I know for sure is that people who try and track him down always end up dead.' He paused again. 'I've heard some things, but they're all spook stories.'

Crossland leant forward in his chair, urging Denic to continue.

'I did a job once with a guy, a con from Marseilles. He heard a story from a lifer he did a prison stretch with. The story goes that the Drakon was adopted into a wealthy family near Sarajevo. He was still a child when the Yugoslavian war broke out. During the siege for the city, an officer deserting from the Bosnian Serb army broke into the family home and did some crazy shit to the boy's guardians before butchering them with a hunting knife.'

'Crazy shit? What do you mean?'

'Tortured them, real twisted. Anyway, the boy escaped and hid out alone in the bombed-out remains of the university library. He survived for over a year by scavenging tins of food in the rubble of the library canteen and killing rats and stray dogs. Alone with the books he began to read, I mean for the whole damn year. Fucked-up books, about magic and Satan worship and stuff. Whatever the boy learned in the rubble of that library turned him into a real sick piece of work.' Denic rubbed the back of his neck. 'And that's not all.'

'Go on,' said Crossland.

'Well, the war came to an end. After years of searching, the Drakon finally tracked down the army officer to a town just outside Sofia. The soldier was running guns along the Bulgarian border and was shacked up with a hooker. The Drakon drugged them both with horse tranquiliser, tied them up, and transported them to the sewer under the city. So the story went, the hooker was made to watch as the Drakon acted out his ... revenge.'

'Revenge?' asked Crossland.

'One by one, the Drakon bit off the soldier's fingers. When there were no more fingers left, he bit off his nose, then his nipples and then large chucks out of his thighs. When he was finished, the Drakon poured molasses onto the wounds and then waited for the rats to come. Before long, there were hordes of vermin all wild with hunger. The soldier was eaten alive, his flesh picked clean within hours. Only bones and a few scraps of clothes were left. When it was done, the Drakon let the hooker go. She told her story to a priest before going mad and blowing her brains out with a shotgun. As I said ... a real evil fucker!'

CHAPTER 22

Blake tried to ignore the banging on the front door of his bedsit.

'I know you're in there. You owe me two weeks rent money.'

Blake held his breath.

'End of the week or else,' shouted the landlord in a strong Glaswegian accent.

Finally, the banging stopped. Several seconds later, Blake could hear the sound of his landlord's heavy boots climbing the stairs outside.

Blake lay on his single bed, a thick vein throbbing in his temple. He stared over to the stack of five large packing boxes standing like an island in the centre of a sea of tattered blue carpet. They had stood there unopened for two weeks. To unpack them would mean conceding to the notion that he was staying.

Blake's mobile began to beep. He looked at the vibrating phone for several seconds before picking it up. It was Milton.

'How you doing, Vincent?'

'How am I doing?' said Blake in a forced whisper, conscious that his landlord might still be lurking outside. 'What do you want me to say, Lukas? Everything is great?'

Another long pause.

'Why are you ringing?'

'I went over to your house last night. When did you move out?'

'Two weeks ago. To a bedsit in Shoreditch. Before you ask, it's a dump. I moved because I need cash for Sarah's hospital bills. Lukas, I don't want to be rude, but I've got things to do.'

The detective gave a hard, obvious swallow, sensing that the conversation was about to be terminated.

'Vincent, I wanted to see you because I promised to keep you in the loop.'

'Right?' said Blake.

'Look, there's something you need to know, and it's best you hear it from me.'

'And what's that?'

'Yesterday, a man was stopped at Dover Ferry Port coming in from Calais. He was stopped because he was travelling on a stolen passport.'

'So?'

'The name on the passport was François Pineau.'

By the silence, Milton knew that Blake had registered the significance of the name.

Finally, Blake spoke. 'The man they stopped, who is he?'

'He escaped.' Milton's words were resigned, almost apologetic.

'Escaped?'

'Yes, and that's not all.'

'Go on,' said Blake.

'He killed two immigration officers busting his way out.'

'Oh my god. Did they get an ID?' asked Blake.

'Nothing firm. He was a pro. Never looked up at the security cameras. He's in the country and we've no idea what he's up to.'

'Isn't it obvious? They're preparing for another robbery,' said Blake in a low voice. 'Hell, for all we know, the man in Dover might even *be* the Drakon.'

Milton said nothing.

'You've got to get me back on the case. I know more about the previous jobs than anyone else. You know it's true.'

'I'm sorry, Vincent, you're just too damn close. That's the problem,' said Milton. 'After you decided to rough up Eight Ball, the Commissioner came down on me like a category-ten shit storm.'

'Forget Eight Ball.' Blake kept pushing. 'Do you want to catch these people or not? For Christ's sake, get me back on the case.'

'Look, man. I'm sorry. My hands are tied. I've got to go.'

The line went dead. There was a sudden bang, and Blake's mobile came to rest by the stack of plastic packing boxes. He got out of bed and began to pace around the room. His pulse was racing. In frustration he kicked out at the lowest crate, sending the tower crashing to the floor.

He stumbled forwards and then, after regaining his balance, brought his heel smashing down onto the nearest upturned box.

'Fuck, fuck, fuck!'

He kicked out again, this time punching a large hole through the side of the crate. He hauled it up to his waist and then hurled it at the back wall of his bedsit. It exploded, sending plastic shrapnel and its contents spilling out across the floor. Blake readied himself for the next crate but stopped in his tracks. With nostrils flaring, he looked down at the small bottle of bright blue nail varnish by his feet. It was given to him at the hospital, along with Sarah's clothes, the day of the accident. Electric blue was Sarah's favourite colour. He picked up the bottle, closed his eyes, and rubbed it against his cheek. He tried to stop himself crying.

The sound of a police siren outside shook him from his thoughts. He put the nail varnish bottle into his pocket and looked around his bedsit. The contents of the upturned packing boxes were strewn all over the floor. CDs, toiletries, books, T-shirts, unopened envelopes, shoes and books of all kinds scattered in all directions. With a resigned breath, he crouched down and started to clear up. His foot began to ache.

A bright red folder rested against the wall, its spine pointing upwards like the apex of a tent, and papers spilled out underneath. He tried to look away, but the word *Newton* stamped on its cardboard jacket wouldn't let him go. He stared at it for a while and then gathered the papers up in his hands.

Looking around Blake located the plastic swivel chair next to the kitchenette. Unceremoniously, he dumped the pile of academic journals stacked on its seat onto the floor. Then he dragged the chair to an area of the carpet away from the mess of the upturned packing boxes. One by one, he laid out the file's contents on the floor in a large semi-circular fan around the chair.

He sat down on the chair, and rubbed his eyes vigorously. After they had returned to focus, he stared down at the arrangement of papers. They were all of differing types and sizes: copies of architectural plans, photographs of museum exhibits, and photocopies of newspaper articles. All were connected in some way to the robberies, and most were collected from police crime scene reports. Blake bounced a curled knuckle against his mouth, searching for a clue.

Since Nomsa's death, he had studied the crime reports time and time again. How many photographs would it take? A missed fact, a figure hidden in the shadows, a small clue that would eventually prove crucial, some interlocking detail, a face in the crowd, an item out of place. Something blowing against the direction of the prevailing wind that he could use as a lever to pry the case open.

Years of assisting the police's Art Crime Squad had made him an expert in recognising the patterns. He knew how documents and mounts evolved over time owing to exposure to sunlight. He could detect the degradation of inks and parchment glues and the oxidisation of oil paints. He could perform a microscopic analysis of signatures and brush strokes. He was familiar with the patterns that made a work of art legitimate or fake. The truth always lay in the patterns.

There was always an answer if you looked close enough. The problem was that the clue was often hidden in the shadows and the cracks, or in a small detail camouflaged amongst its surroundings. The scrap of evidence could be found in the smallest of sounds muffled by the din of the crowd. It had to be there: the key that would lead him to Nomsa's killer.

With the toe of his shoe, Blake slowly spun himself around on his chair. The outline of the papers on the floor started to whirl in his head. Abruptly his foot came down onto the carpet. The chair stopped. He crouched down and shuffled through the haphazard collection of documents and selected three photographs from the carpet. He stood up, walked over to his desk by the wall, and carefully placed each photograph side by side onto the desk. Still looking at the pictures, he reached out for the bottle balanced upright on the radiator next to the desk and filled a mug with another generous measure of whisky. He took a long sip and breathed out the vapours through his teeth. Three photographs, three police crime scenes, three robberies all linked by the same name: the Drakon. The name haunted him. As he rubbed his thick stubble, a brooding intensity filled his eyes.

Blake had been the obvious choice to assist DCI Milton, head of the police's Art Crime Unit, with the investigations. A man with a double first from Oxford University, the eye of a detective, and an unparalleled understanding of the black market in rare art and stolen manuscripts, Blake had been the obvious choice, but now he was high and dry and shut out.

He bit his lip staring at the three photographs, one from each robbery. Blake had studied the *modus operandi* of each job carefully. They all had a consistent signature: all were tightly choreographed and meticulously planned lightning-strike robberies that usually lasted no more than a few minutes. Over the last eighteen months, the gang had pulled off heists from museums and private collections across the world. The target of each robbery had been the same: artefacts once belonging to the celebrated scientist Isaac Newton.

With his thumbnail, Blake traced a line around the perimeter of the first photograph. It was a grainy black-and-white image with a series of Japanese letter symbols displayed in its top right corner along with a date. The photograph was of a man riding a bicycle.

The first robbery had taken place in the heart of Tokyo's Yohogi district. The events had been caught on CCTV, and when the police made several clips public, the footage went viral on the Internet. Three individuals disguised as businessmen on their usual early morning commute to the office, their faces covered by anti-pollution facemasks, had approached Japan's Token Hakubutsukan sword museum on bicycles. The safe room of the museum was being used as a temporary storage facility for a collection of Newton's early papers, which were in transit to the Jewish National and University Library in Jerusalem. The businessmen made their way calmly to the front door of the museum and used tear gas to subdue the museum staff. The museum director was shown a picture of his wife and children along with a note written in red ink, saying that, if he didn't comply completely with their demands, they would be executed. The doors to the safe room were unchained and the Newton papers taken. The gang then simply left the building, locking the front doors behind them, and melted back into the commuter crowds on their bicycles. Two Samurai swords considered to be national Japanese treasures were left untouched in the safe room, and subsequently police found that there had never been any hostages. They found the wife and children of the museum director playing happily in the local park. All investigations by the Tokyo police force had drawn a blank.

Blake picked up the second photograph from the desk and, in deep thought, brought it up to his mouth. The sharp edge of the picture scratched his lower lip. Annoyed, he threw it back down onto the desktop. It was a colour picture of an ambulance car taken from an overhead gantry camera at the entrance of St James Park, London.

This heist had taken place on a cloudless summer day. A BMW 330i, painted in green-and-yellow-checked paramedic livery, had stopped outside the Royal Society's office building in Carlton House Terrace, just off the Mall in Central London. Three men dressed as medics had walked unchallenged into the document room of the Society's archive wing and, in seconds, had located their target: a rare 1596 first edition of Villalpando's biblical commentary on the prophet Ezekiel, known as the *Ezechielem Explanationes*. Tradition had it that the commentary had once formed the centrepiece of Isaac Newton's own personal library. After placing the volume in a medical bag, the paramedics made their way back through the reception area to their waiting vehicle while brushing off questions from concerned staff. Within seconds, the ambulance car was speeding its way down the Mall, eventually disappearing into an underground car park near Victoria. DCI Milton had been in charge of the case. His investigations quickly came up against a brick wall.

The third picture stared up at Blake from his desk. It was a high-resolution police photograph of a satellite phone handset. Blake had studied the picture for months, and its image was burned into his brain.

The third heist took place on an unusually warm late autumn afternoon in Cannes. The robbery had targeted the private collection of the French industrialist Didier Clerot. The gang, dressed as holidaymakers, smashed their way through the front door of Mr Clerot's exclusive waterfront residence. Brandishing automatic weapons, the thieves broke into the document safe and took several of Newton's notebooks and a leather binder containing a collection of his personal letters. The collection had been catalogued for insurance purposes as the 'F' collection, as Newton had addressed each letter to the same individual: a Mr F. The exact identity of Mr F had remained a mystery since the discovery of the papers in 1936.

However, Clerot's gardener, who had seen the felons enter the building, took quick action, and armed officers arrived at the scene within minutes. A firefight ensued, which resulted in the death of a member of the local gendarmerie. After a chase through the tourist-filled waterfront, an area impassable to police cars, the felons escaped via speedboat, but not before one of the gang dropped a secure satellite phone during their getaway.

After days of sophisticated forensic work, Interpol's telecommunications unit in Grenoble had managed to decrypt two messages on the phone's hard drive. The first message read: *'50% of fees transferred, 50% on safe delivery.'* The second stated, *'Document drop, 1st Dec, Faversham, Marshall Street, London.'* Both messages had originated in London.

Despite the treasure trove of valuable books within the safe—including a 1623 first folio of Shakespeare's works and early books by Ptolemy and Nicolaus Copernicus—only the Newton notebooks and letters had been taken. An hour before the heist, the gang had painted all the public benches outside Mr Clerot's house to discourage anyone from sitting on them and observing their entry and exit into the building.

By the time details of the heist broke on the evening news, DCI Milton had received the call from Interpol requesting his urgent involvement in the case. Several days later, the Chief of Police of Cannes informed Milton of the contents of the decrypted phone messages. A week later, the DCI was sitting in a surveillance van in Marshall Street waiting for the drop-off. Unbeknown to Milton, so was the Drakon. Aware that Vinka's satellite phone was now in police hands, the Drakon had taken no chances. At the first sign of the police, the drop-off had been terminated with a single sniper bullet to the back of Vinka's head.

Three photographs, three jobs, one name: the Drakon.

Blake refilled his mug and carried it over to his single unmade bed. After taking a long draw of whisky, he rested the mug on his chest and closed his eyes. He willed himself to remember Nomsa's smile, but the memory refused to take shape in his mind. He tried again, fighting hard to bring her face back. Finally, images began to return: the outline of her lips, the sweep of her neck, the shape of her hands. For over five minutes, Blake lay motionless, lost in thought, only the constant sound of traffic outside disturbing the silence.

CHAPTER 23

Wednesday 25 November

The back doors of the white transit van slammed shut, and the sound was taken up through the trees swaying their goodbye to the fading afternoon sun. Max Crossland pressed a button on the key fob, and the van's central locking mechanism kicked into life, pulling the locking pins down into each door. He walked to the front of the vehicle and carefully placed the keys under the arch of the front right wheel. He walked over to Denic, who was already astride one of the two BMW R1200RT police motorcycles parked further up the forest track. His comrade snapped shut the tinted visor of his police bike helmet and gave him the thumbs up.

Transporting the bikes in the van had been easy. The two-hour drive from the Drakon's secure freight container in the Isle of Dogs to the deserted farm in the Gog and Magog Hills, just five miles outside Cambridge, had gone without a hitch. The farm provided excellent cover from the air and from the traffic speeding close by on the A1307, one of the main highways in and out of the historic city.

In unison, the two men, both clad in police leathers, started their powerful four-stroke boxer engines and kicked away the bike stands. One after the other, the two police motorbikes pulled away from the seclusion of the trees and started the short climb up the farm track to join the main road. Over the integrated helmet radio system, Crossland reminded Denic of the UK speed limit.

CHAPTER 24

Dr Carla Sabatini looked at Brother Nathan sitting in the car passenger seat, his large frame slightly too big for the available cabin space. She smiled.

'Well Nathan, we've arrived in good time. I agreed with Henry that we'd meet him inside the library. I'll give him a call to say we're here.' Sabatini started to rummage around in her handbag to find her mobile phone.

'Carla, I will be ever in your debt,' Brother Nathan said earnestly. He pressed the bright red button by his side, and his seat belt quickly retracted. The priest gave out a laboured groan as if some great pressure had just been released from his chest. Sabatini leaned over to her old friend and squeezed his knee, attempting to lighten the mood.

'Happy birthday, Nathan,' said Sabatini.

'I'm sorry, Carla. My chest is sore. I guess I'm finally becoming an old man.'

Today was the priest's seventieth birthday, but instead of appearing his usual jovial self, Brother Nathan seemed unusually preoccupied. Over the years, they had travelled together many times, but the drive they had just made from Heathrow to the spires of Trinity College, Cambridge, had been different. Something had changed in his spirit, as if he were carrying a heavy weight upon his shoulders.

Sabatini was talking into her mobile.

'... a visitor's pass from the main building? No problem. We'll be with you in fifteen minutes. Ciao.'

Sabatini looked over to her passenger.

'Nathan, you stay in the car. I need to collect our passes from security over there.' She pointed to a large red-brick building several hundred metres away from the edge of the car park. 'I won't be long.' With that, she opened the car door and started along the gravel path.

After clearing the condensation from the car window with the back of his hand, the priest followed the progress of his old student towards the building. Moments later, he searched through the pockets of his overcoat in the footwell. He quickly found the two objects he was looking for. The larger of the items was the crimson book of Gérard de Ridefort. Pressing back into his seat, Brother Nathan scanned the car park in both directions. Satisfied he wasn't being overlooked, he opened the crimson book at a page marked by the stub of his Alitalia boarding pass and started reading. Even though he had read the words time and time again, his heart pounded like a steam train. Newton's handwritten annotations to the illuminated volume shouted out from the pages.

In the darkness of night, I rode to my lodgings in Whitechapel and retired to my room to consider the knowledge that Mr F had imparted. If I hadn't been an eyewitness to the curious happenings of the previous hours, I should have apprehended it as some delusion of the senses, but I knew in the depths of my heart that it was true. Henceforth my world seemed quite altered. I fell to my knees and tried to make my peace with God. I asked Him to remove this colossal yoke from my shoulders, but the more I examined my life, the more I had the strong apprehension that some extraordinary event was unfolding.

After many hours in prayer, I passed into a deep and heavy sleep. A curious dream came to me whose particulars were so lucid that I was shocked to find myself in the room of my lodgings when I awoke. I dreamt that Mr F had met me at Ludgate Hill and whilst sitting under St Paul's Cross he showed me an object from the breast pocket of his jacket. It was an amalgam of gold metal, which I took for the twisted remains of his star-shaped amulet. He told me that the charm had just preserved his life by receiving the shot from a pistol and stifling its flight before it had penetrated his chest. So abruptly had the golden amulet deadened the force of the projectile that it had deformed the charm into a single distorted mass. I outstretched my hand to touch the object, but then I awoke upright in bed in my lodgings in Whitechapel.

I dressed immediately and, being so afflicted by what Mr F had imparted to me hours before, I set out again for my learned friend's house in Devil's Ditch. I arrived at his residence at around seven o'clock and knocked on his door to bid him greetings. All was silent. With the door unbolted I ventured in, and stealing a look into the kitchen, I saw Mr F sitting alone in silence with his back to me. As I approached, I saw that the poor man was stripped to his shirt with arms and legs bound to a chair, all his books and manuscripts scattered everywhere. There was a great effusion of blood on his person. Only the golden amulet around his neck seemed to be free from the red stain. Even to this day, I cannot forget the sight of his bared chest. A single word had been carved into the flesh with a blade.

'Mastema'.

My learned teacher had been slain by some terrible malevolence. I was taken with such terror and the spectacle was so dreadful, that I was not able to stand the sight for another second. I was utterly undone. Remembering my dream from the previous night, I seized the amulet from around his neck, snapping its leather thong in my haste. Fearing for my very life, I took flight, and as I stumbled towards the door, I noticed the corner of the crimson journal signalling to me from under several sheets of vellum strewn on the floor. I picked it up and hid it in my cloak. After fleeing to my horse, I set spurs and rode north with great speed. Before long I was in Shoreditch and then onto the road for Cambridge.

As I rode back to Cambridge, I surveyed the horizon frequently, as I was most concerned that I was being followed by cut-throats. I arrived back to my quarters at the start of a great hailstorm, which broke many windows at the University. The next days were so blustery that not a leaf stayed on a tree. I resolved to devote my time to studying the scriptures, but I was frequently diverted with thoughts of the hideous murder of my friend and the crimson book that I had taken. I opened Gérard de Ridefort's journal, and my gaze fell upon a map showing the floor plan of St Paul's Cathedral and the position of the hidden crypt that Dr Wren's excavations had inadvertently breached. The journal was also filled with other Templar secrets and alchemic knowledge, written in code to hide them from the sight of men. The truth which this writing reveals, I will not divulge here, as it will only add to the confusion of things.

I requested a discharge from my duties at the University, shut up my house and evaded all idle conversation. Keeping all windows, shutters and curtains closed, I set about to study and pray to God with great fervency and devotion. I kept within the walls and never stirred out, deep in study of the sacred books for some insight into the matter.

I sat at my desk burdened greatly with the weight of the task and turned the pages of my Bible. In desperation to discover God's will, I cried out: 'Lord, help me. I am lost. Show me your bidding!' At that very juncture, I looked down at the book of scripture and saw my finger stopped over the forty-third chapter of the book of the Prophet Ezekiel. My eyes were drawn to verses ten and eleven.

> *'Son of man, describe the temple ... consider the plan ... make known to them the design of the temple — its arrangement, its exits and entrances — its whole design and all of its regulations and laws. Write these down before them so that they may be faithful to its design ...'*

In these words, God spoke to my heart with such clarity that henceforth I had no doubt as to the course of my future undertakings. I had to discern the exact dimensions of the inner sanctuary of the Temple of Solomon. Once established, its sacred geometry was to be rebuilt in the great Cathedral of St Paul's and the rod interned there once again, sanctified in the holy triangle of churches that the patriarch consecrated, preserved until Judgement Day.

In the retirement of that evening, I resolved to do God's will. I sat at my desk in solemn study of the Book of Ezekiel, not even pausing for nourishment except a little bread and water. I translated the text from Coptic, Hebrew and Latin, and slowly decoded the dimensions, arrangement and relations of the floor plan of Solomon's Temple. I stirred not out of my squalid den, and became mad with calculations and model-making. After some time I had reconstituted the exact mathematics of the temple and set it down on paper for the good Architect. Once completed, I broke my miserable confinement and sent word to Dr Wren that I would be attending the next meeting of the Royal Society at Gresham College, and I would be bringing knowledge of great worth and urgency.

Brother Nathan was shaken by the sound of gravel being walked upon close by. Startled by the sound, he dropped the Alitalia stub bookmark back into the crimson volume, and hurriedly returned the book into the pocket of his overcoat. Seconds later, Sabatini was sitting back down into the driver's seat and clutching two plastic visitor security passes in her hand. With a gentle nod of her head, she signalled to her companion that it was time to leave the shelter of the car. Taking her prompt, Brother Nathan began to struggle to put on his overcoat. His hand was unable to successfully locate the right armhole, as the arm of the coat was pinned between the car seat and his back. Seeing his predicament, Sabatini reached over, released the trapped material and presented the once-concealed armhole to his still waving hand.

'My hummingbird seems to be flapping his wings too fast again.' Sabatini restrained a chuckle and set about collecting up the contents of the priest's pockets that had fallen into the footwell of the car.

Outside, the wind shook the bare branches of the trees that bordered the neatly maintained lawn. Before them stood the magnificent Wren Library building, its Rutland stone exterior giving off a pinkish tinge in the dying light. Completed in 1695 and designed by Christopher Wren, England's genius architect, the building and its rows of perfectly proportioned windows stood statesman-like above the surrounding lawn.

'I've known Henry for years. He can be a bit odd sometimes, but he is very well regarded,' explained Sabatini. She took Brother Nathan by the arm and walked him towards an entrance flanked on either side by impressive stone columns. 'When I explained to Henry your interest in the exhibits, and that today is your birthday, he was only too happy to help.'

'Thank you. You have always been so kind to me,' he said. The priest paused, and Sabatini thought she could see moisture forming in his eyes. 'I am getting old. I pray God will look after you when I am gone.'

'Don't be ridiculous! There is plenty of life in my hummingbird yet,' said Sabatini, laughing off his comment.

As they made their way towards the entrance, they were intercepted by a smartly dressed middle-aged man sporting a regimental moustache and a black bowler hat. Sabatini recognised the black bowler hat as part of the official uniform worn by every Trinity College porter.

'Can I be of assistance?' the porter asked in a way that was neither friendly nor hostile: a skill that he had obviously developed over years of vetting the general public, who strayed accidentally onto the college grounds.

'Thank you. That would be extremely helpful. I am Dr Carla Sabatini and this is Brother Nathan Vittori. We are ...'

'You are guests of Dr Henry Jenkins. He is expecting you. Let me take you up to the library.' The porter smiled, enjoying the brief sensation of authority as he led the visitors through the entrance archway to a large door kept ajar by an ornate metal doorstop.

The porter ushered the two visitors through the door and, in a hushed voice, reminded them that they were entering a place of quiet academic study.

'Dr Jenkins is waiting for you at the top of the stairs. I will bid you goodbye here. Enjoy the rest of your day.'

CHAPTER 25

At the top of the staircase, the grey stone steps changed into a chequerboard-style marble floor. Brother Nathan's stout brogue shoes echoed down the corridor as he walked towards the library. Soon, the narrow passageway led to a closed door with a paper sign taped to it that read 'LIBRARY CLOSED FOR PRIVATE FUNCTION'.

'That must be us,' said Sabatini, trying the handle. The door opened with the kind of unforgiving creak that reminded Brother Nathan of the vertebrae in his back. The sound of straining hinges caused the man standing on the other side of the door to spin round.

'My dear, Carla, it's wonderful to see you. This must be Father Vittori. Come in, come in. You are very welcome. I believe congratulations are in order, Father Vittori. Happy birthday!'

The man kissed Sabatini enthusiastically on the cheek and then extended a hand to the clergyman. It felt cold and clammy in Brother Nathan's grip, like a fish hooked from a winter stream. Sabatini had first met Dr Jenkins while collecting research material for her book, *The Divine Prism: Seeing God in Science and Religion.* An expert in the history of European Enlightenment science, he and his expansive mind had proved an invaluable resource for her academic research. His physical appearance, however, was less impressive than his scholarly knowledge. He was tall and thin, and his chest seemed to cave in underneath his well-worn shirt; unruly tufts of greying hair sprang from his head. Sabatini had long suspected that he had taken to cutting his hair himself.

'I took the liberty of ordering some sparkling wine to celebrate. Will you join me in a glass?' Jenkins strolled over to the small wooden side table standing next to the door on which sat an ice bucket. Their host rescued a drowning bottle of wine from the pool of melting ice, and, as he poured three glasses of fizzy liquid, Brother Nathan took in the wonder of his surroundings.

They were standing at one end of the library, a large hall with rows of tall windows running along its entire length. Below each classically proportioned window stood a number of wooden bookcases, each holding shelves of antique books. At the end of each bookcase was an elaborate lime wood carving: a number were shaped into intricate coats of arms, while others were busts of classical characters and several more looked like the profiles of animals.

Jenkins handed each of his visitors an overfilled glass of sparkling wine and proposed a toast to birthdays and to friends, old and new. Brother Nathan raised his glass and stared at the bubbles dancing above the rim.

'So, I understand from Carla that you share our passion for Mr Newton.'

'Oh yes,' said the priest, 'You see, in a small way, I share Newton's vision.'

'Sounds interesting,' said Jenkins, 'Go on.'

'I mean to uncover the works of God in the world.'

'Oh, I see,' said Jenkins, taking a sip of wine.

'I do not know of any other individual who has journeyed further and more deeply into the mysteries of God's purposes than Mr Newton.'

Jenkins nodded, thinking about the priest's statement. Sabatini smiled at his side.

Brother Nathan then raised his glass and proposed a toast. 'The true God is a living, intelligent and powerful being. His duration reaches from eternity to eternity; his presence from infinity to infinity. He governs all things.'

'Excellent quote my friend. I'll drink to that.' Jenkins recognised the lines from Newton's first masterwork, the *Philosophiae Naturalis Principia Mathematica*, the book that formed the centre point of the exhibit.

'Let's finish our wine, and then I will take you over to see the *Principia*. For obvious reasons, we can't take liquids close to the exhibition case, just in case there's an accident.' Jenkins playfully swayed his glass from side to side and then took a long draft, downing its remaining contents. 'Carla tells me that this is your first visit to Cambridge?'

'Yes, it is. What I have seen so far through the car window looks very pleasant.'

'It can be,' sighed Jenkins, 'but when Newton came to study at this college in 1661, Cambridge was an altogether different place. In fact, it was a very dangerous place to be. The town was squashed into an area of less than half a square mile and had a population of some 8,000 people, about 3,000 of whom were affiliated in some way to the University. The streets were narrow and filthy, and at night they were almost completely dark except for the lanterns of people who dared to walk them.'

Jenkins continued, 'A new student would need to keep close to the walled safety of the college grounds so as not to fall victim to the thieves and vagabonds that stalked the town. There was real animosity between the local population and the perceived wealth of the academic population, and tensions often spilled over into violence.' He paused, looking at the remaining bubbles coalescing at the bottom of the glass. 'Fortunately, today, relationships between the locals and the University are much more cordial. Do you like the wine, by the way?'

Sabatini and Brother Nathan nodded their approval. They drained their glasses and returned them to the side table. Jenkins handed each of his guests a pair of white cotton gloves. They walked over to the wooden display case at the foot of the bookcases and watched their host remove the cloth covering that protected the exhibit from light-induced fading.

The solid oak display case had a thick glass viewing panel forming its surface. Set within the front panel was a large brass lock, which Jenkins opened with a key that he then returned to the back pocket of his trousers with a reassuring pat. On being released from its locking mechanism, the glass viewing panel raised itself effortlessly on well-oiled hinges to expose the objects beneath. Jenkins ushered his guests to move closer to the exhibit. He cleared his throat and pulled his cotton gloves tight against his hands. 'First published on 5 July 1687, this is Isaac Newton's personal copy of the original edition of the *Principia*.' Brother

Nathan nodded his confirmation, but his attention was quickly drawn to the silver pocket watch positioned at one end of the display case.

The Cambridge academic carefully lifted the open volume from its cradle and offered it to the priest. The book was bound in dark brown leather and measured approximately eight inches by twelve inches. Sabatini looked at Brother Nathan, his eyes now fixed on the *Principia*. His gloved hands trembled slightly, like a convert taking Holy Communion for the first time.

'Throughout the volume, you can see Newton's handwritten notes in the margins,' said Jenkins.

In his capacity as Chief Librarian at the Vatican Observatory Library, Nathan had spent the last seven years surrounded by important rare books. Some had almost become surrogate children to him. The trustees of the library had often joked that the old man spent more time speaking to the books on the shelves than he did talking to his staff. But to Brother Nathan, they were more than mere collections of parchment and paper gathering dust; they were tangible connections to the great men and women of history. As he touched the old texts, he would in some small way summon a trace of the author's spirit into his mind, touching human greatness through the pages.

'Is the condition of the book suitable for me to turn the pages?' Brother Nathan enquired with a hushed reverence.

'It's in excellent condition. The spine is completely undamaged. Please, feel free.'

As he turned the pages, Brother Nathan could clearly see the small neat lettering written by the great scientist. The radical ideas expressed in these pages had changed the world. As he tried to decipher Newton's handwritten notes—some composed in classical Latin and others in strange coded English—, Brother Nathan could almost feel the presence of the author transcending the centuries. He closed his eyes and asked God to reveal His purposes to him.

After several minutes of discussion about Newton and his great work, the priest returned the priceless book to his host, who carefully replaced it in its cradle. Noticing that the priest's gaze had returned to the other contents of the display case, Jenkins cleared his throat.

'We have a truly exceptional collection of Newton's objects for you to see.'

Stationed around the *Principia* like the numbers of a clock face were an assortment of other exhibits.

'First, we have Newton's very own walking stick,' said Jenkins.

The walking stick lay at twelve o'clock position and was fixed by a series of pins that zigzagged down its length. The stick's bone handle was carved into the shape of a face and attached to a long wooden cane. The facial features of the handle had been worn down through use and had the effect of freezing the face into a disfigured scream.

'Then, we have Newton's pocket watch, a lock of his hair from the Earl of Portsmouth's collection; his Latin exercise book from his time at school in Grantham; and his famous letter to Robert Hook, which—'

'Forgive me, Dr Jenkins, would it be possible to see the pocket watch?' said Brother Nathan.

'The pocket watch? Yes, of course,' replied Jenkins with a slightly puzzled expression across his face.

Jenkins complied with the priest's request and carefully handed the timepiece to the priest. A thrill of excitement shot down Brother Nathan's backbone. The watch felt heavy in his hand, like a large metal pebble. Slowly rotating the timepiece in his palm, he studied its exterior. His distorted reflection reared up on the surface of the metal casing as his fingertips turned the object. Brother Nathan flicked open the silver casing that protected the glass front and examined the simple white watch face.

It must be here. It must be here. Lord God show me.

Bringing the object closer to his face, the priest's eyes darted around the circle of Roman numerals that formed the perimeter of the face, looking for a sign that would reveal its secret. Suddenly, he became aware that both Sabatini and Jenkins were staring quizzically at him.

'Next, shall we have a look at the lock of Newton's very own hair?' said Jenkins. He directed his guest's attention to a small silver locket, which contained a thin loop of white hair held together by a bow of fine material.

'You know, Mr Newton had quite a reputation with regard to his hair. According to the records, he went completely grey at a very early age. It is said that he often went out in public without a wig, something quite unusual for a gentleman to do at that time.'

Whilst the academic continued his exposition, Brother Nathan rummaged through the pocket of his overcoat.

'Many people have speculated that the premature whitening of his hair was a result of quicksilver poisoning. Quicksilver, or mercury as it is known today, was a much sought-after alchemic ingredient that, while relatively safe in its liquid form, could cause some very unpleasant physiological effects when inhaled as a vapour. In fact, King Charles II, who himself was a great dabbler in chemical experimentation, was thought to have been poisoned by—'

Jenkins was cut off in mid-flow by the presence of the two police officers who had just entered the library. Both were wearing motorcycle leathers and full-face helmets, their features obscured by tinted visors. Looking up, Sabatini noticed that one of the police officers was carrying a canvas bag and the other had a long metal tube container slung across his back. Closing the door behind them, the two policemen then approached the group, who were all standing around the display case like doting parents around a baby's cot.

'Is there something wrong, officer?' Jenkins asked.

In unison, the two men raised their Glock 22 semi-automatic pistols, one aiming directly at Jenkin's head and the other pointing towards his stunned guests.

'Not if you do exactly as we say.'

CHAPTER 26

'Step away from the display case!' commanded one of the policemen, waving the barrel of his pistol as he did so. The three figures obeyed immediately and moved away from the open exhibit.

'This is a robbery. You have a simple choice. Follow every word we tell you and you will live to see the end of the day. Do not, and I will shoot you dead. Do I make myself clear?'

Without waiting to exhale, both Jenkins and Sabatini slowly nodded their heads in confirmation. Brother Nathan stood perfectly still and started to recite prayers under his breath. Slowly, the fingertips of his right hand began to travel down the lining of his overcoat pocket.

'This is how it's going to work. You,' the policeman pointed to Brother Nathan threateningly, 'are going to take the objects from the case and place them in this bag.' As he spoke, he removed the canvas bag from his shoulder and threw it in the direction of the priest. The other policeman, his pistol now trained squarely on Brother Nathan, took the long metal tube slung across his back and jabbed one end of it into the clergyman's shoulder. 'This is for the walking stick.' Pointing to Sabatini and Jenkins, he continued. 'You two, turn around and face the wall. Fuck with me and I swear I will put a bullet in the back of your heads!'

As Sabatini turned to face the wall, she glanced over to her old mentor. For an instant, he looked much younger than his seventy years, like he did in the photographs on his desk at the Observatory Library. The priest acknowledged her in his eyes and then, instead of following the assailants' instructions, he turned to face the policeman who was pointing the pistol at his face.

'You have no idea what you are doing. I will not let you take it from this place!'

Shaking his head, Brother Nathan swung his fist down onto the open lid of the display case. It slammed shut, firmly locking itself in the process. Jenkins gasped in horror.

'You stupid old man. Get out of the way!' said the policeman closest to the priest. He took a step forwards and cocked his pistol. 'You fucking idiot! Is this stuff really worth dying for?'

Brother Nathan placed his hand defiantly on top of the locked display case. From behind the visor of his motorcycle helmet, Crossland felt a bead of sweat run down his forehead. *What the hell is this old man doing?* The policeman pushed the priest back while driving the barrel of his Glock into his temple. Brother Nathan stumbled backwards, and the back of his head hit the wall.

'I'm warning you, old man.'

Taking a step back, Crossland unzipped his leather jacket to reveal a collection of tools clipped to a harness across his chest. He unfastened the large hammer that hung like a cross at the centre of the webbing and slipped his hand through the loop of material attached to its handle. Crossland marched to the display case with the hammer raised above his head. Jenkins managed to turn his face before the full force of the hammer came down onto the glass top, shattering it into a thousand pieces.

Brother Nathan lurched forwards. His outstretched hands plunged into the sea of glass fragments covering the inside of the case, sending them flying into the air. Exhibits fell off their stands. He grasped at something and then a burst of light flashed from Crossland's pistol. The back of the priest's skull exploded in a crimson supernova of blood and bone. The kinetic energy of the 0.40-calibre bullet entering his head spun his body on its axis, sending lines of pulped brain and shards of skull out like a Catherine wheel. His body fell to the ground in a bloody heap.

For a moment, time stood still. Denic looked over to Crossland, a wisp of smoke still rising from the barrel of his weapon. Sabatini felt her body start to shake uncontrollably. She closed her eyes in the futile hope that it would transport her away from the carnage, but instead it just intensified the sound of glass being crushed underfoot as Denic moved over to Brother Nathan's body.

After a quick inspection of Brother Nathan's shattered skull with the toe of his boot, Denic exploded into action. 'Move!' he commanded at the top of his voice.

Crossland aimed his pistol at Sabatini with one hand, while his other hand swept glass chips from the exposed artefacts. One by one, he quickly placed the exhibits into the canvas bag that was lying on the ground next to Brother Nathan's lifeless body. Gently, he freed the walking stick from its mounting, loaded it into the long metal tube and secured its end with a metal stopper.

'Down on the ground! Now!' Denic stabbed the air menacingly with his Glock 22. As Jenkins crouched down, he tried to make out the face of the killer behind the tinted visor.

'Get your face down!' The handle of Denic's pistol struck the side of Jenkins's face. The academic collapsed to the ground, curling up in a protective position to prepare himself for another blow. As he fought to catch his breath, blood flooded into his mouth. Crossland threw the bag and metal tube over to his partner, who slung them quickly over his shoulder and nodded back a signal.

'You get up or call for help, you will die!' Denic ordered through his helmet. 'You fuck with me, and I will hunt you both down and cut you into pieces! Do you understand?'

Sabatini was trembling prostrate on the floor, her cheek lying against the cold floor tiles damp with her own tears and saliva. She forced her eyes shut and in her mind cried out to God. Was she to die like this?

'Do you understand?' the command roared out again, even more terrifying than before.

'Yes, yes,' whimpered Jenkins, his tongue protruding through the bloody gaps where his teeth used to be. Sabatini nodded her head frantically in acknowledgement. She held her breath and dug her fingernails deep into her clenched palms. To her left, she could hear the sound of footsteps moving quickly across the library floor and then all was silent. She opened her eyes and stared directly into the mutilated face of Brother Nathan.

Still clutched tight in his hand was Newton's pocket watch.

CHAPTER 27

Blake stepped over the unopened brown envelopes lying on the doormat of his bedsit and put the carrier bag from the off-licence on the floor. As a pulse returned to his fingertips, he wondered who was phoning him at this time of night? Reluctantly, Blake answered his mobile phone. As soon as the line connected, a torrent of words roared through the speaker.

'Lukas, can you please slow down. The line isn't very good. Did you say something about Cambridge?'

'Yes, there's been another robbery ... the Wren Library at Cambridge University.' Milton's voice abruptly became clear, as if he had stepped from a busy street into a quiet room.

'You were right. It's the Drakon. His men have struck again: a two-man team dressed as police motorcycle officers.'

'What did they get?'

'They cleared out an exhibition case full of Newton stuff, but not before shooting a tourist in the head. A priest.'

'Dead?'

'Very dead. Forensics are picking bits of his skull out of the bookshelves as we speak. I've just got here. It's a real mess.' Milton cleared his throat loudly and then continued. 'The Commissioner is being summoned to the Home Office. It's going to be all over the press.'

'I guess this is going to be big news. Any witnesses?' asked Blake.

'Two, but they're pretty shaken up.'

'I bet.'

'Hold on,' said Milton.

The detective shouted orders to someone else in earshot.

'Sorry about that. Look, I've just come off the phone with the boss and I've got it cleared.'

'Cleared? What?' asked Blake.

'You.'

Blake's stomach muscles tightened.

'I've got it cleared with the Commissioner for you to rejoin the investigation. I mean, if you still want it?'

'I want it,' Blake answered. 'Email me everything you've got. I'll be in Cambridge before lunch.'

PART 2

THE SECOND LAW OF MOTION

The change of momentum of a body is proportional to the impulse impressed on the body, and happens along the straight line on which that impulse is impressed.

CHAPTER 28

Thursday 26 November

Mary awoke from her fitful night's sleep with the fearful recollection of a dream. The dream was always the same.

She found herself running along a narrow passageway, following the path of a golden line painted onto a granite floor. The further she ran, the more luminous the line became, until the light illuminated the entire corridor. Suddenly, she found the way blocked by a circular stone door. She reached out to touch the elaborate rim of gilded bees cut into its border, and all by itself the door opened just wide enough for her to step through.

She found herself standing in a large room, its walls inlaid with exotic wood. To one side stood a lamp stand and next to it a table made of solid gold. At the far end of the room hung a large purple curtain that seemed to billow as if caught by a gust of wind, but the air all around was perfectly still. At the centre of the room was a magnificent altar of the finest white marble, set high on a platform of many steps. As she climbed the steps, the altar burst into flames. From the heart of the fire appeared a great phoenix of burning gold, its massive wings fanning the flames higher. Soon the outline of the mighty bird was consumed in the blaze, and Mary found herself teetering on the top step of the platform, trying to shield herself from the intensity of the heat. Then, as abruptly as the conflagration had appeared, it was gone. Looking down at the altar, Mary could see that the phoenix had disappeared and in its place was a wooden rod, several feet in length. Trembling, she reached out to touch it, fearing that its heat would burn her. Instead, it felt cold.

Immediately, she was taken over by the compulsion to touch it with her lips, but as she brought the sacred object close to her face, the ground began to shake with such ferocity that she believed she was at the centre of some great earthquake. Gripping the side of the altar with one hand, the rod grasped firmly in the other, she tried to steady herself against the tremors convulsing through the ground. With her eyes fixed upon the altar, Mary became aware of dots of crimson appearing against the virgin white of the marble. The circles of red became numerous in number, and she was gripped by the realisation that it was raining; raining blood. In terror, she looked up at the ceiling, her eyes squinting against the warm deluge against her face.

Mary was shaken from her dream by the tongue of a dog licking her face, its breath hot against her freezing skin. With her body still recoiling from the terror of the dream, she hugged and kissed the animal as if it were a long-lost child.

CHAPTER 29

The large blue refuse bin in the back courtyard of the Mount Mills block of flats looked slightly different to the rest of the bins awaiting collection. It was set apart, secured to the railings by a thick black chain, and a small cross of red insulation tape had been stuck onto its lid. The Mount Mills tower block, just off Goswell Road, was also unusual because it was bordered by an open area of undeveloped land: a valuable commodity in that part of Central London. However, it had remained unbuilt upon for centuries.

The Drakon peered through the gap between the curtains of Flat 406 and tracked the arrival of a dark green Range Rover. The vehicle came to rest just outside the perimeter of the courtyard. From their vantage point high above ground level, the Drakon peered through long-range binoculars. It didn't take long for a well-built man to appear from the passenger door, his face all but obscured by a beige cap and a pair of dark sunglasses. With the engine of the car still running, the man moved quickly towards the bin marked with the red cross, opened its lid, and carefully deposited a black refuse sack inside. The man jumped back into the passenger seat, and before he had time to shut the door, the car was already reversing at speed out of the cul-de-sac, its tyres squealing as it went. The drop was complete.

The Drakon put the binoculars into the rucksack lying on the floor and looked out past the courtyard to the unkempt derelict land beyond. It was sacred land, and only a few residents were aware of the terrifying history of the place and the secret that lay in its soil. The loose ground that surrounded Mount Mills contained the remains of thousands of bodies dumped there during the Great Plague that had ravaged London between 1665 and 1666. Cartloads of diseased bodies were dumped and buried in shallow graves, and the houses of the diseased were marked with red crosses.

CHAPTER 30

Detective Lukas Milton was shouting into his mobile phone in front of the Mobile Crime Scene Command Centre when Blake arrived by taxi. The forty-foot state-of-the-art police transporter was the centrepiece of the Special Crime Unit, and it was parked on the manicured lawn in front of the Wren Library. Two deep furrows of brown mud trailed behind it, and the small sign warning visitors to keep off the grass had been driven deep into the soil under one of its immense wheels. The Command Centre served as a fully equipped mobile laboratory for the processing and documentation of forensic evidence. With its on-board generator and communications equipment, it provided a rapid response to a serious crime and allowed for 24/7 operations at a single location.

On seeing Blake emerge from the taxi, Milton brought his diatribe on his mobile to a close and began to stride across the lawn towards the car. The arrival of the powerfully built detective at Blake's shoulder had the effect of pacifying the taxi driver, whose fare had just been paid with a large assortment of coins. Milton placed his heavy hand on Blake's shoulder.

'It's good to see you, my friend. Thank you for coming up. You okay?' The policeman's voice was as deep as a lion's.

Blake turned around and reciprocated the greeting.

'I'm fine, Lukas. Let's go to work.'

As they walked to the entrance of the library, Milton described the crime scene that had greeted him the previous evening.

'The Italian priest, a Nathan Vittori, was shot in the head at point-blank range. He was celebrating his seventieth birthday with a tour of the library when ... bang!' Milton shot a pretend bullet from the end of his finger. 'Some birthday present! The forensics boys are still trying to clear things up.'

'Last night you mentioned witnesses?' Blake asked, staring up at Milton's tinted glasses.

'Yes, Dr Carla Sabatini, a friend of the priest, and Dr Henry Jenkins, the guy who was giving the tour of the library.'

As the two men approached the foot of the grey stone staircase leading to the library, Milton handed Blake a pair of blue plastic shoe covers and a pair of surgical gloves.

'The forensics team have been in here for most of the night and the morning, but we need to put these on to protect the crime scene.'

Blake nodded, bent down, and slipped the plastic coverings over his shoes.

'They went specifically for the display case containing the exhibits,' said Milton. He rubbed his fingertips through his wiry, shortly cropped hair and then rummaged deep in his jacket pocket. His hand resurfaced moments later holding a small white plastic tube. It wasn't until Milton placed the object between his teeth that Blake realised the plastic cylinder was actually an anti-smoking inhalator and not some new piece of evidence.

'You know, chewing plastic will kill you in the end.'

'Fuck off!' Milton countered tight-lipped like a ventriloquist.

The two men walked stride by stride.

'How many times is that now?' Blake didn't need to ask the question. He knew the score exactly. 'With this one, it makes four in the last eighteen months.'

Milton stopped walking and looked at the ground.

'And now with this shooting added to the list, a holy nightmare is about to be unleashed from on high.' As Milton spoke, he fidgeted with the large gold sovereign ring around his finger. 'The Home Office and Interpol are already requesting updates. It's going to get very nasty if we don't get these bastards and get them soon.'

Blake and Detective Milton climbed the stairs slowly, both trying to order their thoughts. As he gripped the iron handrail, Blake could feel his heat being drawn into the cold metal. He shuddered and released his hand.

'Lukas, you do realise what we're dealing with here?' Blake stopped on the stairs causing Milton to turn around. 'We've got ourselves a "Dr No". He's probably got the same Caribbean island mansion ornamented with stolen works of art, just like the James Bond villain. Mark my words, Lukas. Four jobs, all targeting Newton. We're dealing with a private collector who won't be trying to sell them on.'

Milton stroked the plain blue tie that dangled loosely around his substantial neck, hoping somehow that the action would make the implications of Blake's hypothesis disappear.

'Maybe,' said Milton.

'Lukas, you know as well as I do, that because of their portability, rare books are either stolen for sale at a private auction or used as payment or collateral for drug deals. We've found no evidence that this gang is using them in this way. None of the stolen items have resurfaced with a dealer, auction house, or fence for that matter. They must have all headed for a private collection somewhere.'

Deciding not to answer, Milton nodded a greeting to the uniformed officer on sentry duty outside the entrance to the library. Dutifully, the officer unhooked the drooping length of cordon tape safeguarding the crime scene. At the far end of the hall, a forensics technician dressed in a blue semi-transparent plastic overall was taking photographs of the shattered display case. The light from the flash glared under the brilliant whitewashed ceiling. On the floor, like a giant scab, a black pool of congealed blood spread out from the white outline marking the position of the victim's body.

'Okay, so what do we know so far?' asked Blake.

'The CCTV cameras placed around the university campus show that two police motorcycles approached from the back of the university grounds and parked up outside the library at 5.14 p.m. last night. As I explained on the phone, Dr Jenkins was conducting a private tour of the Newton display case for his guests, Dr Sabatini and the priest, Father Vittori, when the men stormed in. According to Sabatini, the priest decided to play the hero and was rewarded with a hole in the head; a case of being in the wrong place at the wrong time. The forensics boys found the slug embedded in the bookcase over there.'

Milton pointed to a dark wooden bookcase just beyond the shattered remains of the display case. The bullet had narrowly missed an elaborate wooden carving of a phoenix and lodged itself deep within the end of the bookshelf. Blake stared at the carving of the mythical bird, its head tilted to one side as if consciously dodging the path of the oncoming projectile. The bullet hole had the shape of a distorted star caused by the forensics team gouging the surrounding wood to recover the bullet.

'The ballistics report confirmed that it's a 0.40-calibre Smith & Wesson round.'

'The same calibre the French police found in Cannes with the Clerot robbery.' Blake glanced at Milton looking for some recognition for his hypothesis, but found none in Milton's dour features.

'So, what did they take?'

Milton retrieved the small black notebook from the inside pocket of his charcoal flannel jacket and located the relevant page that detailed the inventory of stolen objects.

'A first edition of a book called the *Principia*, apparently it was Newton's own personal copy. His walking stick ...' Milton paused to decipher his handwriting, 'a lock of Newton's own hair displayed in a silver locket, and a notebook ... I'll get Sergeant Peck to drop off a copy of the case notes to you.'

Milton paused. 'There's one last thing, Vincent. They didn't get everything. The priest was still clasping this in this hand when the medics arrived.' From deep within his pocket, Milton produced a clear plastic evidence bag and handed it to Blake, who held the bag up to the light.

Inside was a pocket watch.

CHAPTER 31

Dr Carla Sabatini and Dr Henry Jenkins sat at opposite ends of the medical consulting room, both lost in their own private thoughts. The room was warm, but an icy shiver kept travelling down the sides of Sabatini's body. She pulled her chocolate-brown cardigan tight around her shoulders and stared blankly into the centre of the large room. Every so often, the horror of the last twenty-four hours would crash into her thoughts, making her face tighten in her effort not to cry. But there were no more tears, just a darkness that surrounded her.

After whispering some words of comfort, the uniformed policewoman relieved her of the cup of coffee that had sat untouched in her lap for the last twenty minutes. She barely noticed the officer's intervention, her senses deadened by exhaustion. Having safely secured the cup on the table, the officer placed her hand on Sabatini's shoulder and then returned to the incident report on her laptop.

Jenkins sat at the other end of the table. He looked like a defeated boxer nursing his wounds, a thick crust of dried blood clinging to his swollen lips. His wiry grey hair had gravitated to one side of his head as if it had been blown over by a strong wind. Hesitantly, his hand explored the changed landscape of his bruised face, but the pain from his stitches made him stop. He recoiled back into his chair and waited for the pain to subside. As he did so, the ball of his foot began to bounce on the floor.

There was a loud knock at the door, and Blake entered the room. He was acknowledged by the policewoman and then by the seated witnesses.

'Dr Sabatini, Dr Jenkins, this is Dr Blake. He's assisting the police with our enquiries and would like to ask you a few questions. Afterwards, I'll drive you both to your hotel,' the policewoman explained.

Blake offered Jenkins his hand. He took it and eyed up the new arrival.

'It must have been terrible for you both,' said Blake, 'I promise not to keep you unnecessarily, but you must both understand that time is of the essence. Every hour that goes by reduces our chances of catching the people who did this to your friend. I'm sorry to say, but it looks like Father Vittori was just in the wrong place at the wrong time. Rest assured that his murder makes this a top priority case for the police, and that's why I've been called in as a special adviser on the investigation.'

'So, what do you advise on?' questioned Jenkins as he started to pick at an angry patch of eczema around the nail of his forefinger. Blake gripped the back of a chair.

'My business is the recovery of stolen historical artefacts: documents, paintings, rare books. The items that were stolen yesterday will be heading for somewhere specific, and it's my job to find out where.' He released his grip on the back of the chair. 'I believe we are dealing with an international gang who are systematically targeting objects that are linked to Isaac Newton. There have been similar jobs in France, Japan and London, all committed over the last eighteen months. I have good reasons to believe that all the robberies are connected and have been carried out by the same gang.'

Sabatini looked up at Blake. 'Have they murdered before?'

Blake's hands returned to the back of the chair. A surge of emotion began to rise from deep within. He drew in a breath and released it before answering.

'Yes, and very recently.' He paused, 'I suspect that they're ex-military.'

Sabatini began to nod, as Blake's proposition concurred with the blitzkrieg offensive she had endured and barely survived.

Jenkins continued to scratch at his finger to the obvious irritation of the policewoman sitting next to him.

'So why on earth would two ex-soldiers commit cold-blooded murder in order to steal some old scientific artefacts?' said Sabatini.

'That's what I'm here to find out.' Blake answered. 'Both of your witness statements say that Father Vittori refused to comply with the thieves' demands, and this is why he was shot. I must say it puzzles me,' Blake continued. 'Why on earth would he risk his own life in this way?'

Sabatini reached over to her cup of coffee and took a small sip. The bitter taste of the lukewarm liquid made her feel instantly nauseous, and she returned it to the table without a second taste. She cleared her throat to speak.

'Dr Blake, Nathan lived for books. Earlier in his career, he was a very successful scientist but was called from front-line research by his Holiness to oversee the Vatican's astronomical library at Castel Gandolfo,' said Sabatini. 'As Chief Librarian, he dedicated himself to studying historical documents and preserving them for future generations. He often said that they were his children.' Sabatini's eyes began to fill up as she fought to regain her composure.

'Nathan was especially interested in the works of the natural philosophers of the Enlightenment, particularly Newton. He desperately wanted to come to Cambridge and examine Newton's personal possessions for himself. Recently, it had become something of an obsession with him. He had been quite insistent on making this trip and seeing the exhibits. His seventieth birthday was approaching and I wanted to help him. You know ... something like a birthday present ... and now, he's ... he's dead.' She buried her face in her hands and tears dropped onto the surface of the table. The policewoman stood up and placed a small packet of tissues in her hand. Sabatini squeezed it. The action seemed to release some of the tension around her eyes. Blake took a seat and directed his next enquiry to Jenkins.

'Tell me about the *Principia*,' said Blake. 'I've seen later copies for sale at auction houses over the years, but why is it so special?'

Jenkins stopped scratching his finger and leant forward in his chair with an air of evident superiority. 'The *Principia Mathematica* is quite simply the most important scientific book ever written. Those of us who aren't of a religious persuasion might even argue it is the most important book ever written. It is a masterpiece of breath-taking genius. The *Principia* is the rulebook of the universe. It codifies mathematically the laws of motion and the theory of universal gravity.' Jenkins looked over to Blake, making sure that his words were registering with the substitute policeman. He wasn't convinced.

'Look, it proved for the first time that the force that makes an apple fall from a tree is the same force that keeps the planets moving in their orbits. Think about it for a moment. It is a truly profound notion: a force operating over gigantic interstellar distances that connects every object in the universe together. The pages of the *Principia* provided the first evidence that mathematics govern the behaviour of the very universe.'

Blake decided not to think about it. To his mind, the bullet that had entered Vittori's skull may have followed Newton's laws of motion, but his corpse wouldn't be moving anywhere in the near future.

'And this particular volume, it's special?'

'It's unique,' said Jenkins. 'It's Newton's own copy of the first edition. I simply couldn't put a value on it.' Jenkins swallowed down the returning taste of blood in his mouth.

'It's the same for the other objects they stole.' Sabatini rejoined the conversation, her voice less fragile than before.

'Yes, the other objects,' said Blake firing up his smartphone. He quickly found Milton's report of the stolen objects emailed to him just hours before.

'First edition of the *Principia Mathematica,* 1687. Walking stick belonging to Isaac Newton: carved bone handle, hickory wood stick. Lock of Isaac Newton's hair presented in a silver locket, allegedly part of a larger lock in the possession of the Earl of Portsmouth. Newton's personal notebook, used firstly as a Latin exercise book from his time as a schoolboy at Grantham School, and later as an account book recording his expenses as an undergraduate at Trinity College, 1661. A letter authored by Isaac Newton, Professor of Mathematics, University of Cambridge, to Robert Hooke, Curator of Experiments, Royal Society, London, dated 28 November 1679. Ah yes ... and, finally, the pocket watch.'

Blake could feel the large smooth object weighing down the material of his jacket breast pocket. It had already undergone detailed fingerprint and DNA testing in the mobile forensic laboratory parked in the grounds of the college, and Milton had requested Blake to cross-reference it against the list of rare stolen timepieces on Blake's personal database. It was unlikely, but his database might uncover a connection to another stolen watch. Blake took it from his pocket and placed the transparent plastic evidence bag with the watch on the table. It made a small thud as the metal made contact with the hard surface, causing Jenkins to send Blake a disapproving look.

'Dr Jenkins, can you remember anything out of the ordinary in the days leading up to yesterday's events? Anything at all, no matter how small: perhaps an out-of-the-ordinary request to see the Newton exhibits, or a tour of the college grounds?'

Jenkins had been asked the same question by at least three police officers and the novelty had thoroughly worn off.

'Mr Blake, if there had been, Detective Milton would have been the first to know.'

With that, Blake got up from his seat. 'Thank you both for your cooperation. I won't keep you any longer, but if you do think of anything, please don't hesitate to give me a call, day or night.'

Blake picked up the evidence bag containing the pocket watch from the table and held it up to the light, like a child staring at a goldfish just won at a fair. As he turned the object 360 degrees, his eye caught the glint of something engraved on the outer edge of its back casing. Trying to improve his angle of view, he pulled the bag closer to his face and stretched the plastic tight around the smooth surface of the watch.

The closer he looked, the more convinced he became that there were three small engravings grouped close to the rim. He slowly rotated the watch under the ceiling light, stopping at the precise angle to reveal an area of tiny lettering. The slightest movement obscured it again in shadow. Blake turned his body a fraction and the engraving became clear. He slowly read the characters aloud: 'D2.25. No it's a 7, that's it. D7.25, D12.7 and R12.14.'

Blake peered over the transparent plastic bag to Jenkins, who returned a quizzical look. Jenkins had been curator of the library exhibits for over three years, but this was the first time he had been made aware of any kind of inscription pertaining to the watch.

'Have a look for yourself. It's on the inner rim of the back plate, just beneath the winder. It's very easy to miss.' He handed Jenkins the evidence bag containing the pocket watch and looked as the academic studied its reverse side under the bright ceiling light.

'Well, I'll be damned. You're absolutely right. Extraordinary! It must be a manufacturer's mark of some kind, perhaps a silver mark?'

'No, I know exactly what it is,' said Sabatini staring into mid-air. Blake and Jenkins looked at her. 'They're verses from the Bible: Daniel 7:25, Daniel 12:7 and Revelation 12:14.'

'Dr Sabatini, what makes you so sure?' said Blake, slightly taken aback.

She turned to Blake. 'They are verses that Nathan obsessed over. He even had them written on the inside cover of his bible.'

'Obsessed over? What do you mean?'

'Recently, Nathan had become preoccupied with Newton's religious writings and was convinced that these particular verses were of special significance.'

'Newton's religious writings?' Blake felt himself wading out far beyond his depth.

'Today, it surprises a lot of people to know, but Newton was a deeply religious man and a devout believer in God. During a good part of the 1670s, he shunned the scientific world and focused his energies on a massive programme of biblical research. He taught himself Hebrew and set out to decode the writings of the great biblical prophets, especially Ezekiel, Daniel and St John the Divine, directly from their oldest sources. He wrote more about theology than any other subject, well over a million words, and it wouldn't surprise me if Nathan had read every one of them,' said Sabatini. 'According to Nathan, Newton thought that these three scriptures were important to unlocking the truth about God's ultimate plan.'

'So what are they about?'

'What are they about? I wish I knew. They are the visions of prophets who lived a couple of thousand years ago.'

CHAPTER 32

Friday 27 November

The three men stood in a room adjacent to where the press conference would be taking place. Blake, Milton and Chief Constable Peter Lewis from the Cambridgeshire Constabulary all stood silently by the door, waiting for the signal to enter. Lewis, a man who had carved out a formidable reputation during his meteoric rise through the force, was the embodiment of a new breed of policeman and the antithesis of the two men who flanked him. Milton trusted him as far as he could throw him, and whilst the notion was appealing, it wouldn't be very far.

Blake looked down at his hands and noticed how much they looked like his father's. The dark red band of discolouration surrounding his left index finger, a birthmark that he shared with his father, seemed to have become more pronounced over the last month. The notion made him feel strangely uneasy.

Earlier, a make-up woman had offered him her services 'to make him look his best in front of the cameras.' She had installed a temporary mirror on the wall and had been armed with a bag of cosmetics and brushes. Following the path of least resistance, Blake had complied with her instructions and sat in her chair. He stared at his reflection in the mirror. He knew it wasn't going to be good, but he was still taken aback by what he saw. Though his eyes were bright and clear, the flesh around them looked like it had started to melt. His skin was on a downward trajectory, its progress only temporarily retarded by the bones of his face. Blake watched as the make-up lady struggled to find a complementary tone to his pale skin colour. He asked her if they made a blusher called 'off-white,' but before she had time to register the comment, Blake had vacated the chair.

The din coming from the other side of the door gradually fell silent. Lewis sent Milton a nod signalling that proceedings were about to start. After several firm knocks, the door opened slowly and in stepped the same policewoman who had attended yesterday's interview with Sabatini and Jenkins. She looked tired and was not relishing the role of chaperoning the head of Cambridgeshire's police force through a tense media event.

'It's time, sir,' she said.

The press conference was packed. The room, the size of a large railway waiting room, was creaking at the edges with photographers, journalists, and film crews, all jostling each other for the best positions. In the short time since the incident had been announced to the press, the story had gained such momentum that it had drawn interest from all over the world. A murder committed under the hallowed spires of the University of Cambridge was sensational enough, but the murder of a Vatican priest, committed during the heist of rare artefacts belonging to Sir Isaac Newton, was journalistic dynamite. Blake hated press conferences with a vengeance, and as he walked into the crammed room, he sensed a feeding frenzy about to happen.

The three men sat close together in the middle of a long table situated at one end of the room. A bank of microphones along with three bottles of water and three glasses were stationed next to them. Milton noticed that a large thumbprint had been left on the side of the glass closest to Lewis. For a split second, it lifted his mood.

Blake had only been partially successful in resurrecting his spare suit from the bottom of his bag after breakfast. He had hung it in the bathroom whilst the steam from his bath had permeated the creases. However, compared to the smartly dressed policemen to his right, his suit looked crumpled and clung strangely to his body.

Lewis looked out to the audience and cleared his throat. Even before he said a word, a series of camera flashes went off metres away from his face. He paused, regained his composure and started reading from a prepared statement.

'Good morning, ladies and gentlemen. Thank you for coming. I am Chief Constable Peter Lewis. To my right is Detective Lukas Milton and to my left Dr Vincent Blake. I have called this press conference to give an update on our investigations surrounding the murder of Father Nathan Vittori at Trinity College, Cambridge. Father Vittori died from a fatal gunshot wound to the head, sustained during a robbery at the Wren Library. Our investigations have now entered a critical phase, and today we are asking for assistance from the public with our enquiries. This was a particularly callous crime, and my officers will not rest until these criminals are brought to justice.'

Lewis clicked the end of his Cambridgeshire Constabulary police pen, signalling the end of his introduction.

'Let me now hand you over to Detective Milton, the officer in charge of the case.'

Milton looked like a heavyweight prize-fighter preparing to announce his retirement from the sport. His heavy physical frame, several years past top fighting condition, still looked formidable. In contrast to his powerful physique, Milton spoke to the audience in a quiet and measured way, delivering each word in a rich baritone voice. The assembled media listened intently to the particulars of the case as he read aloud from his notes. All the time, he was acutely aware that his every movement was being recorded by the collection of television cameras stationed around the room. After a few minutes, he came to the end of his report and squared his papers on the table top before placing them in front of him. Milton looked directly into the BBC television camera positioned between the chairs on the front row.

'If there are members of the general public who have any information regarding the robbery, anything at all, we are requesting that they come forward as soon as possible. I cannot overstress the urgency. Every hour is critical to our investigations.' Milton looked over to Lewis to see if he wanted to add anything else and was greeted with a subtle but unmistakable shake of the head. Milton moved about in his seat and felt a cold drop of sweat run down the centre of his back. His mouth felt dry and he had a strong urge to light a cigarette.

'Are there any questions?' Milton's request was immediately met by a forest of hands waving back at him. Milton picked a familiar face.

'Leonard Rowling, *Channel 4 News*. What is the estimated monetary value of the stolen objects?' It was always the first question a journalist asked about a robbery, even in a robbery involving a murder. A headline needed a figure, even more than it needed the name of a victim. Blake was ready with the standard answer and Milton was only too happy for his associate to field the question.

'Each item taken is unique. They were the personal property of Isaac Newton and are highly sought after by collectors. In an open auction, they would probably fetch in excess of a million pounds. However, each object has been meticulously catalogued by the library, and we would be quickly aware of their existence if they were sold through a legitimate auction house.' From behind the table, Milton pointed to a portly middle-aged journalist whom he knew to be a criminal correspondent.

'David Myers, *The Times*. So, if it is impossible to sell these objects on the legitimate open market, are we dealing with a private collector stealing to order?' Out of the corner of his eye, Milton was aware that Blake's body language had changed.

'Mr Myers, because of their intrinsic value and their relatively small size, objects of this type are often used as collateral in drug deals. At this time, we are investigating this line of enquiry, along with all other possible avenues.'

Before Milton had time to change to another journalist, Myers had put another question to the table.

'Do the police believe the robbery is connected to the others?'

Milton shifted uncomfortably in his seat.

'Others?'

While consulting his notebook, the journalist continued. 'The strong room at the Token Hakubutsukan sword museum in Japan; the Royal Society in London; and most recently, in Cannes, the private collection of Didier Clerot: each robbery targeted manuscripts relating to Newton. There must be a connection, don't you think?'

The three men blinked at the blizzard of camera flashes.

'As I have said, we are investigating all lines of enquiry. We have good channels of communication with our colleagues in Interpol and Japan's Criminal Investigation Bureau.' As Milton leant forward in his chair, his biceps strained the fabric of his suit. 'But rest assured, the people who carried out yesterday's brutal robbery will be caught and brought to justice.'

A new voice shouted out from behind a cacophony of camera flashes. Milton struggled to locate its position in the crowd.

'Reeta Hakim, Reuters. Detective Milton, you said that yesterday's robbery seemed to be centred on a single display case in the Wren Library. Did they get away with everything?'

Attempting to bring the questioning to a close, Lewis stepped in. 'I'm sure you all understand that because of the urgency of our investigations, this really does need to be the final question.' He paused. 'No, not everything that was in the display case was taken. A pocket watch belonging to Newton remains in our possession.' Lewis nodded across the table to Blake who retrieved the evidence bag containing the silver watch from deep within his pocket. Standing up, Blake raised the evidence bag for all to see and another storm of camera flashes went off all around.

CHAPTER 33

The Drakon began to shake the contents of the canvas bag onto the solid oak table. Once released from the folds of the bag, a silver pocket watch landed onto the wood with a dull thump and came to rest next to the haphazard collection of stolen objects. With a sense of reverence, the Drakon picked up the silver timepiece and began to examine its casing under a large magnifying glass. The heavy object felt strangely cold in the climate-controlled conditions of the underground strongroom. The trace of a smile appeared from the side of the Drakon's mouth.

Without warning, an audible alert sounded from the laptop stationed at one end of the table. Scanning the screen for the reason for the alarm, the Drakon began to type quickly on the keyboard. A few seconds later, a window displaying a BBC newsfeed began to play. A sombre-faced presenter announced that the next item would be rescheduled owing to the following coverage of a police press conference. A red banner running across the bottom of the screen read: 'Live: Newton Murder. Special Update'. The picture cut to three men sitting behind a table, their profiles partially obscured by the bank of microphones positioned in front of them. The Drakon watched in silence as the detective in charge of the investigation described the details of a shooting at Trinity College, Cambridge.

The television camera tracked the black police detective in charge of the case as he fielded questions from the assembled crowd of journalists. *Don't kid yourselves. You haven't got a clue.* The television coverage cut to a close-up of one of the other men sitting at the table. The subtitle at the bottom of the screen identified the speaker as Vincent Blake. His face was familiar. The picture zoomed in closer. Something in Blake's hand made the Drakon sit up.

With several rapid clicks of the mouse, the Drakon rewound the television clip and paused it, freezing the image of Blake in mid-sentence, a transparent evidence bag suspended from his hand. *The pocket watch! He's got Newton's watch!* Panicking, the Drakon picked up the silver timepiece from the jumble of objects strewn across the tabletop. A large space at the centre of the table was cleared with a sweep of an arm, sending Netwon's walking stick clattering to the floor.

Long bony fingers began to rotate the pocket watch under the convex lens of the magnifying glass, its burnished silver casing glinting under the ceiling strip light. The watch's surface was perfectly smooth and unblemished. A long moment passed. Not looking up from the magnifying glass, the Drakon clicked open the front cover to expose the hands of the timepiece. After adjusting to the new focal distance of the object, the Drakon could pick out small lettering printed onto the white watch face. A second later, a dreadful cry reverberated around the subterranean strongroom. White flecks of spittle erupted from the sides of the Drakon's mouth. The enraged figure hurled the timepiece against the wall. It exploded on impact, sending a shower of watch innards raining down onto the floor. Like a spinning coin, the white watch face finally came to rest next to a table leg. Just below the central hole where the watch hands were once attached, a single inscription was printed.

Roma, 1993.

CHAPTER 34

From the moment his new tenant's rent cheque had bounced, the landlord knew Blake was going to be trouble. According to his 'golden rule,' Blake would have until the end of week to come up with the cash voluntarily, or he would set the bailiffs on him. He would get his back rent, one way or another.

The landlord listened intently behind the front door. He strained his ears, trying to hear for the faintest signs of life, but all was quiet. Moving back, he clenched his fist and brought it down hard onto the centre of the door. A sharp jab of pain shot across his knuckles as his three large signet rings nipped the flesh between his fingers. The pain just made him even more determined, and he started kicking the bottom of the door with his boot.

'You in there, Blake? I need my rent. I need it now. Do you hear me?' The kicking intensified for several seconds before finishing in a frustrated crescendo. 'I'll be back with the bailiffs if I don't get my money!' The landlord waited for a response, but was greeted with silence. Frustrated, he stormed off back upstairs.

CHAPTER 35

Mary looked up at the fearsome outline of the dragon against the darkening sky.

A worker at the shelter had told her about the dragon statues when booking her in for the night. As she led Mary to the dormitory, she explained that they were located at significant places along the edge of the City, to mark its boundary with the rest of Central London. That evening, over a dinner of pasta and garlic bread, she had asked the volunteer to tell her more about the City. She listened intently as she shovelled the piping hot food into her empty stomach. The shelter worker went on to explain that the City, an area of just over a square mile, was the ancient centre from which the modern metropolis had grown. Apparently, its perimeter had remained unchanged since medieval times, and only relatively recently had the mythical creatures been installed to guard its borders.

Mary didn't see the volunteer again, but when she left the shelter the next morning, the man behind the reception desk presented her with an ex-army sleeping bag that had been left as a gift for her by the volunteer. The sleeping bag was now one of her only possessions, and she shared it every night with her black dog.

Mary felt an overwhelming urge to touch the statue's serpent-like skin, but she feared that doing so might bring it to life. Its body, dark and almost metallic, reared up on powerful hind legs, whilst upswept wings cast a terrible shadow over Mary's face below. An arrowhead tongue darted between blackened fangs, and its nostrils flared a warning to those seeking to attack the ancient city. She moved out of its shadow and blinked up at the strong street light, half-imagining that the beast had just turned on its granite plinth.

Passing by the sentinel, she could feel the energy of the City pulsing beneath her feet. To Mary, the City of London was a vast magnetic horizon of surging and ebbing currents. As she walked from street to street, she experienced the energy fluctuations through her body. She hunted out places where the energy seemed to surge and flow unhindered: Fountain Court in the Temple district; the yard of St Bride's Church; or the earth surrounding Christopher Wren's clock tower in the gardens of St Dunstan's Church in the east.

As she charted this invisible topography in her mind, she also became aware of many desolate places where the energy seemed to stagnate, tainted as they were with a strange sense of darkness. No matter how much the local authorities tried to regenerate these areas of permanent disharmony, the feeling of decay always seeped to the surface.

Over time, as Mary became more attuned to the forces resonating through these places, she began to notice an odd quality to the light falling around them. To Mary's eye, the shadows that formed in these areas—such as St Pancras Old Church, Centre Point, and Farringdon Road—all seemed to fall at curious angles, as though they were disconnected from the entity originating them. She could only stay momentarily in such places, just long enough to mark their location on her map.

Whilst waiting to see the visiting dentist in the shelter at the back of St Leonard's Church in Shoreditch, she had once stumbled upon a newspaper article on the numerous reports of a low-pitched background noise being heard by residents all over the capital. The article postulated that the sound was possibly a result of the ubiquitous distribution of fluorescent lighting throughout the city, or perhaps due to the great networks of coaxial cables that criss-crossed underground. But Mary knew exactly where the sound came from: the energy etched into the ground itself. With her black dog by her side, she spent her days dowsing the forces that flowed beneath the streets.

Mary crossed the busy road and followed the line of energy that surged under her feet. Like the bow of a boat, her black dog trotted several feet in front, clearing a way through the tourists that filled Middle Temple Lane. The humming intensified in her ears as she closed in on the source. Driven by the invisible force, she quickly turned the corner and entered a wide spacious courtyard. Abruptly, she stopped walking, her gaze dropping towards the pavement under her feet. Shifting her weight from side to side, she started to pray aloud. Reaching a crescendo, she dropped to her knees and then fell silent.

Minutes later, framed by the dark outline of Temple Church, Mary searched for the needle hidden in her shoe.

It was the day of her twelfth birthday when Mary had first talked about the auras she could see around people. Her parents had dismissed it as mere attention-seeking, but her grandmother had taken a special interest in her ability, describing it as a gift from the spirit world. The auras usually appeared as a coloured field surrounding the head, or a haze pulsing gently from the extremities of the body. She quickly realised that far from looking upon her ability as a gift, the outside world labelled it a mental aberration at best and something bordering on possession at worst.

Everyone possessed an aura, no matter how faint. Mary just needed to stare long enough and it would eventually become visible. At first, she thought that the colours were essentially fixed, except for some slight variations in intensity and form. But as time passed, she realised that the colours did change, albeit incredibly slowly. Only after many years did she realise that the colours of her parents' auras moved through a definite sequence. Her earliest memories were of beautiful shimmering greens, like the waters she had seen off the Dorset coast, but as the years passed she began to perceive changes: firstly into blue, and then into a strange, almost crystalline indigo. Mary had concluded that the colour migration must occur naturally over time, like the colours turning on the leaves of a tree.

Four years ago, on 12 September, Mary's father had woken earlier than usual. What Mary witnessed that morning when she met him sitting at the kitchen table had startled her so profoundly that she couldn't speak properly for hours afterwards. Pulsing like a heartbeat around her father's entire body was a brilliant violet luminescent glow. She circled around her father, touching the air close to his body, wondering if the aura had actually taken on a physical form. Mary's father didn't hide his annoyance, believing that, once again, his daughter was playing one of her imaginary games.

Two days later, he was dead, killed at work in a machinery accident.

As Mary began to understand the language of the colours, she withdrew inside herself and locked the door behind her.

CHAPTER 36

Saturday 28 November

Millions of tiny ice crystals sparkled over the surface of the only car parked in the visitor bay of the Wren Library. Although the sun was still bright, it struggled to impart warmth from its low position in the winter sky. Sabatini shivered and pulled her long coat close against her body. She wondered if she would ever be truly warm again. With the key fob buried deep within her coat pocket, her fingers managed to locate the unlock button and the side lights of the vehicle flashed back a greeting in pale yellow light.

The calls from the car hire company had been clear. If the car wasn't returned to an allotted drop-off location in the next twenty-four hours, she would incur a significant penalty charge, and the car's details would be given to the police and treated as stolen. In the chaos of the last few days, Sabatini had completely forgotten about returning the car that she and Brother Nathan had travelled up in from Heathrow just days before. She had started to explain her situation to the representative on the other end of the phone, but had quickly given up; it was just too painful. Now, she felt that dealing with such mundane matters, so quickly after the brutal murder of a close friend, was somehow sullying his memory. She stood over the driver's door with tears forming in her eyes.

She tried the door handle but the ice had frozen it shut, and the cold metal stuck to her bare fingers. Again she heaved at the handle, this time with both hands, and finally the door relented with a sharp cracking sound. The vehicle's interior was bitterly cold, and her breath materialised in the air in front of her as she manoeuvred her body into the driver's seat. The windscreen had frozen up on the inside, a translucent coating of ice obscuring any view outside. The car felt dark and closed-in. She hated the feeling. After mumbling several expletives in Italian, she tried the ignition key. A bank of lights blinked simultaneously from the dashboard, and the engine rattled into life. A minute later, warm air began to emerge from the air vents and, little by little, Sabatini started to feel the life return to her chilled bones.

The representative from the car hire company had explained that the nearest drop-off point to Trinity College was the railway station, and Sabatini had arranged to hand over the car between two and three that afternoon. It was now 1.44 p.m., which left her plenty of time to make the trip across the city centre and deliver the car. Remembering the map of Cambridge that she had picked up from the car rental office at Heathrow Airport, she reached over to the glove compartment, but her attention was quickly taken by something lying in the footwell. What looked like a small red notebook was partially lodged under the passenger's seat. Straining forwards, she scooped the object up from the floor and pulled herself upright in the seat.

The book was quite striking in appearance with a thick red velvety cover. She examined it closely and stared at the occultist design on the exterior. It fell open in her hand to a page bookmarked by the stub of an Alitalia boarding pass. Apart from a few sheets towards the back, the gilded calligraphy on its pages was mirrored on the opposite side with Isaac Newton's distinctive penmanship. Sabatini snapped the book shut and started to cry. She imagined Brother Nathan reading the book at his desk at the Observatory Library. Sabatini pulled the notebook close to her face and breathed in its smell, trying to detect some scent of her dear friend captured within its pages.

It must have dropped out of his pocket when I helped him with his overcoat.

With the back of her hand, she wiped away the tears running down her cheeks. After a series of long deep breaths, she opened the book and started to read. The words echoed in her head, as if Nathan were sitting right next to her. Sabatini's reddened eyes darted from page to page. It was Newton's handwriting, but she couldn't believe what she was reading. There was no doubt that this was the Gérard de Ridefort volume from Lot 249 of the Sotheby's sale: the one that Nathan had sworn was missing. *My god, Nathan, what had you got yourself into?* Sabatini quickly turned the page.

The day before the meeting of the Royal Society at Gresham College, I took the wagon for London. On my approach to Shoreditch, there fell such a storm of rain and darkness as never I had seen before. It was as if London were drowning. Caught in the midst of it caused a great impediment to my journey, and I had to take shelter for several hours, keeping my documents and the holy relic close to my person, afraid some ruthless villain would securely rob me.

By and by, I arrived at Gresham College and made an urgent request to see my learned friend the Architect, Dr Wren, but whilst waiting I was met by the loathsome Curator of Experiments; a man of tricking temper and smooth of tongue. He said he was much concerned with my pale and sickly countenance and wanted to take my luggage from my person, which I stoutly refused. After some discourse relating to several particulars of the Society, he gossiped about the murder of an alchemist who lodged close to Devil's Ditch. Rumours were rife that he had determined the secret for multiplying gold and was killed for the knowledge. How he knew these things he spoke not of, nor did I make much inquiry after it, in fear of my involvement being exposed. His constant snooping and prying into my affairs were part of some bloody design, of that I am sure.

In no time Dr Wren arrived, and after leaving the Curator to his duties, we took to the Architect's private quarters. I wasted no time in giving him a full account of the events that had passed and warning of the grievous jeopardy that we now lived under. He sat and listened, his face wracked with a tremendous worry. I then showed him the plans for the temple that God had revealed to me through the Book of Ezekiel, and the solemn purpose that He had instructed me to follow. No sooner had his eye cast upon my work than he was profoundly moved, sensing the Almighty's hand in its invention. I exhibited to my worthy friend the floor plan of the inner sanctuary and he did not disdain my advice on some particulars of its potential construction. After much consideration, this virtuous and excellent man had formulated a method by which he could petition the King for resources and yet keep our purpose obscured from sight. Being extremely ruined by the Great Fire, the fabric of the Cathedral had been demolished and new foundations were being readied. On that night, we sealed an earnest vow to rebuild Solomon's inner temple under St Paul's, and not to slacken the diligence of our endeavours until it was done.

And so the great work began. Dr Wren directed the laying of the foundations personally, keeping the overall plans for the Cathedral secret. By this means, and by only imparting a small view of the total design to his masons, he protected the true intent of our endeavour. Though the ground was waterlogged owing to inclement weather, the work advanced quickly with innumerable hands and incomparable inventions, such as pumps and bucket pulleys, designed by the genius Architect to drain the waters out. When the Royal Society came to meet once a month at Gresham College, I would go up to Ludgate Hill to view the progress and survey the trenches, cuts and mounds of earth around the site. There were no idle hands; every man was busy in building to my secret design.

On the 1 June 1675, Dr Wren sent word to me in Cambridge that the work had been completed, and he urgently requested my presence in London to seal the holy relic once again in the foundations of the great Cathedral of St Paul's. I arrived the next day and, with the rod in my possession and under the darkness of night, accompanied the good Architect to the site of the rebuilding. Wisely, Dr Wren had placed a sentinel on the highest point of the ruins of the Cathedral with orders, if he saw any stranger approach, to fire his piece into the air and ring his bell.

Directed by the light our torches afforded, we eventually came to the room housing the ingenious door fashioned from my design. We stepped into the chamber and set our torches next to the wall. The locking mechanism was accomplished indeed. The locking pointer was formed into the shape of a beehive which ran on a circular metal runner along the perimeter of a large flat stone, exactly as instructed in my drawings. Around the edges were a number of beautifully executed gilded bees; twelve in all. For its craftsmanship and carving, it was a masterpiece.

Guided by our torches, we climbed through the door, entered a passageway and crept a good depth into the bowels of the earth. It was not more than the height of a man; a strange and fearful corridor indeed.

Dr Wren had built the sanctuary room precisely to the design I had decoded from the scriptures. A large golden candlestick, projecting seven sockets from the middle stem stood in the corner, next to a gilt table, which glittered in the torchlight. The pieces were exquisitely polished, and glorious to look upon. At one end of the room hung a heavy purple curtain, its length spanning from roof to floor. In the centre of the sanctuary stood an elevated plinth mounted on three steps hewn from the finest white marble. On the mount of the plinth was carved a hexagram, representing the union of the Old and the New Jerusalem; the Old Jerusalem in the Holy Land, marked by the triangle of the Temple Mount, the Holy Sepulchre and St James Cathedral; and the New Jerusalem in London, marked by the Knights' configuration of churches, the Temple, St Paul's and St John's. Two perfect triangles joined in one Holy design.

The good Architect nodded his head, indicating that the time had come to perform the ceremony; the ceremony that would seal the holy relic in the foundations of the great Cathedral until the end times. From beneath my cloak I retrieved a package wrapped in crimson velvet, along with a Bible and the amulet that I had taken from Mr F's neck. With profound reverence, I set the bundle on the plinth and unwrapped the sacred object. Standing on the elevated platform of the plinth, I read from the books of Daniel, Ezekiel and Revelation, then I anointed Dr Wren with oil, first in the palms of his hands and then across the forehead in the sign of a cross. The particulars of the ceremony I will not share here.

After private prayer, we swore an oath to each other and then made preparations to seal the door of the chamber. The great door of stone was shut and on the very moment of setting the lock, a supernatural wind spread out from it, like the undulations of the water in a pond when a weighty stone is cast upon its surface. Dr Wren and I were thrown to the ground with such violence as to beat the breath out of our bodies, so as I could not speak nor fetch my breath for many minutes. During this instant, my senses seemed quite altered, unbounded by time, with all places lying together in one point of the compass. But it pleased God to deliver us out *of this affliction, for which we rendered to Him much praise. As we passed once more down the dark passageway, our lungs became choked with smoke from our torches and we were mightily relieved to see the moon again over our heads. I heartily thanked the good Architect and we both gave praise to God for His mercy in preserving us. I came from the place with infinite satisfaction, knowing we had done God's work.*

I heard nothing more from Dr Wren until several weeks later when a letter arrived to my quarters in Cambridge. In it he relayed the following account. Work laying the foundations of the Cathedral had progressed at speed and on the 21st of June, 1675, almost nine years after the dreadful conflagration, Dr Wren and his Master Mason undertook to mark out on the ground where the central point of the dome should be. He ordered a common labourer to search out a large stone from the piles of rubbish that lay all around and return it back to him without delay. The worker arrived back carrying a portion of a gravestone, which simply bore a single word carved in large letters, RESURGAM: 'I will rise again'. I was heartily gladdened on hearing such a good omen.

In the city of London, new buildings are always rising, highways repaired, churches and public buildings erected, fires and other calamites happening, but the Temple must not be disturbed until we are living through the end times and the rod is brought back to the Holy Land. When it will be so, only heaven pleases, for Christ comes as a thief in the night and it is not for us to know the times and seasons which God hath put into his own breast.

In the narrow compass of this writing, I have set down the history of my actions. I have concealed Gérard de Ridefort's map showing the location of the holy rod in the hope that a righteous man will use it well. Only God can search hearts of men and discover the truth, and to Him it must be left. I pray to God, that He gives you the grace to make the right use of it. It is a treasure greater than all the conquests of Alexander and the Caesars; for these are mere trifles compared to the power of the rod.

Sabatini eagerly turned over the page in trembling expectation. On the reverse side of the next page, Newton's final words formed the shape of a perfect equilateral triangle.

I have taken from this book the map revealing the rod's location in the great Cathedral of St Paul's and hidden it until the chosen time. For the parts of Prophecy are like the separated parts of a watch. They appear confused and must be compared and put together before they can be useful. Descend the eighty-eight steps and unlock the stone door, as all will be revealed in a time, times and half a time.

Jeova Sanctus Unus

Sabatini quickly turned the last few pages of Gérard de Ridefort's journal. Newton's cryptic instructions meticulously laid out in the shape of a triangle were, indeed, his final annotation to the crimson book.

The academic slumped back in the driver's car seat, her brain working furiously like a revving engine slipped out of gear. Abruptly she retrieved the book from her lap and then very deliberately let the pages fall open in her outstretched hands. From the way the pages fell away from the back cover, it was obvious that something had been removed from the back of the book. Sabatini closely examined the spine. A jagged edge of parchment protruding from the book's binding was all that remained of the last page. It had been carefully removed from the book and with it the map describing the possible location of the most important religious relic in all of history. For a long while, she stared into space feeling like the wind had been sucked out of her lungs.

At 3.17 p.m., the vehicle returns coordinator left a message on Dr Sabatini's mobile phone to ascertain her whereabouts and those of the bright red Volkswagen Passat. A vehicle matching that description remained parked outside the Wren Library as it had been for the previous three days. A woman sat in the driver's seat. Her world had just been turned upside down.

CHAPTER 37

Blake finished clearing his makeshift desk on the third floor of the central Cambridge police station. After looking over his shoulder to make sure he hadn't left something behind, he retraced his steps back down the corridor to the lift. His thoughts had turned to the train journey home and the off-licence next to Farringdon Tube Station that stocked his favourite whisky. He pressed the button next to the lift doors and waited. The winding mechanism made a strange whirring noise that seemed to intensify and wane with no predictable pattern. The doors opened to reveal a policewoman thumbing through the pages of an incident report. Without looking up, she moved to one side to make room, but Blake didn't move. He was lost in thought.

The doors of the lift clunked shut and it continued downwards, with the policewoman oblivious to the fact that the man in the corridor hadn't stepped in. Blake stared blankly at the dividing line between the closed lift doors, his eyes focusing on the chipped enamel paint running down the junction.

Even with Blake's phone set to silent, he was all too aware of the arrival of the incoming call by the insistent vibration against his leg. He accepted the call and pressed the handset against his ear. On the other end of the line, Milton's voice sounded serious.

'Vincent, it's Lukas. I'm with the pathologist. I've sent a patrol car over to collect you. You still at the police station? Good, good. It'll be with you in fifteen minutes. You need to be here—'

Milton's voice was cut off mid-sentence, as for no obvious reason, Blake's phone started to reboot itself.

Shit!

Blake resisted the temptation to press any buttons whilst the device performed its start-up operation. His intervention with electronic gadgets always seemed to make things worse. As he stared at the spinning wheel icon on the screen, he tried to imagine what Lukas could possibly have found that necessitated sending a car. He would know quickly enough. As soon as his phone finished booting up, it started ringing again. It was Lukas.

'I'm sorry about that, Lukas. My phone just died.'

'You taking the piss? Mine's just gone as well.' There was a brief silence; then the conversation picked up from where it had left off.

'You're sending a car to the station?' said Blake, 'Why, what have you found?'

'It's hard to explain,' There was a long pause. Blake could hear Milton breathing down the receiver. 'It looks ... satanic.'

CHAPTER 38

'No dogs!' The voice of the security guard patrolling the entrance to the British Library was distinctly unfriendly. The patrolman had joined Portcullis Protection Services following his discharge from the army. He had returned home from his third tour of Afghanistan in a Hercules air transport plane, lying on his back and nursing a fractured pelvis. His injury from an insurgent sniper round had been complicated by the fact that the bullet had come to rest less than a centimetre away from his spine. After several months of convalescence at the army's rehabilitation centre at Headley Court, it had become clear that his days of active service were well and truly over. On hearing of his condition, an ex-sergeant major, who had served with him in the bandit country of Kandahar, managed to pull a few strings and landed him the security job. He started with Portcullis the day after his official discharge from the army. The job posed its own challenges, but it certainly beat dodging bullets from the Taliban.

The only trouble came from the undesirables who would wander the streets searching for a warm place to sleep off a belly full of strong cider, or the after-effects of a crack pipe. He would arrive at the library just before the doors opened to the public at 9.30 a.m. and leave just as the last readers left the building at about 6.00 p.m. The security guard had quickly got to know the names of the regular academics and researchers who would make their daily pilgrimage through the entrance doors of the massive red-brick building.

He stared at the dishevelled female tramp and black stray dog standing in front of him and knew he would never have the desire to know their names. Vagrants only meant one thing: trouble. He caught a strong whiff of something unpleasant and wondered whether it was coming from the woman, the dog or both.

'No dogs allowed in the library. Unless you lose the dog, you won't be able to come in,' said the security guard sternly.

The woman scratched at her matted hair. The guard began to wonder if she might be stoned.

'Unless you are here to use the reading facilities, I will have to move you on. Do you understand?'

Mary tried to force a smile to placate the officious security guard in her path. She had never quite got used to people's reaction to her. The usual combination of fear and loathing towards the homeless was never far from the surface.

'You stay here, boy, Try not bite anyone while I'm gone,' said the woman. She gave the dog a vigorous rub under its chin and shuffled past the security man and through the airport-style metal detector.

'I'll be watching you, madam. Mark my words; any trouble and your feet won't touch the ground.'

The entrance foyer to the library was a wide space opening out into a series of multi-layered terraces. Each terrace served a different function: some housed the astonishing collections of printed material available at the library; some were set aside as dedicated reading rooms; others were filled with computer terminals for online searches; whilst another was used as a business centre. Mary quickly located a sign of the building layout. It showed that the subject area she was interested in was located on one of the upper terraces.

Whilst the escalator took her slowly up to the required level, she could feel the many pairs of eyes following her progress. As she approached the top, she pulled up the hem of her long threadbare skirt and gave a little hop off the moving walkway. The sign that greeted her confirmed she had arrived at the right floor: 'Philosophy & Religion'. Four small arrows beneath the sign guided the visitor to a particular subject area: 'Bibles, Philosophy, Theology, Jewish Studies'. Mary pondered the options for a while, and then followed the modern whitewashed corridor bending off to the right. The notice attached to the double doors at the end of the walkway pronounced that Mary had reached the reading room dedicated to Jewish Studies. Apart from the elderly woman working the desk next to the door, the room was completely empty. To avoid attracting the woman's attention, Mary disappeared amongst the line of shelves that occupied one end of the room.

She eventually found the section entitled 'Non-canonical scriptures', next to the narrow rectangular window at the end of the first line of shelves. Using her finger as a guide, she scanned the titles of the tightly packed volumes. Much to her delight, she hit upon a small scholarly commentary on the Book of Enoch within a matter of seconds. The volume had a stout leather jacket and was no more than 150 pages long. Bonded onto the inside cover was the distinctive raised profile of the computer alarm tag that would set off the metal detectors positioned at all exits of the library. She flicked through the first few blank pages before settling herself on the floor to read the introduction.

The Book of Enoch

Traditionally attributed to Enoch (the great-grandfather of Noah), the Book of Enoch is an important Jewish religious narrative, and it is thought to have been written somewhere between 300 and 100 BCE. Though not part of official Jewish or Christian scriptural cannons, the text has undoubtedly had an important effect on the development of both. Fragments of the Book of Enoch form part of the Dead Sea Scrolls, and the book is referred to in several places in the Christian Bible.

The first Book of Enoch, commonly known as the 'The Book of the Watchers', contains the unsettling account of a group of rebellious angels lusting after human women down on earth. After an unholy pact is struck between them, 200 angels descend onto Mount Hermon in order to take human wives. Rejecting heaven for the carnal delights of human women, the fallen 'Watchers' had crossed over a forbidden boundary. The defiled women bore monstrous children: great giants (the 'Nephilim') and demons of many kinds, which perpetrated despicable sins against God. Mastema, the leader of the demons, transmitted great evil across the earth (see note) ...

Mary snapped the book shut, as if trying to stop the words from escaping into the outside world. She held the book tightly to her chest. At first, Mary tried to resist the urge, but finally she relented. Still sitting cross-legged on the floor and under the cover of two long rows of shelving, she rolled up the sleeve of her coat and looked at the tattoo etched deep into her forearm. Though the lettering was crude and obviously the result of an amateurish procedure, the word was clear enough: 'Mastema'.

It all made sense: the lines linking the churches, the prophecies, and her part in the great unfolding. It all made dreadful sense. She had been chosen.

Out of the blue, she heard the sound of footsteps approaching. Through a small gap between an irregular stack of books, she peered in the direction of the sound. She recognised the owner of the boots immediately. It was the same security guard who had given her a hard time at the library entrance. She guessed that he was now making his rounds and probably trying to locate her in the process. From her vantage point between the books, Mary watched the security guard stop at the librarian's desk. Without diverting her gaze from the large computer screen, the librarian nodded and then pointed in the direction of the book racks. Seeing the approaching danger, Mary worked quickly. Using her thumbnail, she managed to unpick a corner of the inside cover of the book. With several tugs of the now separated corner, she carefully peeled off the paper lining along with the bonded security tag. Sensing that the footsteps were now nearly upon her, she placed the small book inside her coat pocket.

As the security guard turned the corner, he was stopped in his tracks by the sight of the vagrant woman splayed out on the floor.

'Ah, there you are.' His voice managed to combine a sense of relief and disdain. 'About to lie down and have a kip, were you? I don't think so. I told you, any nonsense and you'd be out. Come on, up you get.'

Against his better judgement, the security guard leant forward and offered the homeless woman his arm for support. She took it and used it as an anchor to haul herself to her feet. As the guard steadied himself against the metal shelving, he became aware of the pungent odour wafting from the filthy overcoat wrapped around her body. What he was completely oblivious to, however, was the screwed up ball of paper that had just been dropped into his jacket pocket. Not wanting to aggravate the tramp, he held his breath and corralled her first through the double doors of the reading room and then down into the lobby of the library. Mary noticed that her progress towards the main entrance doors was now being tracked by a number of additional security guards keeping a safe distance behind her.

'I'm going. I'm going. You don't need to see me out. Thank you for your hospitality,' she said sarcastically.

As Mary was about to cross the threshold into the cold air outside, she stopped and turned around. In unison the assembled security team readied themselves for trouble. Instead, the tramp raised her gaze up to the ceiling and genuflected.

'Bless you all!'

With that, she was gone.

The security guard was late home that evening. He had been delayed for over an hour, explaining to his manager how a British Library anti-theft tag had been found in his jacket pocket. The offending tag kept setting off the library's alarm system until a colleague made the correlation between his proximity to the entrance metal detectors and the alarms. As his manager opened the tight ball of paper, he realised that it was, in fact, the cover lining to one of the library's books. A single footnote was printed just above the raised edge of the security device: 'Note: *Mastema*, derived from the Hebrew word *mastemah*, meaning hatred'.

CHAPTER 39

Blake had expected to be greeted with the smell of death, but instead his nostrils were filled with a pungent cocktail of chemical disinfectant and formaldehyde. He tried not to touch anything, imagining plagues of bacteria, viruses and fungi mutating invisibly on every surface.

'Vincent, this is Dr Sullivan, the forensic pathologist.' Milton nodded in the direction of a squat man in his mid-fifties whose cheeks boasted a ruddy complexion that looked conspicuously out of place in a morgue. He and Milton stood on either side of a shiny steel autopsy table. By the shape of the large sheet that hung around its edges, Blake guessed that the table was already occupied.

'I asked Dr Sullivan to delay certain aspects of Vittori's post-mortem until you'd seen the body intact.'

'Intact?' said Blake.

'Once the skin is cut, its form will be lost,' Sullivan answered impatiently. 'We really must get started.'

Blake steadied himself as he imagined the effects of a 0.40-calibre bullet shot in the face at point-blank range. The pathologist lifted back the sheet to expose Vittori's naked body up to the neck.

'My god!' Blake took a few steps forward to get a better view.

'Obviously, it's been photographed from several angles already,' added Milton, in an attempt to break the spell of morbid interest that had come over Blake's face.

'It looks satanic, don't you think? Some kind of sign of the devil?'

'Can I get more light?'

Sullivan tugged gently at a white cord hanging down from the ceiling. Immediately, a block of powerful spotlights lit the cadaver from above and showed the full extent of the tattoo that extended over Vittori's chest.

'I wanted you to see it because I know you've studied these kinds of things before.' Lukas was referring to a case that Blake had spent years trying to forget; a case that had started as an investigation of a break-in at the British Museum and the theft of several wax discs dating back to Elizabethan times. Blake had later discovered that the seemingly innocuous circles of wax had been used for casting spells. The case had ended in the uncovering of a satanic network spread across Greater London.

The design tattooed across Vittori's chest looked distinctly homemade and recent, but the motif was unmistakable: the two overlapping equilateral triangles of the six-pointed star had been carved into the skin. An uneven line of black tattoo ink ran across the corpse's upper body from nipple to nipple. This formed the base of the downward pointing triangle, whose apex terminated at Vittori's navel. The tip of the upward-pointing triangle ended at the very top of the sternum, just below the collar line. Each of the six smaller triangular compartments that formed the outer wings of the star had a single tattooed symbol; each different, but all prominent against the cadaver's white skin.

'God knows what Father Vittori was into, but it looks bad. This devil stuff freaks me out,' said the detective. He took a step away from the body, feeling that although its host had died, the tattoo somehow retained a life-force all of its own.

'What do you make of it?' Milton asked Blake.

Blake was now copying the design of the tattoo as best as he could on the palm of his hand. He studied each of the symbols in turn.

'Lukas, you're right in some respects. This has to do with the devil.'

'I knew it.' Milton started to rock from foot to foot.

'I didn't know you believed in all that,' said Blake.

'My cousin got into some bad shit as a teenager in Jamaica. Really bad things happened; things that couldn't be explained,' said the policeman.

The pathologist looked on as Blake and Milton stared at each other, hoping that they would both soon leave so he could get on with his work.

'Lukas, I don't think this is a symbol of the devil. If I'm not mistaken, this is the Magen David, or the Shield of David. It's meant to *protect* the wearer from the devil. The same design crops up time and time again in Jewish amulets. It's also sometimes referred to as the Seal of Solomon.'

Milton looked blank.

'According to some Jewish legend, the Seal of Solomon was a magical signet ring possessed by King David's son, Solomon, which gave him the power to control demons. I've heard stories of exorcists tattooing this symbol onto their bodies to protect themselves against inhabitation by expelled evil spirits. It looks like Father Vittori might have been concerned for his safety.'

'Well it didn't save him from a bullet through his head,' said Milton. 'And the symbols around the edge?'

'I'm not sure, but some of them are in Hebrew. Email me the photos and I'll have a look at them when I get back to London.'

'Have you gentlemen finished?' asked the pathologist.

Milton threw Sullivan a nod and the pathologist snapped down the visor of his face mask. After selecting the largest scalpel from the trolley stationed next to the wall, Sullivan leant over Vittori's body and made a long vertical incision down the chest.

The seal had been broken.

CHAPTER 40

The Bedford Hotel was located in the middle of North London's fashionable borough of Islington. A friend had recommended it to Sabatini, and on paper it appeared to be good value for money; a rarity for a London hotel. She had made the reservation for her and Nathan to spend several nights there after their visit to Cambridge. They had hoped to do some leisurely sightseeing in the city before flying back to Rome. But since making the reservation several weeks ago, her entire world had collapsed around her.

'And your guest, Mr Vittori, is he checking in with you?' asked the hotel receptionist before her eyes returned to the computer screen.

Sabatini stared up to the lobby ceiling, blinking rapidly and fighting down the emotion rising up from within.

'No, he isn't,' she said finally, her hand squeezing tightly the handle of her trolley bag.

'Not to worry,' said the receptionist, not looking up from the screen. Fingers tapped loudly on the keyboard.

Moments later, Sabatini received her door card key and directions to the lift to her sixth-floor room.

A wall of stifling warm air met Sabatini's face as she entered her room. She opened the window and then ordered a pot of coffee and sandwiches from room service. Carefully, she slid her laptop from her bag and placed it on the small writing desk at the foot of her bed. She opened the computer and its processor began to whir. After calling down to reception for the password to the hotel's Wi-Fi, she settled into her chair and logged into her email account. She picked out several emails from the large number of condolence messages she had received from colleagues, all shocked by the tragic news of Nathan's death. It was all too much. She closed the mail application and clicked open an Internet search browser window.

For a while, she just stared at the empty search panel. Finally she typed in two words, '*Vincent Blake*', and then hit enter. In a fraction of a second, the first page of some half a million possible matches was returned, which she scanned through. The first three pages were mainly entries concerning the messy break-up of a Californian film director, nicknamed *Blakey*, and his glamorous pop star girlfriend, but the last entry in the list stood out from the rest.

Displayed in the short description of its contents was the title of a news article: '*Dr Vincent Blake receives award from the Vatican*'. Sabatini moved the cursor over the web link, quickly pressed the return key and waited for the page to build. Flicking from left to right, Sabatini's eyes scanned the article written two years before.

The latest winner of the Julius Prize was announced on Thursday by the Holy See Press Office. This year's winner was a surprising and somewhat unusual choice. Dr Vincent Blake was honoured today by the Vatican for his role in recovering priceless stolen manuscripts belonging to the Vatican archives in Rome. As reported in the international media, the documents were stolen by a Russian criminal gang whilst in transit from the Vatican archives to a document preservation laboratory in Orvieto. Through his resolute detective work and speedy actions, Dr Blake managed to trace the documents to the United Kingdom. At considerable danger to his own life, Dr Blake tracked down the gang to a cargo plane heading for Saint Petersburg. The plane was stopped by the British authorities on the runway at Heathrow airport and, after a stand-off that lasted more than twenty-four hours, the gang was finally apprehended and the documents recovered.

Dr Blake will be officially presented with the prize next month at a private ceremony in the Vatican City by Cardinal Giuseppe Andretti, President of the Document Committee in Rome. In a Vatican Radio interview, Cardinal Andretti spoke of the committee's reasons for awarding Dr Blake the prestigious prize: '*Through Dr Blake's tireless detective work, priceless documents that have been part of the Vatican's collections for centuries were saved. The award is a tangible way for the Pope to express his thanks. Today, we unfortunately experience multiple threats to the work of the Holy See. For this reason it is very important to constantly acknowledge people who have helped protect the Church's legacy. We are all very grateful to Dr Blake.*

Sabatini scrolled down to the footnote of the article.

Dr Blake has written numerous scholarly articles in the field of document authentication and is also an expert on religious iconography and the history of the Royal Society, Great Britain's learned institute of science. He is the first non-theologian to win the Julius Prize.

A knock at the door jolted Sabatini from her thoughts. She stood up and walked over to the door. After squinting through the spy hole, she opened it and was greeted by a tall French Algerian waiter in a well-worn white jacket who was carrying a large flask of coffee in one hand and balancing a large tray of sandwiches in the other. The hotel attendant deposited the tray and flask on the small luggage table next to the door, requested Sabatini's signature on a slip of paper, and loitered momentarily for a tip. Sabatini obliged on both counts and shut the door firmly behind her.

Quickly Sabatini returned to her laptop and clicked back to the search results. Directly under the news article summary about Blake's Julius Prize was a short description of an obituary.

Nomsa Blake: Obituary
Internationally Respected Human Rights Lawyer
Nomsa Adimu Blake, who died tragically at the age of thirty-eight after a hit-and-run car accident, was an internationally

respected human rights lawyer and academic. She had recently taken up a visiting lectureship at the London School of Economics and was a leading adviser to Amnesty, Africa. Nomsa was a practising barrister and brought many human rights cases before the Europe Commission and Court of Human Rights.

She was born and lived in Bulawayo before moving to the UK to study law at Cambridge. After completing a master's degree in criminology, she joined the Civil Rights Association, of which she became an executive director. None of her high-profile activity diminished Nomsa's commitment to her family and students.

Sadly, the accident that took her life also critically injured her daughter, Sarah.

She is survived by husband Vincent and daughter Sarah.

Sabatini got up from the desk and walked over to the window. As she stared out across the city, her thoughts started to form like the freezing fog gathering over the London rooftops.

CHAPTER 41

Sunday 29 November

'This is a security announcement. Unattended luggage will be removed from the platform and destroyed.' Blake sat in the shopping concourse of London's Paddington railway station sipping his espresso. He liked his coffee piping hot. This particular cup of coffee, however, was rapidly losing its heat in the cold London air, and he decided to abandon it to the vacant table next to his.

He had spent the hour-and-a-half trip back from Cambridge researching the background to the stolen library exhibits and making calls to his contacts in London's antique market. Perhaps one of the fences that owed him a favour might have heard something on the grapevine. It was a long shot, but it was worth a try.

The station was busy and the sound of the passing commuters echoed high in the magnificent glass-and-steel Victorian roof, which covered the fourteen platforms in a single span. He noticed a figure standing perfectly still on the other side of the concourse, like an island in the middle of a fast-flowing river. From where he sat outside the coffee shop, Blake couldn't make out whether the figure was male or female, but he guessed by the state of their clothes that they were sleeping rough. Any of the usual visual clues suggesting the gender of the individual—the curve of the hip, the length of the hair, the size of the frame—were all hidden under layers of shabby clothing. The person was constructing a cigarette from a bag of tobacco and a packet of cigarette papers. From his seat, Blake studied the figure rolling the shredded leaves into a thin uneven tube of paper ready for lighting. Something about the tramp was vaguely familiar. Then, like a footprint on a beach being washed away by a wave, the figure was lost in the crowd of passengers decamping onto the platform from a train that had just arrived.

Blake's mobile began to ring. If he hadn't been expecting a call from Milton, he would have probably ignored it, but Milton was a stickler about people answering the phone, day or night.

'Is that Dr Blake?' said the voice. It belonged to a woman.

'Speaking.' Blake couldn't quite place the voice on the other end of the line.

'Thank goodness! Dr Blake, I need to see you urgently.' The voice took a breath. 'It's Carla Sabatini. I've found something, something of Father Vittori's. I don't know who else to go to.' Sabatini sounded desperate.

'Okay, what exactly have you found?' said Blake.

'I can't really explain. I need to show you. It's very strange; something of great importance.'

'Have you talked to Detective Milton about it?' asked Blake.

'I don't really want to get the police involved. I need to protect the memory and reputation of Brother Nathan.'

'Reputation? What do you mean?'

'Dr Blake, are you a religious person?' asked Sabatini.

'Religious? Is that relevant?'

'It may be,' said Sabatini.

'I used to be, but not anymore.'

'You don't believe in God?'

Blake sighed. He was getting irritated.

'If you mean, do I believe in a god that intervenes in the world, then the answer is no. I haven't seen any evidence of it. I don't want to be rude, but how can I help you?'

'Dr Blake, I believe Nathan had become obsessed with something very dangerous; something that his Holiness would have found abhorrent. If I go to the police, I know it would be over the front pages within hours.'

'Are you still in Cambridge?'

'No, I'm in London. I have a flight tomorrow back to Italy. I am going to see Nathan's sister in Rome to start making funeral arrangements, but I need to see you. I know it's short notice, but can I meet you this afternoon?'

Slightly taken aback, Blake tried to remember his appointments for the day. He could possibly meet Sabatini after his visit to Sarah at the hospital.

'Okay, how about two o'clock? There's a pub close to where I live ...' Blake immediately corrected himself, 'where I *used* to live. It's quiet and I know the landlady. We'll be able to talk undisturbed. It's called the Jerusalem Tavern, close to Farringdon Tube Station. I'll text you the address.'

'The Jerusalem Tavern?' said Sabatini strangely.

'Yes, is that okay?' said Blake.

'Yes, that's fine. Thank you so much.'

'Okay, I'll see you later,' said Blake before terminating the call.

Blake sat back in his chair and gazed blankly across the station concourse. Before long, he started to get an unsettled feeling that he was being watched. He spun around in his chair to locate the source of his unease.

Despite being some distance away, the eyes that finally met his from across the busy platform made the hairs on the back of his neck stand up. The vagrant that he had spotted minutes before was now staring directly at him, the face vacant and absolutely still. Blake became aware that the shadows around the figure were shifting as the clouds outside moved across the sun. Like a giant spotlight being turned on from above, an area of the station concourse was illuminated in brilliant sunlight. A disc of light travelled quickly across the platform floor as the clouds were blown across the sky high above the glass roof. Blake watched as the floor surrounding the vagrant became bathed in sunlight. As the perimeter of the white disc passed over the vagrant's body, the network of tattoos covering the person's forearms became visible. As quickly as the sun had appeared from behind the clouds, it was lost again. So was the vagrant ... lost in the crowd.

Blake twisted around on his chair to locate the tramp, but failed to spot her. He thought for a moment and then dialled Milton's number. The line took a long while to connect. Finally, Milton's deep baritone voice echoed in Blake's earpiece.

'Milton.'

'Lukas, it's Vincent' said Blake.

'You got anything for me? Any leads on that watch?' asked Milton without pausing for breath.

'I'm still looking into it.'

'You'd better hurry up. I need it back tomorrow. The library is getting twitchy about it being away. Not that they know how to secure their exhibits by the look of those display cabinets they had in there,' said the detective. 'One thing though, I just got a call from the forensics boys. It looks like they might be able to enhance a couple of CCTV pictures taken in Dover. We might yet get a mug shot of the bastard who killed those immigration officers.'

'Okay, that's good ... that's good,' said Blake. 'Anyway, the reason I called is that I wanted to let you know about the design of the tattoo on the priest's chest.'

'Go on,' said Milton.

'I was right. It's the Seal of Solomon. It's a talisman. The design is meant to give the wearer protection against evil forces. The seal is formed by two interlocking triangles, the top one representing the Trinity in heaven and the bottom one the Trinity working on earth. It shows that changes in one world can be reflected in the other.'

'Okay, anything else?' said Milton.

'Yes, there is something. You remember that the priest had carved symbols in the spaces formed between the triangles?'

'Some kind of magic writing, right?' said Milton.

'Many people believe in the power of written or spoken words. The symbols tattooed on Nathan Vittori's body are very unusual.'

'Unusual? In what way?'

'They're Aramaic: the language spoken by Christ.'

'What do they say?' asked Milton.

'You need to understand that seals of this type are always inscribed with words specific to their purpose. It's a prayer to God, asking for protection against a specific evil force.' Blake paused.

'What evil force?'

'A specific demon stalking the earth.'

'Right,' Milton's voice sounded incredulous. 'And this demon ... does it have a name?'

'Yes ... Mastema.'

CHAPTER 42

Blake waited for the Filipina nurse to finish her usual checks of Sarah's ventilator. After diligently adding another column of small ticks to the bottom of the patient chart, she smiled her goodbye and quickly left the hospital room. As the door clicked shut, Blake walked over to the chart at the end of Sarah's bed and started to idly thumb through its pages.

Blake had tried to sleep on the train back from Cambridge, but his swirling thoughts wouldn't let him settle. The Drakon had struck again: another person brutally murdered, all because of some dusty exhibits that once belonged to a scientist who had been dead for nearly 300 years. All roads led back to the Drakon: Nomsa's killing, Sarah's coma, the four Newton robberies, and the dead bodies that lay in their wake. Whilst his mind drifted in and out of semi-consciousness and his head tapped gently against the window of the railway carriage, something had become sealed deep in his being, as if the darkness shrouding his life had become illuminated by the possibility of nailing the Drakon for good.

An announcement on the hospital's public address system caused Blake to return Sarah's patient chart to the hanger at the foot of her bed. Before sitting down, he took a small bottle from his pocket: the bottle of nail varnish that Nomsa bought Sarah the day of the hit and run, and the same one that had dropped out from the packing case a couple of days before. Blake pushed his chair next to his daughter's bed and strained to unscrew the top of the bottle. Finally, it gave way. The smell of solvent vapours quickly filled his nostrils.

He placed the nail varnish bottle carefully down on the side of the bed, leant over, and brought Sarah's hand close to his chest. Though the room temperature was stiflingly warm, Sarah's fingers felt cold, like the surface of a marble statue. Gently he tried to spread out his daughter's contorted fingers on the white cotton sheets of the bed, but as soon as he removed the slight pressure of his hand, they quickly returned to their original twisted configuration. Unperturbed, he dipped the thin brush into the bottle and, after wiping away the excess liquid, began to paint Sarah's little finger. Tiny flecks of silver glitter suspended within the bright blue lacquer sparkled under the strong ceiling lights of the hospital room. Once Blake had finished with the little finger, he repositioned the angle of Sarah's hand on the bed and moved onto the next. Minutes later, all of Sarah's finger nails were painted in electric blue.

There you go, my darling, just a year late.

Blake moved in his chair and felt something hard dig into his back. Shifting his weight to the side, he tried to locate the offending article in his jacket hung over the back of the chair. He quickly found the object and, after slipping it out of the police evidence bag, placed it next to the bottle of nail varnish at the edge of Sarah's bed. Blake studied Newton's pocket watch sitting proudly like a silver egg on a nest of white cotton hospital sheets.

After several moments, he picked up the smooth pebble-like object and placed it in his open hand. Somehow its dimensions fitted perfectly into the curve of his palm as if had been designed specifically for that purpose. Turning the pocket watch over onto its reverse side, he traced a slow line around its perimeter with his fingertip and felt the raised lettering that he had discovered during his interview of Sabatini and Jenkins. *What did Sabatini say about the three tiny inscriptions? References to Bible verses that, according to Sabatini, Father Vittori had become obsessed with.*

Blake recalled Sabatini's look when she had offered up this piece of information. The muscles of her face had turned rigid, her features frozen in an expression of deep concern. Blake leant forward and reached out to the wooden cabinet at the head of the bed. He opened its simple drawer to locate the Gideon Bible that he had placed there before. He removed it from the drawer and opened it on his lap. Next he retrieved a pen from his jacket.

Using the blank inside cover of the bible as notepaper, Blake copied down the three tiny symbols inscribed on the outer perimeter of the timepiece: *D7.25, D12.7* and *R12.14.* Keeping one finger inside the front cover of the bible, he quickly flicked through the pages until he found the first reference.

> *Daniel 7:25. He will speak against the Most High and oppress his saints and try to change the set times and laws. The saints will be handed over to him for a time, times and half a time.*

He read the verse and then reread it, pausing on each small section, searching for meaning within its words. Flicking back to the text as he did so, Blake faithfully transcribed the verse onto the inside front cover with his pen. The next reference, chapter 12, verse 7, was located just two pages further along in the bible. By the time he had transcribed the second reference from the book of Daniel onto the inside front cover, a pattern had become visible.

> *Daniel 12:7. The man clothed in linen, who was above the waters of the river, lifted his right hand and his left hand to heaven, and I heard him swear who lives forever, saying 'It will be for a time, times and half a time ...'*

Quickly, his fingers pulled at the thin pages to find the third reference located in Revelation, the final apocalyptic book of the Bible.

> *Revelation 12:14. The woman was given the two wings of a great eagle, so that she might fly to the place prepared for her in the desert, where she would be taken care of for a time, times and half a time out of the serpent's reach.*

As Blake read out each verse in turn, the pattern screamed off the page.

A time, times and half a time. What the hell did that mean? Why would Newton have commissioned someone to engrave these particular verses onto his pocket watch?

As Blake stared at the impenetrable scriptures, his fingers ran over the thin furrows made by his pen tip on the soft cardboard cover of the bible. He searched his mind for inspiration, but nothing came. After five minutes of trying to find a way into the hidden meaning of the verses, he abandoned the endeavour, stood up and walked over to window. Before long he was pacing around Sarah's bed. After several circumnavigations, he stopped. Standing perfectly still in the middle of the room, Blake started repeating the phrase common to all three verses over and over again like a mantra. *A time, times and half a time. A time, times and half a time. A time, times and half a time* ...

Blake's eyes widened. He scooped up the pocket watch from the bed and started to examine the winder at the top of the timepiece. Pinching the winder stem between his thumb and forefinger, he gently pulled the crown several millimetres upwards, releasing the winding mechanism with a click and resetting both hands of the clock to the twelve o'clock position. *Could this be the meaning?* Blake carefully wound the stem through one full rotation, its completion marked by the sound of a click originating deep within the mechanism. He looked at the open white face and saw that its thin black hands were now displaying one o'clock exactly. *Okay, that's a time, and now for the times.* He inhaled deeply and held his breath as he rotated the winder stem through two full revolutions. As before, the full extent of the movement was pronounced with a clear click just as the minute hand reached the vertical position. The dial now displayed a time of three o'clock precisely. *And now for half a time.* Keeping the face of the pocket watch in view, Blake now rotated the winder stem through a half a turn. As the delicate minute hand greeted the Roman numeral number six at the bottom of the face, some internal mechanism released, causing the back case of the watch to spring open. Startled by the unexpected movement, Blake nearly lost grip on the pocket watch, his shaking hand dislodging something from inside the timepiece.

He watched in slow motion as a square piece of folded paper fell onto Sarah's bed like a leaf falling from a tree.

CHAPTER 43

The cavernous space echoed to the sounds of straining ropes and a body moving quickly through the air. Like a self-propelled pendulum, the man on the trapeze increased his momentum with every swing until his body was raised high above the step-off board. The wires supporting the trapeze rig strained under the weight of fifteen stones of bone and muscle pulling against it. As the man reached the bottom of the arc, he kicked his legs forward and injected even more speed into the long sweep of the trapeze. Again his body passed the step-off board, the sinews in his forearms relaxing momentarily before gravity once again pulled him downwards. At the bottom of the swing, Denic kicked his legs forward and let go of the bar. Grabbing his knees with his hands, he executed a tight somersault before landing perfectly on the net.

The old Shoreditch Electric Light Station had been designed to generate electricity for the needs of the local community. Powered by the burning of local refuse, its turbines had turned from 1896 until its demise in the second half of the twentieth century. The large industrial halls that had once housed the power plant's generation and combustion equipment had stood derelict for more than forty years until they had been saved and converted into one of the best circus schools in Europe. The full-size trapeze rig occupied one end of the vast generating hall.

Denic grabbed hold of the edge of the safety net and dismounted the apparatus. Crossland was waiting for him next to his blue kitbag.

'You should try it, Max. It would do wonders for your back,' said Denic. Crossland had sustained a compression fracture during a low-altitude drop over Baghdad, and from time to time it burned like a shrapnel wound.

'Sarge, I came as fast as I could. We've got some serious trouble. I guess you haven't seen the Drakon's latest message?' Denic's face turned

THE HISTORY OF THINGS TO COME

serious as he shook open the neatly folded towel lying between the worn leather handles of his kitbag.

'The Drakon? What's going on?' He patted his brow, but as soon as the towel left his forehead a new constellation of sweat droplets had appeared.

'If we fuck this up, we're going to end up with a bullet in our heads. You saw what happened to Vinka. Fuck!'

Without saying another word, Crossland handed over his secure satellite phone and watched his comrade study the message displayed on the screen.

URGENT!
JOB INCOMPLETE!
The priest switched the pocket watch with a fake. Get the original. Currently in possession of Dr Vincent Blake; address to be sent separately. The pocket watch is likely to be returned to the police within the next 24 hours. Locate it immediately.
NO LOOSE ENDS!
Drakon

CHAPTER 44

Mary's eyes were shut and her eyeballs moved rapidly beneath her eyelids, as if she were caught in a dream. The source of the line of dark energy travelling from the church stationed at the riverbank was now directly under her feet. Feeling the loose sand shifting in the Thames tide, she tried to steady herself by shifting her stance. For a second she couldn't move, as the mud under the thin layer of surface sand was sucking her down and refusing to submit to her movements. She began to rock from side to side, pulling her legs upwards as if marching on the spot. With each stride she was able to move a little more, until eventually she broke the vacuum and freed her legs. Squatting ankle-deep in the freezing water, Mary clawed at the area around her submerged feet, transforming the once-clear water into a cloud of brown sediment. She made a long sweep under the water with her right arm and then stopped. The dark silt oozed through Mary's frozen fingers as the morning tide of the Thames exerted its irresistible pull back out to sea. Despite being numbed by the cold, she could feel something hard scraping against her fingernails. Her eyes opened wide as if startled from her dream, and she shouted back to the black dog lying patiently on the wharf steps. The dog rose to its feet in anticipation of something about to happen. Another slight swell and then the waters surrounding her feet were quickly drawn away.

First, the outline of a rectangular block of stone became visible through the cloud of silt, followed by several lines of lettering. Mary stopped moving her hands and allowed the sediment to clear. Gradually, the black words of an inscription became clear:

'And the great dragon was cast out, that old serpent, called the Devil, and Satan, which deceiveth the whole world: he was

cast out into the earth, and his angels were cast out with him.'
Revelation 12:9.

From the shore Mary's screams were clearly audible against the lapping sound of the water and the frenzied barks of the black dog nearby. Another swell of water and the inscription disappeared once again under a cloud of black sediment.

It took several minutes for Mary to drag herself up the mud bank to the steps leading to the wharf. During that time, a pretty Indian girl about seven years old had squeezed herself next to the black dog on the third step of the jetty. She was insulated from the cold wind by a thick coat, jeans and a pair of dark brown boots, and she began to whisper to the animal as she slowly stroked its long matted hair. Mary strained a smile at the young girl and beckoned her to join her on the lowest step. The child accepted the invitation and shuffled her bottom down the stairs.

'Is this your dog?' the girl asked, her wide eyes forming perfect black circles against the whites of her eye.

'The dog has no owner,' Mary replied in a gentle voice. 'We have been best friends for a very long time.'

'Hmmm.' The girl thought carefully about what Mary had said and then tightened her scarf around neck.

'Have you been paddling?'

Mary nodded and pulled on the sheepskin gloves that she kept in the pockets of her outer coat. She possessed three coats, and today she was wearing all of them.

'It's too cold to paddle,' said the girl.

Mary smiled back at the girl.

'You're right. It is very cold, brrrrrrr,' said Mary.

'What are those things?' The girl pointed to the black symbols tattooed on Mary's feet.

Mary focused on the blue aura pulsing around the girl's head and whispered, 'They tell me where I've been, and guide me to where I'm going. Can I ask your name?'

'Noorjehan,' answered the girl, adding. 'It means "light of the world".'

Mary nodded.

'Why were you shouting?' asked the girl.

'Oh, I'm sorry. I didn't mean to frighten you. I followed a line of energy from that church over on the bank to an energy centre out there in the river. It was very strong dark energy.'

'Those marks on your feet, are they to do with the energy?' asked the girl, her face turning curious.

Mary nodded. 'It's my map. It shows me where the good and dark energy is.'

From behind the railings bordering the wharf, angry shouts broke the sanctity of the moment.

'Noorjehan, get here this very second! I've been worried sick!'

Even hidden under her layers of clothing, Mary could detect the shrug of Noorjehan's shoulders.

'That's my mum. I've got to go.'

'Before you go, let me bless you.'

Mary leant forward and touched the girl's forehead with the still wet tip of her finger.

'Noorjehan, *you will be* the light of the world.'

CHAPTER 45

With his ear to the door, Blake's landlord strained to listen above the constant drone of traffic passing close by. He had been waiting outside the basement flat for less than thirty seconds, but he had already become impatient. He stepped away from the door and peered through the small crack between the curtains of the window, his hands square to his forehead as if he were looking out to sea. Slowly, his vision became accustomed to the shadowy interior. Even in the gloom, the bedsit looked a mess, with packing cases strewn across the floor. It was the sight not only of the disorder but also the Panasonic music system perched on the kitchen sink that strengthened the landlord's resolve to act. *So you think you can treat my house like a bloody landfill site, do you? Right then, it's about time I took a deposit in lieu of your rental arrears, and that music system will do very nicely.*

Glancing over his shoulder, he unclipped the large ring of keys from his belt and searched for the silver Yale key that fitted the lock. Still unsure whether his tenant was sleeping soundly under the duvet heaped by the side of the bed, he turned the key gently, eased the door open and waited by the threshold, listening out for signs of life. Nothing stirred and he stepped inside.

The door slammed shut behind him as if caught by a sudden gust of wind. Before his brain could compute the origin of the changing shadows to his right, the landlord felt a crushing pain at the side of his face. His legs buckled and he crashed to the floor.

Crossland looked down at his captive's moaning body and wiped the blood from the handle of his pistol.

CHAPTER 46

The ground floor of the Jerusalem Tavern was comprised of five separate rooms, each decorated in wood panelling and faded paintwork on which hung a hotchpotch of paintings, framed cartoons and newspaper cuttings. Running down the entire length of the largest room was a well-stocked bar. There were slightly too many wooden tables and chairs set out for the space available, forcing Blake to weave a zigzag route to the bar.

Blake smiled at the landlady pulling a pint at the bar and waited for the drink to be handed over to an expectant customer before he started talking.

'How you doin', Frida?' Blake didn't wait for a reply before continuing. 'A pint of the usual, when you have a moment.'

'Vincent, it's good to see you. You've been a stranger. I thought you'd disappeared.'

The landlady of the Jerusalem Tavern was a chirpy forty-four-year-old woman with a deep tan that contrasted with the pallid skin of most of her customers. She had a wide face with high cheekbones, and along the top of her left eyebrow was the faint trace of a scar. Instead of violating the symmetry of her face, the blemish seemed somehow to enhance her appearance.

'Yes, I've been away,' said Blake.

The landlady began to pull a pint of brown frothy ale from the hand pump.

'I'm meeting a lady here, but I'm a bit late. Have you seen anyone?'

Frida's eyebrows raised inquisitively.

'No, it's not like that,' said Blake.

'I see,' replied Frida playfully. She delivered Blake's pint to the bar. 'There's a woman in the snug sitting by herself. She's been there for half an hour or so.' The landlady nodded to the open doorway at the other end of the bar.

Sabatini sat alone behind one of the three wooden tables that occupied the small side room of the Jerusalem Tavern. Clasped in her hand was a simple silver crucifix. Brother Nathan had given it to her at the airport as a thank-you gift for organising the trip to Cambridge. She was squeezing it tightly when Blake walked into the room.

'Dr Blake, thank goodness you're here,' said Sabatini.

'Please, call me Vincent.'

Sabatini forced a smile. 'Okay, then please call me Carla.'

She looked exhausted and, by the redness around her eyes, Blake guessed she had been crying.

'I'm sorry I'm late. Can I get you a drink?' said Blake.

The small remnants of ice floating in the glass of water in front of her confirmed that Sabatini had been there for quite some time.

'No, no, thank you,' said Sabatini.

Blake sat down opposite Sabatini and took a small sip of his drink.

'What can I do for you?' asked Blake.

'Vincent, before I start, you need to understand the implications of what I am about to show you.'

Blake was disorientated by the intensity of her expression.

'I understand you were brought up in the Faith.'

Sabatini was now staring directly into Blake's eyes.

'Please forgive me, Carla, but that was then. Things have changed. I think we've talked about this before.'

'You mean because of your wife and daughter?' said Sabatini.

The corners of Blake's mouth dropped like a guillotine.

'I don't want to be rude, Carla, but that's a private matter.' Blake felt slightly embarrassed by the directness of her question and the terseness of his response.

'I didn't mean to offend you,' she said. 'What I mean is that you understand the work of the Church and what it means to millions of people.'

'I don't follow,' said Blake.

'What I'm about to show you must remain completely confidential. You must understand that Brother Nathan was a good man. He was a second father to me.'

Sabatini opened up the leather handbag resting on her lap and took out a red book. She handed it to him.

'Brother Nathan dropped this in my car on our journey up to Cambridge.'

Blake gave the volume a cursory external examination. 'What is it?' he said.

'It's the reason why Nathan was murdered and the reason for the robbery.' She had Blake's attention.

'I had my suspicions that things hadn't been quite right with Nathan for the past few weeks. He'd been acting rather strangely in the run-up to his visit to Cambridge. When I heard from a mutual friend at the library that he had started to miss morning mass, I wondered if his angina had been troubling him again.'

'Go on,' said Blake.

'Then he started ringing me, time and time again, about the arrangements for our trip. I remember he sounded very preoccupied, almost nervous. He desperately wanted to examine the Newton exhibits with his own hands. I knew that his old colleagues at the library were arranging a dinner for him for his seventieth birthday, so I originally scheduled the trip for early in the New Year, but he was insistent. He wanted to come to Cambridge at the earliest opportunity. Now I understand the reason for his urgency.' Fighting back the tears, Sabatini motioned for Blake to start reading.

Blake rested the spine of the vivid red book in the palm of his hand. It was no bigger than a small paperback, with a cover of crimson velvet. Unusually, for a book of such obvious antiquity, the velvet cover was in excellent condition, as was the elaborate golden border that ran around its perimeter. However, what caught Blake's attention, more than its physical condition, was the strange hexagram design on its cover; the same design had been cut into Brother Nathan's chest at the mortuary. He opened the book and with a gentle puff of breath carefully separated the delicate leaves. Quietly he made a cursory examination of its contents.

It appeared that each facing page was written in elaborate gold lettering, the language an almost impenetrable mix of medieval French and Hebrew. Periodically, the writing was interspersed with a series of strange symbols, probably alchemical in design. On the opposite pages was a narration written in neat copperplate lettering. Though very small in dimension, each word could be easily made out. Blake recognised Newton's handwriting immediately. Without asking Sabatini for confirmation, he started reading.

Thirty minutes later, Sabatini felt ready to explode with anticipation. Since reading the crimson notebook, she had been consumed by the revelation contained within its pages and had longed to share its existence and burden with another person. She hovered at Blake's side, waiting for his eyes to reach the bottom of each delicate page before turning to the next, longing him to reach the end of the dense copperplate narrative. Blake read on in complete silence. Finally, he reached the last page, Newton's handwritten commentary eventually taking the form of a perfect equilateral triangle.

In the narrow compass of this writing, I have set down the history of my actions. I have concealed Gérard de Ridefort's map showing the location of the holy rod in the hope that a righteous man will use it well. Only God can search hearts of men and discover the truth, and to Him it must be left. I pray to God, that He gives you the grace to make the right use of it. It is a treasure greater than all the conquests of Alexander and the Caesars; for these are mere trifles compared to the power of the rod.

I have taken from this book the map revealing the rod's location in the great Cathedral of St Paul's and hidden it until the chosen time. For the parts of Prophecy are like the separated parts of a watch. They appear confused and must be compared and put together before they can be useful. Descend

*the eighty-eight steps and unlock the stone door, as all will be
revealed in a time, times and half a time.*

Jeova Sanctus Unus

Sabatini looked down at her hand. As she unclenched her fist, her
face grimaced from the pain now throbbing in her palm. She had been
grasping Brother Nathan's silver cross so tightly that it had punctured
her skin. As she slowly opened her hand, she saw that a small pool of
blood had collected in the well of her palm.

CHAPTER 47

Blake's landlord tensed his body in a supreme effort to free his arms and legs from their restraints, but he quickly realised that his struggle was hopeless. At first, he questioned whether he was actually dreaming, but the pain blazing across his jaw and the overpowering metallic taste of blood on his tongue gave him no doubt. Though his eyes were now fully open, he could see nothing except for the smallest shaft of light coming up from an area around his neck. All of a sudden he felt as if he were suffocating, and panic took hold of his body. He started to shake violently, his wrists and ankles straining against an unyielding force. He tried to scream out, but the pain in his jaw exploded with an excruciating intensity. In all but near darkness, tears and sweat began to stream down his face.

Hearing a sound to his left, the landlord froze. His senses strained to lock onto the noise that appeared to be moving slowly towards him. Then the backs of his hands felt a rush of wind before a massive crash detonated close by. The shock of the sound sent the captive into a fit of uncontrollable sobbing, his brain unable to cope with the sudden jolts of sensory input. Another sound, this time moving behind him, shook him back to his senses. He tried to slow his breathing and avoid visualizing what was happening around him. For a second, all was perfectly still and then his eyes were filled with a brilliant white light. Blinded, he tried to raise his hands, but no matter how hard he struggled to get them free, they remained pinned to the armrest of the chair.

Slowly unscrewing his eyes, the landlord became aware of his surroundings. His vision quickly resolved the diffuse shape in front of him into the outline of a large man. For the first time he could see the nature of his restraints. His wrists and ankles had been bound to the chair with electrical insulation tape. Again, he jerked his body in an attempt to set himself free, but this only had the effect of tightening the tape even further.

'There's no point in struggling,' said the figure.

Squinting, the prisoner looked up at the man towering above him. The man was swinging a thick white and red canvas sack, about the size of a cushion, close to his face. 'Any more and I'll tape your mouth up and put this back on your head.'

Struggling to focus on the object in front of him, he slowly followed the movement of the sack like a patient following a hypnotist's watch. It took him a short while to register that the crimson colour that permeated the sack fibres was still damp, its surface giving off a dark glossy sheen. The moment he realised that the pigment was in fact his own blood, sheer terror took hold of his body. His chair began to shake.

Why? Why is this happening? His mind raced, trying to find a connection that would provide an answer to this unfolding nightmare. *He had taken the law into his own hands a few times, but business was business.* The landlord tried to avert his gaze from the face of the man now standing just a metre from his sweat-drenched body.

'Look at me. Look at me!' shouted the man, his voice full of menace. The landlord complied with the instruction as best as he could, but as he slowly raised his head to meet the eyeline of his persecutor, the vision in his right eye started to blur. 'You have something I want and I can assure you, I will get it. Do you understand?'

A glimmer of recognition quickly solidified in the landlord's mind. *The Albanians!* The previous month, the landlord had to evict an Albanian family from one of the flats upstairs. They hadn't been able to keep up with their rent payments and had been causing trouble. Waiting until the family of four had left the flat, he and a hired hand from the betting shop had set about changing the locks and clearing the premises of their possessions, but not before helping themselves to anything of value. He might have used a little too much force, but they owed him and he wasn't going to stand around while they took the piss. *They've set the Albanian mafia on me ... all for a crappy camera and a handful of old jewellery.*

Grabbing a handful of the target's hair, Crossland yanked his head back, causing an agonising scream to echo around the walls of the bedsit. The cause of the pain was obvious. The handle of Crossland's pistol had done a lot more than incapacitate his target; it had shattered the right side of his jaw, leaving it hanging limply as if he had just suffered a stroke. A long pendulum of dark red slaver swung from the end of his chin. Crossland moved closer, his lips now almost touching the target's ear.

'Listen to me very carefully. I know who you are and that you are working for the police. I know what you have in your possession. We can do this quickly or slowly, and rest assured, I can cause you an unimaginable amount of pain.' Crossland tilted his head slightly and gently blew on the side of the landlord's cheek. Pain ricocheted through his eye socket.

Crossland's demeanour turned even more threatening.

'Where is the watch?' he said. 'Have you given it back to the police?'

The landlord tried to answer, but his shattered jaw mutated his words into a series of incomprehensible grunts. Crossland shouted the question again, his mouth now inches away from his hostage's face. Again his prisoner tried to answer, but now he was fighting desperately for breath. With every shallow intake of air he could feel a pressure, like a band of steel, tighten around his chest and move down his left arm. A series of violent tremors convulsed through his body like powerful waves smashing onto a beach. With each intense shock, his hands writhed against their restraints, the tape cutting deep into his wrists. The pain in his chest was unbearable. He tried to scream, but he didn't have enough breath in his lungs. The landlord could feel a pressure building in his head, as if his brain were expanding against the rigid walls of his skull. He started to see shooting lines of colours. There was a feeling of momentary release and then a burning sensation between his eyes, as if a trail of gunpowder had been lit deep within his brain and was now burning a channel of white-hot phosphorus through his head, consuming everything in its path. The landlord's last conscious thought was a memory of his mother cutting his father's hair, before everything turned a terrifying black.

Crossland knew exactly what had just occurred. He had seen it happen enough times during periods of interrogation at the internment facilities in Baghdad. Heart attacks were an unfortunate risk of enhanced interrogation techniques, but the timing of this one couldn't have been worse. Although he had spent the last couple of hours turning the flat upside down, the pocket watch wasn't in his possession.

In sheer frustration, Crossland launched the heel of his biker boot onto the side of the chair, sending it and the landlord's body crashing to the floor. There was now only one thing to do. Walking over the scattered contents of several upturned packing cases, Crossland headed towards the kitchen area. From the sink he retrieved a blue petrol canister. As he hauled it against himself, the weight of the canister shifted from side to side like a boat listing in a heavy sea.

Even before he had unscrewed the black plastic cap from its nozzle, the sickly sweet smell of petrol swirled around his head. He stood over the corpse. It stared back up at him, its face frozen with terror. Crossland stepped forward and raised his right foot just a few inches above the dead man's face. Then with a twisting motion of his boot heel, he prised open the lips to form a gaping yawn. Slowly he tilted the fuel can and watched a stream of petrol flow into the landlord's open mouth, as though he were a parched man drinking under a waterfall. Almost immediately the mouth was full and petrol spilled out from its sides, soaking the carpet underneath. Heaving the canister from side to side, Crossland sent out long lines of liquid fuel around the bedsit, first following the back perimeter of the room and then across the centre of the old mattress that was now pushed up against the far wall.

He would have less than a couple of minutes before the first signs of the fire would be noticeable in the flat above. It would have been a lot sooner had he not removed the battery from the old smoke detector that was hanging forlornly from the ceiling. Once the fire was underway, he would stroll calmly to the motorbike parked in the neighbouring street and would soon be lost in the London traffic. With a flick of the wrist he struck a match and tossed it onto the corpse, instantly igniting its petrol-soaked woollen jumper. The pale blue flames quickly enveloped the body, and Crossland watched the loops of electrical tape binding the landlord's body evaporate under the building heat. Free from its physical restraints, the burning corpse slumped forward onto the floor as if it were still alive. Crossland lit another match, tossed it onto the mattress and closed the front door behind him.

By the time Milton had picked up his mobile phone from his locker at the Fitzroy Lodge Boxing Club, it displayed eight missed calls. With sweat still streaming down his face from twenty minutes of hard sparring, he listened gravely to the first recorded message. Before it had finished playing, Milton was sprinting to the car park. Five minutes later, he and two patrol cars were speeding to Blake's bedsit address.

The driver of the leading squad car needn't have punched the postcode into his vehicle's satellite navigation system. The plume of smoke could be seen from miles around.

CHAPTER 48

Blake rested the crimson notebook on his lap and stared up at Sabatini. He was speechless. A tidal wave of questions had just broken into his mind, and his brain was reeling to stay afloat. Sabatini moved her chair closer to his.

'*Jeova Sanctus Unus*: One Holy God. It's the pseudonym that Newton used in his secret alchemic writings. It's an anagram of the Latinised version of his name: *Jsaacus Neuvtonus,*' said Sabatini.

Blake just nodded, still unable to form a sentence for himself.

'Brother Nathan found the book as part of an auction lot that the Vatican purchased in 1936 from Sotheby's, here in London. Inside the back cover is the library's catalogue stamp. It's dated 1936,' said Sabatini. Blake opened the back cover and recognised the faded outline of the Vatican's crossed-keys coat of arms printed in pale blue ink. As he studied the imprint, he noticed that the last page of the volume had been ripped out, leaving a jagged edge close to the binding. Blake moved restlessly in his seat.

'I'm convinced that Nathan wanted to come to Cambridge to examine Newton's pocket watch. You see the sentence *"For the parts of Prophecy are like the separated parts of a watch"*. He must have believed that it somehow held the secret to the rod's location in St Paul's Cathedral.'

Blake's head was swimming. 'Hold on,' he protested, trying to slow Sabatini's exposition. 'You think it was the watch the gang was after too?' said Blake.

'It must have been. There was something that Nathan said in the library just before he was shot. It confused me at the time, but now I understand. He shouted it to the man who shot him. He said, "I won't allow you to take *it* from this place." There were lots of exhibits in the case, but he shouted *it,* not *them.* He knew exactly what they were after, because he was after the same thing.'

'You think that the rod is real and in London?' Blake tried to talk quietly. 'You mean the rod of Aaron, the brother of Moses, the first High Priest of the Israelites? You think that his rod, the one talked about in the Bible, the one God bestowed with miraculous powers, is actually buried somewhere under St Paul's?' said Blake. The lines running across his forehead had now formed into deep furrows. 'You mean the same rod that performed miracles in front of the Pharaoh of Egypt, during the ten plagues of the Exodus?'

'Vincent, since finding the notebook I've done nothing else but think about it,' said Sabatini. 'Tradition says that the rod bore the inscription of the Tetragrammaton, the ineffable name of the God of Israel, along with a word constructed from the ten Hebrew initials of the ten great plagues. This was the inscription that Newton writes about in the notebook. I'm sure of it. According to the scriptures, the holy staff was given to King David and then passed on to his descendants. The rod was used as a royal sceptre by successive Davidic kings and kept in the Ark of the Covenant in the holy temple. Later traditions assert that in order to protect it from the enemies of Israel, King Josiah concealed the rod within the Temple compound, and from that moment on, its whereabouts have remained unknown, until ...'

Blake finished her sentence for her. 'Until today.'

'Gérard de Ridefort was elected Grand Master of the Templars immediately after the consecration of the Temple Church and St John's, here in London. He must have known of the rod's existence and the mission to bring it to London for safe keeping.' There followed a long silence. Sabatini's heart had already accepted the physical existence of the holy relic and now she could feel her reason being drawn to the same incredible conclusion.

'Hold on,' said Blake, 'I haven't been to church for a long time, but you think that this object *actually* exists? Come off it! You mean some magical staff that actually performs the will of God?' Blake took a large swig of his beer. 'You know this thing was meant to have transformed itself into a snake and then swallowed the wands of the Pharaoh's magicians? Oh yes, not to mention it mystically blossomed and then bore fruit in the Tabernacle. It's all religious mumbo-jumbo.'

'I know it sounds incredible, but how do you account for *this?*' Blake looked at Sabatini, who was now holding the crimson notebook in her hand. 'Don't you see? It all makes sense.'

'What exactly makes sense?' Blake fell back into his chair.

'The Star of David. Wren realigning the axis of St Paul's. The crusader knights. The Peasants' Revolt. Newton's obsession with the Temple ... it all makes sense.'

'Slow down, slow down. Can you explain all that to me again, one step at a time?' said Blake.

Sabatini placed the small metal cross onto the table. 'The hexagram of the Star of David only came into common usage as a symbol of Judaism around the seventeenth century. Its origins have always been shrouded in mystery. Some have postulated that the motif derives from the design of medieval Jewish protective amulets, but the notebook suggests a different genesis.'

'I'm sorry, Carla, I didn't read anything about the Star of David. Did I miss something?' Blake could feel himself getting annoyed. It had already been a long day and it was still only mid-afternoon.

'The Star of David is composed of two interlocking equilateral triangles. According to Newton, each triangle represents the location of three churches: the churches of the Old Jerusalem—Temple Mount, the Holy Sepulchre and the old crusader cathedral of St James—interlocked with the three churches of the New Jerusalem here in London—St Paul's Cathedral, Temple Church and the ruins of the Priory of St John. I did some research last night, and the earliest known record of the Star of David comes from a late twelfth century Jewish prayer book; the very time of the consecration of the crusader churches. I've mapped the position of each of the churches on my computer, and they form a perfect equilateral triangle. The pub we are in now is only several hundred metres from the foundations of the Priory of St John. It's strange that it is called the *Jerusalem* Tavern, don't you think?'

Blake felt like the wind had been sucked out of his lungs.

'After the Great Fire of London, Christopher Wren had the axis of the new St Paul's Cathedral moved by eight degrees so that it was in perfect alignment with the Temple Church. The flag of the State of Israel, the Star of David, is actually a map, showing the configuration of the churches.'

Blake tried to rationalise the information that was being dumped into his head, but he had no time to process it. The academic was offloading her hypothesis at full speed. Reading from a note she had saved on her smartphone, Sabatini continued.

'The Peasants' Revolt of 1381 was the most violent and widespread insurrection in England's history. No chronicler of that period has ever given an explanation as to why there was a systematic and vicious targeting of the crusader knights during the rebellion in the city, including the murder of the Prior of St John's, Sir Robert Hales.' Without warning, the screen of Sabatini's phone turned black and the device started rebooting itself. She muttered something under her breath in Italian, and waited impatiently for the phone to restart.

'Every Hospitaller property, from here in Clerkenwell to the Temple area between Fleet Street and the Thames, was ransacked. It all becomes clear in Newton's commentary. The rebels, led by the shadowy figure of Walter the Tyler, were searching for something so precious that they risked civil war to get it. Newton believed that they were searching for Aaron's rod, brought to England by the Patriarch of Jerusalem some 200 years earlier.' She paused to take in breath.

'It still remains a complete mystery today that nothing is known about the leader of England's greatest civil rebellion. How did this man, Walter the Tyler, become appointed to be the uncontested supreme commander of the revolt? And how did he manage to mobilise an army to march on London in a matter of days? I found some references on the Internet last night, suggesting that some scholars believe that his name, "Tyler", refers to a Masonic rank, the Tyler being the sergeant at arms of a Masonic lodge who checks the credentials of visitors and stands guard outside the meeting place with a drawn sword in his hand. The more I look at it, the shadier the historical record becomes.'

Blake felt a caustic plug of acid rise in his throat. He swallowed it and slid his beer glass to the edge of the table.

'Vincent, I know some of this is guesswork, but what is undeniable is that from the 1670s to his death, Newton became obsessed with biblical prophecy. He called biblical prophecy "histories of things to come" and became convinced that they were nothing less than cryptograms of God's plan for the world. He learned Hebrew to read the original sources of the Old Testament and dedicated the rest of his life to decoding their secrets. He became fanatical about the design of Solomon's Temple, believing the details of its layout were ordained by God Himself. His papers show that he used the Book of Ezekiel, which describes its floor plan, to produce a complete architectural drawing of the temple. You can see his plan for the temple in the Hebrew University of Jerusalem today.'

Blake quickly examined Sabatini's face. 'Carla, do you honestly think that is enough reason to murder? People have been killed; lots of people.' Blake then stared into mid-air. 'My wife was killed. You're telling me that they all died because of some archaeological wild goose chase?' Blake could feel his blood pressure rising.

'Vincent, listen to me very carefully. Many people believe that the discovery of Aaron's rod and its arrival back in Jerusalem would fulfil the beginning of the third sign of the Prophecy of the Tribulation.'

'Wait a minute. The prophecy of what?'

'According to the Bible, the Tribulation is a time of great suffering on earth; war, famine and death filling every corner of the world and, afterwards, the eventual ushering in of God's kingdom. The scriptures talk of three signs that will herald the start of the Tribulation.'

'Three signs?' Blake tried to remember Newton's reference to the three signs that he had just read in the crimson notebook, but his mind just couldn't seem to get a foothold.

'The first sign was the restoration of the Nation of Israel. That was fulfilled with the formation of the state of Israel in 1948. The second sign was the return of Jerusalem to the Jewish people. When Israeli paratroopers entered the old city of Jerusalem and captured Temple

Mount during the Six-Day War in 1967, many believed that they had seen the fulfilment of the second sign.'

'And the third sign?' Blake's eyes widened.

'The third sign is the discovery of the rod and then the rebuilding of Solomon's Temple on Temple Mount. Once the building is complete and the rod is reinstalled in the sanctuary, the Tribulation of the world will begin,' said Sabatini.

Blake rubbed his forehead with his fingertips.

'The Tribulation is God's final judgement on the unbelievers of the world. They will experience unimaginable sufferings, and three-quarters of the world's population will be destroyed. Only when these horrors have passed will the Messiah come and establish His kingdom on earth. There are countless people who believe this version of the future, and many who would work to hasten its arrival, believing they would be one of the few chosen by God to be spared from the suffering. The discovery of the rod would be seen as a signal to start rebuilding the Temple in Jerusalem.'

'You mean, on the location where Solomon's Temple once stood?' said Blake.

Sabatini nodded, her brown eyes squinting in the winter sunshine streaming through the window.

Blake understood the implications. He had recently read a newspaper article about a leaked US security memo describing the 37-acre site as the most contested 'real estate' in the world. According to the article, US intelligence chiefs had categorised the tensions surrounding the disputed ownership of the site as the single most likely trigger for a third world war. As he recounted the narrative in his mind, he started to feel sick. Temple Mount was the third holiest place in Islam, where Muhammad had been taken up to heaven to be shown the signs of God, its location marked by the Al-Aqsa Mosque and the golden Dome of the Rock. It was also the exact same place where Jews believe the very foundations of Solomon's Temple were built; the Temple Mount, or the focal point of two sacred revelations and the battleground of two ideologies. Blake held his breath, trying to stop the thoughts that were careering out of control in his head. A realisation gripped him. Something was happening and for whatever reason he was involved. Finally he exhaled.

'Carla, I don't know what any of this means. I don't know whether the rod actually exists, but I think I've got a good idea of the location Newton described in this book. One thing is for certain. We've got to prove it, one way or another, before anyone else gets killed.'

CHAPTER 49

Sabatini released her grip on the armrest of the armchair, leaving a deep imprint of her fingernails in the soft leather. She leant forward, perching her body on the edge of the seat.

'You know where the rod is hidden? How?'

Blake reached into his jacket pocket and carefully placed a silver object onto the table top. Sabatini's eyes widened. It was Newton's pocket watch.

'DCI Milton asked me to see if I could come up with any leads surrounding the watch. Brother Nathan was grasping it in his hand when he was shot. He seemed to be intent on protecting it at all costs,' said Blake.

Sabatini nodded. Blake picked it up. It felt strangely warm. He once again traced a circumference along the edge of its case, its smooth surface only interrupted by the three small inscriptions along its rim. With the Bible verse on his lips, he opened it and started to rotate the hands of the timepiece. He breathed the words: 'For a time, times and half a time.'

As the black minute hand came to rest at the bottom of its sweep, an audible click came from deep within the watch interior. Released from its locking mechanism, the back case opened to reveal a folded piece of paper hidden within. Gasping in amazement, Sabatini rose from the seat.

'Carla, the crimson book ... lay it flat on the table and open it to the last page,' said Blake.

As Sabatini duly complied with his request, Blake carefully unfolded the sheet of paper and positioned it over Gérard de Ridefort's open journal. The physical dimensions and intricate gold bordering of the page exactly matched the other leaves in the notebook. Holding his breath to steady his hand, Blake set the rough margin of the page against the jagged edge protruding from the book's binding. The fit was exact, like the interlocking borders of a jigsaw puzzle.

'Newton must have ripped out the map and placed it in his pocket watch for safe keeping. He would have worn the watch every day, keeping it close to his person at all times,' said Blake.

Sabatini gazed at the intricate design inscribed onto the surface of the page. Despite the ink being badly faded, the form of the drawing was clear. It was a map showing the floor plan of a great church, the distinctive cross motif of the nave intersecting with the north and south transepts clearly visible in outline. Offset to the right of the main entrance was the start of a thin line of gold paint, and its rich lustre was undiminished by the obvious age of the paper. The golden line superimposed an 'L-shape' onto the floor plan. From its beginning at the staircase close to the entrance steps, it moved to the centre of the nave before turning ninety degrees and following the central axis of the cathedral. The line came to an end at the very centre of a great dome, its terminus marked by a delicately painted golden cross.

'It's a map of St Paul's Cathedral. See, Newton has marked the position of the rod,' said Sabatini, her voice trembled with the realisation of the discovery. Her mind was then taken by another thought. She picked up the crimson notebook from the table and quickly thumbed through the pages.

'Here ... here it is.' She read aloud.

'Descend the eighty-eight steps and open the stone door, as all will be revealed in a time, times and half a time.'

'Look, the golden line starts at the centre of a circular staircase. It must lead to the sanctuary that Wren excavated under the cathedral. The rod must be buried somewhere beneath the dome of St Paul's!'

Blake opened his mouth to speak, but his mind just couldn't cling onto a thought long enough to express it in words.

'Vincent, don't you see? It all makes sense. Nathan's strange behaviour; why he was so insistent on coming to Cambridge; why he was murdered: it's all to do with the rod. Someone else knows of its existence and they'll kill to get their hands on it.'

Blake's head was spinning. He began to say something, but the insistent ring of his mobile abruptly curtailed his flow. Milton's name flashed on the phone screen. For a moment he wondered whether to take the call. Eventually he conceded to its persistent ringing.

'Hello,' said Blake.

'Vincent, is that you?'

'Yes, Lukas, who were you expecting?'

'Thank god, thank god!' said the DCI.

'Thank god?'

'Thank god you're safe, man. I thought ... I thought ... you were toast!'

He looked over at Sabatini.

'What the hell are you talking about?' said Blake.

CHAPTER 50

Ema Mats ran her fingertips over the embossed motif at the top of the evening's programme. The modern design decorated in gold leaf displayed the academy's name—*The Mats Academy for Business Science*—set in the centre of a circle of five stars. A constellation of five stars had been the emblem of the academy since its formation thirteen years before. Mats had been somewhat insistent on its adoption; as the founder and major financial donor of the academic establishment, she had certain privileges. After explaining the design's ancient association with the pursuit of knowledge, the Board of Governors had passed it unanimously.

The Mats Academy was a shining beacon of urban renewal. Its vision was simple and ambitious: to seed a world-class business school in the heart of London's deprived East End. The poorest local students who showed aptitude and ambition were given a free education to rival anything elsewhere in the capital. Mats sought out the students herself, spending days interviewing candidates from local schools, churches, foster homes and even local markets to find those who would benefit most from the school's programme. After pledging an oath to the goals of the academy, new students embarked on a programme of studies dedicated to transforming inner-city kids into modern entrepreneurs. Once in the network, 'Mats-incubated' businesses had an uncanny chance of success. Many had become serious commercial enterprises and covered a wide range of industries, including health care, television production, the restaurant business and advertising.

During its thirteen-year existence, the Mats Academy for Business Science had established itself as an outstanding institution. The campus for the business school, a converted housing estate in the centre of Hackney, had been secured from the local council at a time when the borough had been labelled as the poorest in London. Backed by the enormous financial resources of her business empire, Mats had made the council an offer for the site that it simply couldn't refuse. The centrepiece of the campus was the Mats Tower, an eighteen-floor converted block of flats transformed into a state-of-the-art educational facility complete with lecture theatres, library, technology centre, graphic design studios, restaurant, and even a printing press that churned out educational literature under the banner of the Mats Educational Press. Since its opening, the campus had become a nucleus for regeneration in the area, bringing in both private and public capital.

The young man bounding up the steps to the stage to collect his award must have been no more than twenty years old. The name of the stylishly dressed Nigerian man announced over the loudspeaker was Charles Henderson. According to the event's brochure, read aloud by the suited Master of Ceremonies behind a lectern, Henderson had already made his first million in the fashion industry, and with his label about to be sold to a High Street retailer, he was well on the way to becoming seriously wealthy.

After shaking the Master of Ceremonies' hand, Henderson confidently took the microphone from the stand and stepped to the edge of the stage. The only sound in the lecture theatre was the intermittent click of camera shutters.

'Thank you for those kind words.' The man's diction was precise and wouldn't have sounded out of place on the playing fields of Eton. 'Before I accept this prize, I would just like to say a few words about the person who has inspired me more than any other. I will never forget the day, five years ago, when Ema Mats arrived at my foster home.' Henderson beamed a smile over to the seated guest of honour at the side of the stage and beckoned her forward to the lectern. At first, Mats remained resolutely in her chair, but as the spontaneous ripple of applause turned into a thunderous ovation, Mats was left with no option but to join the man at the front of the stage. As she moved to kiss her protégé politely on the cheek, she whispered something into his ear.

'Get ready, the time has nearly come.'

CHAPTER 51

Even though the stairs leading up to the entrance of the Jerusalem Tavern had been gritted, a thin layer of ice had begun to form on the uppermost steps. Milton saw the tell-tale sparkle of ice crystals as he began to climb the stairs. He flattened his stride and steadied the swing of the service revolver under his jacket by clamping it securely under his elbow. As he ascended the marble stairs, his hands, deep in their pockets, pulled his long black overcoat close around his body.

He barged open the large entrance door with his shoulder and stepped into the bar. The pub was already three-quarters full with the usual eclectic mix of city slickers and postal workers from the nearby Mount Pleasant sorting office. Mixed in with the regular clientele was an assortment of flotsam and jetsam washed up from the constant stream of commuters running outside the pub's front door.

The policeman scanned the bar to find Blake and Sabatini. Milton had met Blake at his local many times before, but it was evident that he wasn't sitting in his usual position at the corner of the bar. He began to panic.

Where the hell are you?

At that moment, Milton felt a tap on his shoulder. It was Frida holding a circular metal tray. The detective recognised the pub's landlady.

'If you're looking for Vincent, he's over there in the snug.' Frida nodded to the far end of the bar and then walked off, tapping the tray against her hip like a tambourine.

Milton quickly found Blake and Sabatini sitting around a small wooden table. Blake was staring into mid-air. He looked terrible. Milton retrieved a chair from the table opposite and sat down; his voice was uncharacteristically hesitant when he started to speak.

'Vincent, I am deeply sorry about your place, but I'm afraid I have something really difficult to tell you.'

Blake gave a hesitant nod and then took a breath that seemed to catch in his chest.

'The fire brigade are still putting the fire out, but I'm really sorry to say they've found a body.'

'A body?' Blake looked at Milton, alarm etched over his face.

'Yes. I need you to tell me who was staying with you in your flat,' said Milton in an official way.

Blake felt his heartbeat begin to pound in his ears.

'Staying with me? No one. No one was staying with me,' said Blake.

'Vincent I need you to think very carefully.'

Blake's mind was already working overtime to think through any possibility. Finally, he just shook his head, his eyes reflecting back an expression of total bewilderment.

'What about a key? Did anyone have a spare key?' asked Milton.

'No, no one. I've only been in the flat for two weeks. I've only got one key and it's in my pocket.'

To make the point, Blake retrieved a key ring from his trouser pocket and placed it at the centre of the table.

Milton stared at the silver key for a moment and then gave his thick five o'clock shadow a long scratch.

'So who the hell is it?' he said blankly.

'I've got no idea,' said Blake.

The detective shook his head slowly.

'Man, I'm really sorry about your place. You had me going for a minute. I thought you'd gone up in the building. Things have got really out of hand.'

'It wasn't an accident, was it?' said Blake.

Milton had rehearsed the answer in his mind whilst driving at full speed from the burned-out shell of Blake's bedsit to the Jerusalem Tavern, but the words still got caught in the back of his mouth.

'Vincent, I think ... I think we need to be...careful.'

'Careful? Someone has just tried to kill me, right?'

The look in Milton's face answered Blake's question for him.

'They've burned down my bloody bedsit, thinking I was in it, right?'

A dreadful realisation broke over him.

'Oh fuck! The Drakon. You don't think…?' said Blake his face full of alarm.

Sabatini shot Blake a puzzled look.

'The Drakon?' asked the academic, 'Who or what is the Drakon?'

Milton cut the conversation. 'Look, we'll talk about this in the morning. The important thing is that you're safe. What we've got to do now is get a place for you to stay tonight. I'll get a hotel organised.'

Milton reached for the mobile in his pocket, but before he had time to dial a number, Sabatini made a suggestion.

'Vincent, why don't you stay in my hotel? Nathan and I were booked into rooms tonight ready for our return flight back to Rome; the rooms have already been paid for. It's nothing fancy, a small place called the Bedford. It's only a short taxi ride from here.'

Sabatini shrugged her shoulders, not knowing how her suggestion would be taken. Blake sat there rooted to the spot, paralysed with confusion. It was as if the walls and the ceiling of the pub were closing on in him, inch by inch. Soon there wouldn't be enough air to breathe. He fought to remain calm. Someone had just tried to kill him. His bedsit and his few possessions had been torched. All he could think about were the family photograph albums of Nomsa and Sarah that had just gone up in flames, his memories irrecoverably erased.

Blake was shaken from his thoughts by Sabatini's hand on his arm.

'So, Vincent, what do you think?'

'Okay, thank you. I guess I don't have many options left,' said Blake. Milton rose to his feet.

'I think it's best that we take a few precautions,' said Milton. 'I'll get a squad car stationed outside the hotel during the night. Tomorrow, when you're ready, can I ask you both to come over to the police station and we'll take it from there?' The detective checked his watch. 'I'll drive you both there now. We can pick up some toiletries from a shop along the way.'

Before leaving the bar, Milton patted Blake on the shoulder. 'Man, I'm really sorry for all this shit. We'll get them I promise you.' With that, the policeman stepped out of the bar and started dialling a number on his mobile. By the time Milton had begun talking into his phone, Blake had found Frida. She was stacking glasses behind the bar.

'Frida, I need you to do me a favour,' Blake said hurriedly.

'What's that, Vincent?'

'I need you to look after a couple of things for me.'

CHAPTER 52

With no cloud cover, the evening air temperature had plummeted. As Milton rocked from foot to foot to keep warm, he realised that he hadn't eaten since breakfast and his body was starting to protest. The cumulative effects of the last forty-eight hours, living on strong coffee and infrequent indigestible food, had drained his reserves of energy, and all he wanted to do now was to switch off and refuel. His old friend was safe. Well, at least for now.

Outside the Jerusalem Tavern, Milton made two phone calls. The first call was to his divisional commander to inform him that the charred carcass found in the gutted bedsit wasn't Blake. His second call was to his desk sergeant back at the station to request a protection car outside the Bedford Hotel to safeguard Dr Vincent Blake and Dr Carla Sabatini. As Milton hung up, a strange metallic click echoed in his earpiece.

PART 3

THE THIRD LAW
OF MOTION

For a force there is always an equal and opposite reaction: or the forces of two bodies on each other are equal and directed in opposite directions.

CHAPTER 53

Monday 30 November

Two things were unusual about the appearance of the white-coated doctor who had just opened the door to the private patient's room on the fourth floor of London Bridge hospital.

Firstly, the doctor wore no name badge. Since the hospital's last major redesign in the early 1980s, all medical staff were required to wear identification. Secondly, the doctor was wearing an operating theatre mask and surgical gloves. Hospital protocol was very strict on the issue of cross-contamination between wards, and wearing used protective clothing across sterile boundaries was a serious disciplinary offence.

With the main light switched off, the room was bathed in a subtle red glow from the bank of medical equipment at its far end. For a little while, the Drakon just stared at the slight frame of the patient occupying the hospital bed. It was four o'clock in the morning, but the room was far from silent. The clicking sound of the ventilator piston breathing air into Sarah's lungs and the regular metallic ping of her heart monitor filled the air.

Sarah there you are, you wretched child. Look at you, all twisted and deformed. You know, your father is causing me so much trouble. He is the reason you are lying here, like road kill. I must admit I was surprised to find out that they managed to scrape you off the tarmac still alive.

The Drakon stretched, and a strange percussive sound of clicking vertebrae echoed through the room. The intruder leaned forward and ran a finger through Sarah's matted hair. *Killing your mother was all too quick. I remember the sound of her head slamming onto the bonnet and her limbs being mangled under my wheels, but it was all over too soon. Your demise on the other hand has been all too slow. Look at you, your body slowly putrefying in this bed. Your deformity disgusts me. I have given your father a chance to stop his pointless games, but he continues to defy me. He is ruining everything.*

In a series of short staccato breaths, the Drakon smelt the skin around Sarah's throat. *You rotting excuse of a human being. Your father has dared to keep something very precious from me and he must be made to realise that my retribution for his insolence will have no bounds.*

Sarah's stiff neck was raised off the pillow and two cold, probing fingers were inserted into her ears.

Don't fight me. Surrender to me. A surge of energy flowed across Sarah's temple. *You are very much alive, Sarah. I can feel you. You are struggling to be heard, but no one is listening. Before long they will switch these machines off and you will perish just like your mother. But now you have a use to me.*

The Drakon dropped Sarah's head onto the pillow and then knelt down next to her bed. Without warning, Sarah's hand snapped into a tight fist, sending a shockwave down the IV line connected to her forearm. The Drakon seized the child's hand.

I see you are not as dead as you seem.

Slowly, the Drakon pulled down the facemask and raised Sarah's hand to an open mouth.

The sister sitting at the nurses' station looked up from her magazine and stared at the flashing display. Two alarm lights flashed red, both for Room 4 and both indicating dangerously raised vital signs. For a moment she hesitated, her eyes flicking between the screen and the patient names written on the ward wall chart next to her desk. Then her hand slammed down on the emergency crash alarm button. Twenty seconds later, the sister and a duty doctor burst through the doors of Sarah's room. The sister let out an audible gasp at the sight of the pool of blood surrounding the patient's left hand.

In the basement of the hospital, a laundry bin was open and now filled with three items: a white coat, a pair of latex gloves and a surgical face mask. Two words were stencilled on the side of the laundry bin in dark blue lettering.

For incineration.

CHAPTER 54

Vincent Blake hadn't slept a wink all night. The hotel alarm clock had jolted into action at 6.30 a.m. and had been met immediately by Blake's fist silencing its incessant electronic drone. The implications of the previous day's events bounced around his head like a trapped wasp looking for something to sting: the torching of his bedsit; the body found in its wreckage; Sabatini's crimson book; and the hidden map he had discovered in the back of Newton's pocket watch. He felt like he had been dragged out to sea and was now alone, drifting, off-course in a vast threatening ocean.

He noticed the first signs of daylight breaking through his bedroom curtains and was relieved that the night was finally over. The wooden floor felt cold under his feet as he moved slowly to the bathroom. He looked at his reflection in the mirror. The edge of his greying stubble followed the shape of his sunken cheeks like the contours of a map. As he stared at his reflection, a dark thought invaded his mind: the thought of pulling a trigger and putting a bullet-shaped hole in the head of the Drakon.

Denic adjusted the driver's wing mirror of the blacked-out Mercedes van. From his position just outside the Bedford Hotel, they had both points of entry to the hotel covered. He would see them long before they saw him. Now it was just a matter of waiting. He had already checked that there was a round in the chamber of his Sig Sauer P228 9mm semi-automatic pistol. Its weight felt reassuring against his chest, but he couldn't be too careful, particularly if they needed to make a speedy exit. London's traffic was notorious and they would need options if they were forced to abandon the van and move on foot. They had decided that a quick sprint through Canonbury Square Gardens to the Tube station beyond would be their best option, or, failing that, the labyrinth of Islington Town Hall would afford lots of opportunity for escape.

Through the tinted glass of the van's back window, Crossland noticed the slim profile of a woman crossing the street onto the opposite pavement. Regardless of the cold, she wore no coat and appeared to be rushing from one office to another with a file of papers under her arm. She wore a pair of black woollen tights that disappeared midway up her thighs under a large oversized cashmere jumper. As she came closer, he could make out that she looked Asian, with razor-sharp cheekbones and wide dramatic eyes. He waited until she had passed the car and then studied the shape of her buttocks moving up and down inside the wool of her dress. He watched as her long hair swayed in time with her bottom.

'Don't get distracted,' Denic shouted over his shoulder as he leant over to the passenger's seat and opened the glove compartment. From within, he removed a small plastic zip-lock bag containing several pairs of surgical gloves. He pulled on a pair, stretching the thin synthetic material tight against his fingers. Then, without diverting his gaze from the entrance of the small townhouse hotel, he tossed the bag casually over his shoulder into the back of the van.

'Get them on. You ready?' asked Denic. With his attention now refocused on the job in hand, Crossland unrolled a cloth tool holder on the van's floor. Once fully open, it was clear that the heavy fabric sleeve held a collection of work tools: small chisels, wire-cutters and pliers of different sizes.

'One minute. I just need to get this packed,' said Crossland. Grabbing the headrest of the front passenger seat, Crossland hoisted his great weight upright, and removed a stainless-steel dental drill from the back pocket of his jeans. The car's suspension rocked with the shifting weight.

'Don't worry, Sarge. Give me five minutes with him and he'll be squealing like a pig to tell us where that pocket watch is.'

Denic quietly considered a response and then decided better of it. Crossland had been convinced that he had dealt with Blake the day before, soaking him in petrol and setting him alight. This time he wasn't going to take any chances. They would do the job together. He would make sure it was done right. The tone of the Drakon's latest message informing them of their failure had been chilling in its simplicity. If they fucked up this time, they were dead.

Denic looked over at the small plastic container lying on the passenger seat next to him. Under the Drakon's express instructions, he had collected it from a left-luggage locker at Kings Cross Station three hours before. He'd opened it. He wished he hadn't. Denic looked at his watch. The express train from Paris to Zagreb would be leaving in twenty-three hours, and he planned to be on it.

'Any sign of movement from the hotel?' Crossland asked as his oversized fingers tucked the cylindrical dental drill into the canvas sleeve.

'They're still in there. Just sit tight and be ready.' Denic reached inside his jacket and felt the cool metal of his Sig Sauer. 'You know our instructions; get the watch at any costs. Blake and his Italian girlfriend are about to get an early Christmas present they weren't expecting.'

Sabatini was right on time, which meant that Blake was late, and he knew it. The first ring of the doorbell came while he was cleaning his teeth with the toothbrush that Milton had bought him the night before. The second and third rings were accompanied by a series of raps on the door. The previous evening, Blake had agreed with Sabatini that she would call for him on the way down to breakfast. They would spend the morning talking through the implications of the crimson book and Newton's map, and then decide what to tell Milton. The two messages that had just arrived on Blake's phone had upset his timing: a voicemail message from the hospital and a text from the DCI explaining that the patrol car stationed outside the hotel had just finished its shift and was now leaving for other duties. A replacement car was on its way.

'Just give me a second,' he shouted from the bedroom. Resurrecting his trousers from the floor, Blake hopped to the door, trying to locate the opening to his trouser leg with his foot. He kicked frantically at the material, but it refused to comply. Several seconds passed and then Blake opened the door by a few inches. He looked terrible, like a convict just emerged from a long stretch in solitary confinement. He pulled a towel close around his shoulders.

'Sorry about that,' he panted, trying to regain his equilibrium.

Sabatini, a woman obviously unaccustomed to being greeted in this way, acknowledged Blake with a reserved, 'Oh, good morning.'

'Carla, I'll meet you at breakfast, just give me ten minutes. I've just had a message from the hospital about my daughter. I've got to give them a call.'

Blake's reaction to his conversation with the hospital consultant was immediate and visceral. He ran to the bathroom, the muscles in his abdomen tightening with every step. He got there just in time to retch up the meagre contents of his stomach into the toilet. After steadying himself against the wall, Blake sat down on the edge of the bath and then reached over to the washbasin. A muscle in his cheek began to twitch. He switched on the tap and plunged his head under the ice-cold water.

Sabatini sat alone in the hotel's small dining room nursing an untouched cup of black coffee. Blake arrived at her table in a hurry, his face paler than usual.

'Carla, something happened to my daughter last night. I've got to get to the hospital. I'm sorry. The book, the map, it's all got to wait. I'll give you a call from the hospital.' His words were like bullets being fired from a machine gun. Sabatini tried to grasp what Blake was saying, but he was already turning towards the door. Without thinking, she grabbed her coat from the back of her chair and shouted after him.

'I'll come with you.'

Blake pushed the door handle of the Bedford Hotel and impatiently held it open for Sabatini. It felt loose, worn down by use from thousands of hands. Blake descended the eight large steps down to the pavement in two jumps, quickly followed by Sabatini. About 100 metres further on up the road Blake spotted a taxi rank. At this time in the morning, the ride to the hospital would take about twenty minutes.

Placing a hand behind Sabatini's back, Blake ushered her forward along the pavement.

A little way further along the road, a large man wearing a baseball cap and a well-worn leather jacket walked towards them in the opposite direction. He was moving quickly in the centre of the pavement, his face down, his eyes covered by the visor of his cap. Both Blake and Sabatini had the same notion at approximately the same moment: if the approaching pedestrian didn't alter his current trajectory, Blake would be required to step into the road to prevent a collision. A few seconds later, the person on foot still hadn't looked up, apparently unaware of the oncoming obstacle. Blake gave a quick glance up and down the road for traffic, then dropped away from Sabatini's side and stepped into the road.

As the pedestrian passed, he abruptly changed direction. A fraction of a second later, he had pinned Sabatini up against the wall by the throat. At the same time, Blake felt a hard object jab in the centre of his back. He heard a voice behind his head.

'Don't you fucking think about it,' said the voice. 'You have a gun in your back. Don't make me squeeze the trigger.' The voice was Eastern European and terrifying. A second jab arrived in the square of Blake's lower back, this time its force of delivery was designed to hurt. Blake cursed with pain. Out of the corner of his eye, he could see that Sabatini had been released from the wall. A gun barrel brushed against her side, just above her kidney. A voice behind Blake's ear whispered calmly.

'We are going to cross the road and walk over to that van. We're all going to take a little trip.'

CHAPTER 55

As Blake's unsupported head jerked forward, his mind was thrust back into consciousness. For an instant, he felt his thoughts retreating into sleep like a wave being sucked out to sea, but a noise, sharp and irregular, yanked him back into waking. He moved his head instinctively towards the sound. It came again, this time louder, more insistent. Gradually, Blake's mind began to resolve the dirge of sound into a series of distinct words. Moments later they detonated in his brain with desperate meaning.

'Vincent. Vincent, wake up! They're going to kill us! Vincent, please wake up! Oh god!' Sabatini's voice was hysterical, her words fighting to break through her shallow frantic panting. As Blake slowly opened his eyes, diffuse blurred outlines gradually turned into clear edges. He turned his head to one side. His body tried to follow, but his movement was severely restricted by something cutting into his wrists.

Then he saw Sabatini, and dreadful memories began to flood into his mind: the Bedford Hotel; being bundled into the back of a van at gunpoint; the hypodermic needle. The needle had been plunged deep into his neck and the entry point was still raw. He tried to raise his hand, but he couldn't move. He looked down and took in his awful predicament. Both his wrists and his ankles were tightly bound to a chair with electrical insulation tape. He tried to push against his restraints, but they were too tightly wound. He tried again, this time with his entire body writhing against the bindings, but it made no difference.

As Blake looked over to Sabatini sobbing at his side, he became aware that they were sitting in some sort of derelict building.

'Carla, are you okay?' Blake whispered as his eyes scanned their surroundings.

Sabatini didn't know what to respond. She had regained consciousness minutes before with one of her kidnappers standing over her. He had been holding a kitchen carving knife.

'Vincent, they're going to kill us,' Sabatini moaned through tracks of tears and snot. 'He's got a knife. He's got a ...' The end of her sentence dissolved into a whimper.

'Carla, I need you to think. Have you got any idea where we are?'

Sabatini shrugged her shoulders. The last thing she could remember was being shoved into the back of a van then a sharp scratch on her neck. She had woken up with the blade of a long knife twisting before her eyes.

By the random assortment of shiny nails and off-cuts of electrical wire scattered on the bare wooden floor, Blake guessed that the room had been recently gutted. The walls were stripped back to plasterboard and bore the remnants of many layers of wallpaper. A large window was set into the opposite wall, its frame painted in an incongruous bright yellow gloss, and a single light bulb hung down from the ceiling. From where he was sitting, Blake could see a thin rectangle of dappled daylight shining out from the bottom of the slatted blind. *Maybe trees swaying outside,* he thought. *Maybe we're not on the ground floor.*

An idea flickered in Blake's head. He strained his neck forward and looked down at his watch. Though most of its face had been caught up in the taping around his wrist, Blake could clearly make out the first figures on its digital readout. The digits formed the number ten; the hour was still ten o'clock. Blake had received the call from the hospital a few minutes after ten, which meant that they had been unconscious for less than an hour. If that were the case then Blake guessed that they were probably still in London.

The door flew open. Blake held his breath. Sabatini looked up, her heart beating so fast that it pounded in her ears like a metronome. Slowly two men walked into the room. Both were tall, muscular and formidable: the same men that had confronted them outside the Bedford Hotel.

'What do you want?' Blake pleaded. 'Tell me, please, what do you want with us?'

Crossland sneered at his prisoner. Blake should have been dead, burned to a crisp in that shitty bedsit. *He soon will be*, he thought, as his sneer morphed into a malevolent smile. Out of the side of her eye, Sabatini tracked the other man as he picked up a large cardboard box abandoned in the corner of the room. As the man came closer with the box, her body retreated back into her chair. Once close enough, Denic casually threw the box onto the floor in front of the two prisoners. After making a small adjustment to its position, he placed an open laptop onto it.

Almost immediately an alien voice echoed through the dilapidated house. The voice was not human. Though the laptop's screen was black, a small red light next to its inbuilt webcam indicated that the picture was being streamed live to an unknown location over the Internet.

'Dr Blake, you have become somewhat of a problem to me,' said the voice.

Blake strained against the electrical taping securing his wrists to the chair. Though the voice had been digitally disguised, Blake guessed the name of the person he was listening to.

'Are you the Drakon?'

'Very good, Dr Blake, very good, I see you have been doing your homework,' said the voice.

'You bastard!' Blake spat the words contemptuously from the side of his mouth. Seeing the larger of his two jailers step forward menacingly, Blake checked himself.

'Time is running out,' the voice continued. 'You are in possession of something I want and I need it now.'

'In possession of something? What do you mean?' said Blake.

'Don't play games!' The voice shook the internal speaker of the laptop with obvious frustration. 'Newton's pocket watch; the one that was switched in Cambridge. I need the original.'

'Switched?' Sabatini questioned indignantly.

'Yes, Dr Sabatini. Your friend the priest switched the original with a fake. We ended up with the fake and Dr Blake ended up with the original. Isn't that true Dr Blake?'

'I don't have it. It's back with the police,' said Blake, his fingertips squeezing hard the metal armrest of chair.

A pause followed where the only sound that could be heard came from the static of the laptop's inbuilt loudspeaker. When the Drakon's response arrived, it was seething with rage.

'Listen to me, you little fuck! You will give it to me. Remind Dr Blake what he has at stake.'

Crossland smiled, removed a small, white plastic box from his jacket pocket and placed it next to the laptop on the makeshift cardboard box table.

Blake stared at it, and then a dreadful thought entered his head.

'No, no, please. I'll get it for you. Oh god, please no.' As his wrists writhed against his restraints, his left thumb clawed against the edge of his wedding ring.

'For the love of god, no.'

Tears began to stream down his cheeks, as his head rolled from side to side in anguish. The Drakon's voice started to rage again over the speaker.

'Where is the watch? Nothing will stand in my way. Do you understand?'

Blake began to nod furiously as Crossland quickly grabbed the plastic box from the table, removed its airtight lid and dropped the contents onto Blake's lap. Blake looked down, his face frozen in sheer horror. There, resting between his legs was a severed finger; the finger of a child. The fingernail had recently been painted in nail varnish. Blake recognised the shade: electric blue. It was the finger of his daughter.

Blake's body thrashed against his bindings. A tidal wave of adrenalin surged into his bloodstream.

'You evil bastard! I'll fucking kill you if you go anywhere near my daughter. I swear it, I'll kill you.'

'I doubt that very much. The watch, Dr Blake, where is it?'

'Okay, okay.' Blake's head rolled back against the chair as Crossland gathered up the finger from his lap with the plastic box. 'It's in the back safe of a pub in Clerkenwell called the Jerusalem Tavern. I asked the landlady to keep it safe after you burned down my bloody bedsit.'

Denic nodded in acknowledgement.

'Blake, this is your last chance. If the watch isn't there, I'm going to gut you both alive.'

'It's there, I swear,' cried Blake.

There was a long pause and then the loudspeaker shouted out a final order.

'Gentlemen, I need to talk to you in private about our next move.'

With that, Denic stepped forward, retrieved the laptop and followed Crossland out of the room, shutting the door behind him. Seconds later, the sound of their heavy footsteps could be heard descending a long flight of stairs outside.

A terrible coldness swept over Blake's body, as if the sun itself had gone out.

CHAPTER 56

Hitting out his right shoulder and then his left, Blake managed to make his chair rock. He did it again, this time twisting his body as far as he could to the edge of the chair, using the bindings around his wrists for purchase. Sabatini looked on, her face taut and damp with sweat. This time two legs cleared the floor, teetered for a moment before thumping back down again. Keeping the momentum going, Blake shifted his body weight to the opposite side. The chair rocked again, this time through a bigger arc. It gradually came to rest perfectly balanced on two legs. Sensing the tipping point was close by, Blake yanked his shoulder downwards, every muscle in his neck jarring as he did so. Sabatini held her breath. The small additional force was just enough to send the chair and Blake crashing to the floor. The side of his head smacked onto the ground, his right eye just missing the upturned edge of a discarded paint tin by several inches.

Panting loudly, Blake pulled in his ribcage and tried to raise his shoulder off the floor. After managing to open up a small gap between the top of his arm and the floor, Blake gritted his teeth and jerked his other shoulder forward. Blake and the chair shifted their position on the floor. He steadied himself for a moment and then once again jarred his shoulder forward. This time his body and the chair rotated through some forty-five degrees around an imaginary axis through his pelvis.

With a gasp, Sabatini realised what Blake was doing. 'Vincent, you're really close, just a bit further.' The fingers of Blake's right hand scrambled desperately towards the large shiny nail resting in the gap between two wooden floorboards. An inch now separated his fingertips with the end of the nail. He had to be careful. Too much movement and the nail would be lost under his torso. Too little, then the combined weight of the chair and his body would remain stubbornly anchored in its current position. Blake pulled his head back and then snapped it forward. As the chair shifted slightly, pain fired down the muscles of his back. He let out a gasp, his elbows instinctively pulling themselves into his midriff.

After several deep breaths, the pain had subsided enough for him to re-assess his altered position. Unclenching his tight fist, Blake stretched out his fingers, desperately trying to locate the thin metal spike. At last his fingertips found the groove between the floorboards. Using the furrow between the wooden slats as a guide, he clawed forward with his index finger. Finally, his fingernail touched the head of the nail, the slight downward pressure flipping it onto the back of Blake's hand. His fingers scrambled to get hold of the object. Soon it was secure in his hand. Far from being blunt at one end, the nail head had been fashioned into a pointed wedge, as if it had been struck repeatedly by a hammer. With the nail head pushing down into the well of Blake's right hand, he positioned the sharp tip against the electric tape binding around his wrist. Slowly he closed his hand, the action driving the point of the metal spike into the tape restraint and beyond into the skin of his wrist.

Sabatini watched in silence as Blake grimaced with pain. Squeezing the shaft of the nail, Blake tried to focus on the binding around his wrist. A puncture hole was clearly visible in the plastic. After first repositioning the nail in his palm, Blake once again drove the spike into the plastic tape. "Fuck!" The pain shot through his wrist as if a shard of glass had been jabbed into his forearm. Sabatini tried to find some words of comfort, but all she could manage was to mumble his name into the cold air.

Blake bit into the side of his mouth and willed the image of Sarah lying in her hospital bed back into his mind. Keeping the nail flat to his palm, he angled its sharp tip in the small gap that had just opened between the underside of his wrist and the tape that had come unstuck from his skin. Clenching his hand, he pushed the nail hard into the plastic. Abruptly the tension on the nail gave way as its tip cleanly punctured a hole through the tape. Blake pulled the spike back through the hole with his fingertips. After realigning the tool in his hand, he once again drove it through the tape. Quickly he repeated the operation. Like the merging of several drops of water, the puncture points joined together to form a wider hole. A minute later he had opened up an aperture of over an inch in the binding.

The ligaments in Blake's wrist tightened like wires through his skin as the nail jabbed at the tape. His hand slipped and the head of the metal nail cut deep into his palm. He recoiled in pain, spitting curses through a shower of sweat. With breath bursting in and out of his lungs, Blake carefully repositioned the nail's head away from the stinging flap of skin now hanging from the well of his palm. He shut his eyes and girded himself for the inevitable pain. Mustering all his energy, Blake's hand unleashed a final flurry of stabs with the nail. Abruptly, his bound wrist moved slightly under its restraint. He forced his hand upwards, his biceps and forearm tensing under the pressure. The tape started to tear apart through the perforated edge he had just created.

When the tear broke through to the previously formed aperture, Blake's hand jerked forward. With all his might he pulled his hand backwards. The tape around his wrist ruffled up into a tight edge. Like a wire snare, the tight loop of plastic sliced into the back of Blake's hand. Defying the pain, he pulled it back as hard as he could. The edge of the tape slipped slightly and then cut into the raised profile of his knuckles. He pulled again and then, with a sudden movement, his hand was free.

Blake brought his clenched fist up to his panting mouth and felt a trickle of blood run down his forearm. For a split second, he looked over to Sabatini. She tried to speak, but nothing came out of her mouth. With his right hand now free, Blake easily located the leading edge of the tape restraining his left wrist. He pulled it backwards. It let out a loud ripping sound. Blake unwound the tape with a series of quick tugs. Soon his hand was free, seconds later so were his ankles.

Mustering all his energy, he tried to stand up. For an instant, his mind fell out of sync with the movement of his limbs, as if they were all operating in slightly different dimensions. He waited for his vision and the rest of his senses to reunite. Instead, the room began to spin. He stumbled to the side, his shoulder glancing off the exposed plasterboard of the wall. Cursing, Blake willed the blood to drain into his limbs. Biting hard into the side of his mouth, he stumbled forwards. Seconds later he was tearing at the plastic tape securing Sabatini's wrists.

CHAPTER 57

A solitary torch beam travelled across the bonnet of the Mercedes van parked in the run-down garage adjoining the safe house. The ceiling strip lighting had years since expired, and Denic and Crossland were working by torchlight. The air was filled with the sound of electronic music coming from a small radio balanced in the van's large air intake grille.

The screws fixing the front number plate fell to the floor, and the laminated plastic rectangle dropped into Denic's hand. From behind his shoulder, Crossland handed his partner the replacement plate and repositioned the torch beam onto the now vacant space just above the vehicle's front bumper. They weren't going to risk being picked up on the police's number plate recognition system fed by the battalions of ever-present CCTV cameras standing guard over the city's streets. Substitute number plates were a necessary precaution.

The two men didn't speak, there was nothing left to say. The Drakon's instructions had been unequivocal. Take the Jerusalem Tavern apart, brick by brick, until the pocket watch was found. For leverage, Blake and Sabatini would go along for the ride, but when the timepiece had been located, they would pay dearly for their games. The Drakon didn't care about the method of their execution, but an image was already forming in Crossland's imagination.

Denic tightened the last screw, hauled himself up and switched off the radio. He dropped it, along with the screwdriver into the half-packed canvas bag lying at his feet. He picked up the bag and the two men edged their way around the vehicle towards the door. The next job was to load the prisoners into the van. By the time they had walked under the lean-to that linked the garage to the side entrance of the safe house, Crossland was ready with the key. He turned it in the stiff lock and kicked open the paint-blistered door with his boot. Once inside, the two men headed for the stairs.

Suddenly a loud clattering sound came from the top of the staircase. Denic and Crossland looked at each other, their faces caught between shock and concern. Crossland grabbed two pistols from the canvas bag and threw one to his partner. Denic snatched the Sig Sauer out of mid-air. Without thinking, his index finger slid the safety to the off position. Hugging the side of the wall as they went, the two men slowly climbed the stairs. At the top, Crossland peered around the blind corner to the landing. Through the sights of his weapon, he quickly scanned down the long empty corridor. After nodding a signal to his partner, the two men began to move silently down the hallway.

Again there was a loud clattering sound, this time more violent, as if a poltergeist had taken hold of something and thrown it against the wall. There was no doubt: the source of the noise came from behind the closed door. On the other side of the door were Blake and Sabatini. A single drop of sweat traced a path down Denic's back. He readied himself, squaring his body up with the centre of the door. A moment later, he exploded into action.

The wooden frame surrounding the lock exploded into splinters as Denic's boot came smashing down on it. The force of the impact sent the door flying open on its hinges. As the door handle slammed into the plasterwork of the wall, Crossland burst into the room, his weapon tracking from side to side. Immediately he felt the cold wind on one side of his face. He quickly turned and located the source of the clattering sound. The window was wide open and the slatted metal blinds were crashing on the glass pane.

A large hand slammed down onto the wild blind, silencing it dead. Against the low winter sun in the horizon, a flickering movement caught Crossland's attention. Beyond the brick wall at the end of the garden, high on the roof of a disused lock-up, he could see the two silhouettes. Blinking through the sights of his weapon, he tried to resolve the blurred figures into two distinct targets. He held his breath and tunnelled his concentration through the crosshairs of the sight, his finger feeling for the tension in the trigger. As one of the figures appeared to haul themselves to their feet, Crossland fired a rapid burst from his pistol. The flickering silhouette fell like a stone.

CHAPTER 58

The identification card attached to the taxi's dashboard stated that the driver's name was Gregory Kovac. He had almost paid off the loan on his car and wasn't going to take any chances with the two passengers who had just arrived in the back of his taxi. Kovac pressed a dashboard button and the vehicle's central locking mechanism engaged with a loud snapping sound. Two days ago he had lost out on a sizeable fare when two young American tourists had jumped out of the taxi without paying. They had disappeared without trace down a side street in Holborn, and Kovac's internal warning radar was still on full alert. The condition of the two passengers now sitting in the back of his taxi was also giving him some concern. He looked in his rear-view mirror and repeated his question.

'Is there any direction you want me to head in? I can drive around the city for as long as you like, as long as you have the money to pay me,' he said.

At first there was no answer. His two passengers appeared to be catching their breath following a prolonged sprint. This was not in itself out of the ordinary, but the state of their clothing was. Kovac's eyes flicked from the road ahead to the rear-view mirror to get a clearer picture of the couple on the back seat. The man was tall and slim, in his late thirties and appeared to be wearing a heavily creased suit. He was warming his hands in the heated air flowing through the air-conditioning vent next to his knees, and Kovac could make out a large muddy stain running down the front of his once-white shirt. The woman was younger, good-looking and had a Mediterranean complexion. Spanish or Italian he guessed. Kovac lengthened his back and strained to see if she was wearing a wedding ring, but her hands were buried in the pockets of her coat. Both of them were staring forward, silent and consumed in their own thoughts. Their posture reminded Kovac of his mother and father sitting in the hearse the day they buried his brother; two people set adrift, not knowing how to get back to solid ground.

Then Blake managed an answer: 'Ludgate Hill. Drive us to St Paul's Cathedral on Ludgate Hill, as quickly as you can.'

As the warm air thawed Blake's frozen hands, they began to sting. His brain replayed the sound of bullets whistling past his ear and exploding into the brickwork just metres away from his head. If they hadn't escaped, they would be dead. He was certain of that.

The events of their escape snapped back into his mind. Once they had broken free from their restraints, Blake and Sabatini forced open the window and, with the help of a drainpipe, scaled down the back of the house into the overgrown garden. Blake immediately looked over to the garage adjoining the house and heard loud music coming from inside. He scanned left and right to take in the enclosed space that they had just entered.

The garden was bordered on both sides by high walls and flanked at its rear by a ramshackle storage lock-up of some kind. They started moving across the garden, but when they reached halfway, the music from the garage suddenly stopped. Blake and Sabatini froze. Then they heard heavy footsteps approaching the side of the house.

Terrified, they sprinted towards the end of the garden and the pile of household refuse dumped there. Like a madman, Blake searched through the discarded innards of the house for something to help them get onto the roof of the lock-up. He opened his mouth to say something and then noticed them. Discarded paint cans, lots of them, scattered amongst the weeds and rolls of decaying carpet.

The two of them quickly assembled a makeshift pyramid from the cans three or four feet high that formed just enough of a step for Blake to clamber up onto the roof. Once there, he reached down and hauled Sabatini up to join him.

As Blake stood up and straightened his back, a bullet whizzed by his ear, followed a millisecond later by the crack of a firing gun. He swung round just in time for a second bullet to miss his shoulder by a finger width and ricochet off a lamp post.

He remembered pulling Sabatini down and then crawling on his front to the edge of the felt roof. He looked over the edge and spotted a builder's skip positioned square up against the wall. There was no time to think. He shouted over to Sabatini, who dragged herself to the corner of the roof.

Blake watched in silence as she took hold of the wooden beading strip that kept the felt roof in place and moved over the side. Using the strip as a handhold, she lowered herself just enough to find a toehold in the crumbling brickwork. With her foot secure, she took little time to find a new handhold, and soon her other foot planted itself firmly onto the side of the skip. Seconds later, she made it to the ground. As she called up to him, Blake remembered glancing back to the house, half-expecting to see two men sprinting across the overgrown garden, but they were nowhere to be seen.

Next, it was his turn. Just like Sabatini before him, Blake shuffled his body parallel to the edge of the roof and, using the beading strip to support his weight, swung himself over the edge. Almost immediately, the wooden strip shifted in his hands, and the nails securing it in place bent out of the wall. He remembered his right hand scrambling to re-establish his grip and his arms flailing out to the side to gain purchase against thin air.

Blake grimaced as he relived the events in his mind and how he had landed with a heavy thwack face-up on a bed of cardboard at the bottom of the skip.

Sabatini's recollection of the next few moments was limited to a series of silent frozen images, as if her memories had been truncated to let her brain process them. She remembered Blake's hand pulling at her shoulder and being dragged through the small alleyway that led out to the main road. Then she remembered a flash of light to her side and an eruption of brick dust exploding around her head. After emerging from the shadows of the alleyway into Kilburn High Road, Sabatini recalled

Blake pulling her onto the pavement and shouting for the taxi driver to stop.

After weaving through London traffic for fifteen minutes, the taxi approached Ludgate Hill. Blake looked anxiously out through the back window. Seeing only the usual scrum of tourists and early Christmas shoppers, Blake fell back into his seat.

'Vincent, you're bleeding!' Sabatini's words were full of concern. He looked down and saw a line of crimson dots cutting across the front of his shirt.

'It's my hand,' said Blake. 'I did it with the nail. It slipped whilst I was cutting through the tape on my wrist.' Talking about it made it worse.

Sabatini took Blake's hand and placed it face-up on her lap. Gently she examined the circular cut in the centre of his palm. She took a handkerchief from her coat pocket and placed it over the wound. Blake closed his eyes and tried to hold on to the feeling of warmth, but the respite only lasted for a second. A loud Eastern European voice crackled over the taxi radio and jolted Blake back to reality. As if readying himself for a battle, he slowly made a fist with his injured hand. A sharp pain radiated out across his palm. It reminded him that he was still alive.

Startled by the ringing of his phone, Blake took it from his pocket and glanced down at the caller ID. He reacted, and Sabatini mirrored the alarm in his face. A line of black characters flashed back from the display: VINCENT BLAKE, TAKE THIS CALL! YOUR LIFE DEPENDS ON IT!

He accepted the call and tapped the screen to activate the phone's loudspeaker. Blake and Sabatini both stared at the handset in silence, waiting for a voice. When it came, the sound shook the speaker in its housing.

'Dr Blake, listen to me very carefully.' It was the cold metallic voice of the Drakon, digitally disguised as before. 'I see your reputation for resourcefulness is well placed. You have escaped, but this situation is only temporary. You can run, but you can't hide from me.'

Blake thought quickly. 'I'm sitting in Clerkenwell Police Station with Detective Milton, and I can assure you—'

Blake was cut off mid-sentence by the sharp electronic voice, frustration clearly mounting in its tone.

'Don't be a fool. You are currently in a car heading south. Next to you is Dr Sabatini.' Sabatini's face dropped in horror.

Blake sat up straight in his seat, his eyes briefly meeting those of the taxi driver staring directly at him from the rear-view mirror.

Sabatini silently mouthed something to Blake. He nodded and spoke into the phone. 'What do you want with the watch?'

'I know more than you can possibly imagine,' said the voice. 'This moment was foretold millennia ago in the scriptures. I know what is hidden in the watch.'

'Foretold in the scriptures?' said Blake. Out of the corner of his eye, he could see the shadow of St Paul's Cathedral coming into view.

'Mr Blake, the End Times are coming. You and Dr Sabatini must make way for my master's purposes.' The signal momentarily dropped and then returned even louder than before. 'I can see you have arrived at St Paul's. You have obviously found the map. Give it to me now, or I swear I will drag you both into hell.'

Kovac pulled the black cab into the taxi rank just outside the front steps of Wren's imposing cathedral. He hadn't understood a word of the conversation he had just overheard in the back of his taxi, but he understood one thing: he needed to eject his passengers as quickly as possible. From further up Cannon Street, Kovac could hear the screaming siren of a police car weaving its way at speed through the traffic. *Were the police after them?* As he watched the blue flashing lights of the police car come closer, the most extraordinary feeling of unease washed over him. He flicked the central locking switch and ordered them to get out. Behind his left ear, he heard the sound of a dull click, like the cocking of a gun, and the shocking image of himself slumped over the steering wheel with a hole in his head appeared in his mind. He closed his eyes, uncertain which would arrive first: the bullet in the back of his head or the police car.

It took Kovac several drawn-out seconds to realise that the sirens were not getting closer but were in fact decreasing in pitch. The police car had passed in front of the cathedral and was now speeding down Ludgate Hill.

Gritting his teeth, Kovac opened his eyes and looked into the rear-view mirror. What he saw made him turn around quickly in his seat. Both back doors of the taxi were ajar, and his two passengers were nowhere to be seen. The only evidence that they had ever been there were the two mobile phones abandoned on the back seat.

CHAPTER 59

Mary and her black dog had been sitting on the steps to the cathedral's main entrance since the sun first rose over the horizon. The cold London sky had turned a vivid eggshell blue, and white vapour trails from high-altitude jets were the only marks in the perfectly clear sky. The time had come; she could feel it deep in her being. She looked down at the polished surface of the marble step. The subtle grain of minerals permeating its structure made the stone look like weathered animal bone. She took the needle and scraped it along the stone, blunting its end. She had no more use for it. The map was complete.

Long before Mary heard the police siren above the drone of the traffic, the ears of her dog had risen to attention. She stroked the animal's head, but its ears resolutely resisted the movement of her hand across its fur. From her position high above street level, she could see the speeding blue lights of the police vehicle reflected in the office windows. As her eyes followed the blue light jumping from window to window, her attention was drawn to one of the two figures that had just emerged from a black cab parked at the taxi rank. She was not struck by the urgency with which he and his companion alighted from the vehicle but rather by the purple aura surrounding him. She had seen the man several times before, but today his aura was extraordinary. Like a heat wave shimmering above hot tarmac, the colour seemed to evaporate from the extremities of his body as its source was renewed by a constant source of energy.

Her pulse quickened as she became transfixed by the man and woman running towards her. Mary rose to her feet and felt a wave of expectancy as they came closer. Together they ran up the stairs in front of her, covering two steps with every stride. Mary froze, powerless to move or avert her gaze. As they rushed by, something dropped from the man's hand and fell silently onto the white marble step by her feet.

She looked down, and a tremor of apprehension shook within her body. Contrasting vividly with the pure white marble steps was a blood-stained handkerchief moving gently in the cold breeze. Twisting around, Mary shouted at the top of her voice.

'It has been foretold in the Psalms: *a band of evil men has encircled me, and they have pierced my hand.*'

The force of her words hacked against the back of her throat. She shouted again, the sound echoing high in the doorway of the cathedral's main entrance. Blake stopped in his tracks, and Sabatini quickly followed suit. Slowly he turned, at first uncertain as to the source of the sound. Then he saw the face of the homeless woman staring back at him as if caught in a trance.

'What did you say?' Blake glanced to the woman's dog standing to attention by her side.

The woman's face was framed by a heavy black scarf tied around her head. Apart from her piercing eyes, her features were concealed under layers of dark grime. As he came closer, Blake could see that the junctions between her dense layers of clothes were stuffed with pieces of newspaper to insulate her from the cold.

A faint glimmer of recognition sparked in his eyes.

'I've seen you before,' said Blake.

'Let me see your hand.' The woman's words seemed to neutralise Blake's statement and leave it hanging in the air. Still keeping his distance, Blake slowly outstretched his hand. As his palm opened, he felt the crust of dried blood that had formed in its centre pull at the surrounding skin. He extended his fingers and could feel the layer crack apart and the tension in his palm release.

He repeated his assertion, this time almost whispering. 'I've seen you before, haven't I?'

The woman started speaking in tongues, her words swirling in the air like an incantation. Then her body lurched forward, her eyes focused so intensely upon Blake's open hand that it made him take a step back. Sabatini followed the line of the woman's stare to see a single drop of blood fall from the well of Blake's hand and land on the white marble floor. Mary took a sharp intake of breath as if recoiling from its impact on the ground.

'It has begun.' Mary said, her voice trembling.

'What? What has begun?' said Blake.

The woman stared into his eyes with such intensity, it sent his heart pounding.

'The prophecy is coming to pass. You have both been brought to this place at this time for a reason.'

'What are you talking about? What reason?'

'To decide,' said the woman.

'To decide what?' Blake's tone of voice had now changed to frustration.

'To decide whether the time has come to break the ancient seals. You are standing on holy ground. God's purpose is connected to this place and to you. His spirit has brought you here so that the ancient prophecies can be fulfilled.'

'I'm sorry, I don't understand?' Blake's voice echoed against the high walls.

'It was written in the scriptures and today it has come to pass.'

'The scriptures? What do you mean?'

'You have been marked with His sign.'

As she reached out to take his hands, Blake noticed the elaborate tattoos that covered hers. He scanned the designs, most of which were crude geometrical symbols, some annotated with Hebrew lettering, but all seemed to be connected by a spider's web of lines that disappeared up the sleeves of her coat. Looking directly into his eyes, Mary slowly turned Blake's hands over so that his palms now faced upwards. She positioned her fingertips next to his and then turned over her hands. Standing at Blake's shoulder, Sabatini gasped at what she saw.

Like staring at a reflection on the surface of a pond, Mary's right palm bore a dark tattoo, its six-pointed star the mirror image of the outline drawn in faded pen ink on Blake's left hand. He had drawn the shape of the Seal of Solomon on his hand with a pen whilst at the mortuary, and, though now badly faded, its design was still clear. The outline of the tattoo carved into Brother Nathan's chest was now staring back at him on his hand and was mirrored on the hand of the homeless woman. More shocking still, the small cut Blake had just sustained from the nail head was also perfectly mirrored on the vagrant's palm as a black spot tattooed on her skin.

Blake's hands began to tremble.

'You aren't the only one caught up in God's purpose,' said Mary.

Sabatini grabbed Blake's shoulder. 'Vincent, we've got to move now!' Blake turned on his feet and followed Sabatini's line of sight into the crowd of tourists milling beyond the cathedral steps. Pushing against the flow of people moving along the pavement were two men forcing their way towards the cathedral steps.

'Oh my god! They've followed us here!' shouted Sabatini.

Blake quickly turned to warn the homeless woman of the approaching peril, but she had dropped to her knees and started to pray.

CHAPTER 60

A shockwave pulsed across the surface of Milton's fourth coffee of the day. The heavy brown cardboard file that just landed on his desk had the word 'Dover' scrawled across its front cover in thick black felt pen. Milton raised his head and saw his sergeant looking expectantly at him from the edge of his desk. Hanging from his shoulder was a single strand of thin orange paper, the lonely remnant of a party streamer. Milton had politely declined the invitation to join his colleagues at the pub for the IT manager's birthday. Since the televised press conference, Chief Constable Lewis had been on his back, demanding to see progress in the 'Cambridge University' murder investigation. Several lost hours in the pub would be just the kind of ammunition the Chief would need to make life even more difficult than it was.

'Boss, you've got to see this,' said the sergeant.

Milton saved the email he was writing and leant back in his chair. It creaked as his large frame shifted in the seat.

'I'm listening,' said Milton.

'The CCTV images from the Dover port authority.'

'What about them?'

'The IT guys at Scotland Yard managed to clean up a couple of the Dover images. I cross-referenced them with our friends at Interpol, and what do you know? We've got a possible match.'

After dragging the file closer, Milton spread out its contents on his desk. He recognised the format of the Interpol 'high priority' report attached to the CCTV image of the mystery man. As Milton scanned his way through the pages, the police sergeant summarised aloud.

'Zoran Denic, aka "The Viper". Born in Cetinje, Montenegro, which was real bandit country during the Balkan wars of the early 1990s. He worked up the ranks to head one of the region's largest smuggling rackets, shipping contraband across the Serbian border,' said the sergeant. 'Smuggling was rife then due to a United Nations' embargo. It was a favourite haunt for *saners*.' From Milton's puzzled expression, the sergeant guessed that he had never heard the word before. Neither had he until fifteen minutes ago, but all the same it was nice to put one over on his boss. 'It's a local expression for thieves who only rob outside the borders of Montenegro and then return home to spend their ill-gotten gains.' The sergeant was now in full flow.

'You see, Montenegro used to lack extradition treaties with just about every country in Western Europe, and so it became a safe haven for some real hard nuts. Denic acted as a go-between for several prominent *saners* but had to leave Montenegro in a hurry after an altercation with the leader of a local militia. Like many shady characters coming out of the Balkan wars, he travelled west and ended up in the French Foreign Legion, where apparently he made a name for himself as an interrogator. He served two tours in Iraq but was court-martialled for stabbing an officer in the neck. He escaped from custody and then disappeared before resurfacing in Germany two years later.'

Milton picked up the artificial cigarette resting above the top line of keys on his workstation keyboard and bit into the end. 'Go on,' he said.

'He was arrested at the French-German border last year for travelling on a forged Bulgarian passport. The French police seized his vehicle and found that the boot contained boxes of stun grenades, a satellite phone and three Russian icon paintings that had just been stolen from a Scottish stately home. The day after his arrest, Denic was moved to a holding prison in Lyon, where he was sprung by two other members of his gang. Apparently, they shot out the prison watchtower with machine guns as Denic climbed over the prison wall with a fold-up ladder. One prison guard was killed and one was seriously injured. He's real lowlife shit.'

Milton went for his mobile but then thought better of it. Instead, he shuffled his chair backwards and reached out for the receiver of the desk phone. His mobile had been temperamental over the last few days, and he didn't want the line to go dead mid-conversation. After dialling a number, he scanned the air with his eyes, waiting for the call to be answered. Eventually, the unanswered ringing was cut short by the sound of Blake's answer phone message. He pressed redial and settled himself back in his chair. This time there was no delay. Not waiting for Blake's response, Milton relayed the information he had just gathered from the Interpol report.

'Blake, it's Milton. We've identified the person who killed the immigration officers in Dover. He's on Interpol's high priority list. His name is Zoran Denic, better known as "the Viper", and Vincent, he's a really nasty—'

Milton's flow was cut short by the loud sound of church bells coming from the other end of the line. The voice that eventually came on the line caught Milton completely off guard. The accent was Eastern European, and the voice was struggling to make itself heard over the din of the church bells.

'You a policeman, right?' said the voice.

Milton hesitated. 'Yes.'

'My name is Gregory Kovac. I am taxi driver. I think your friend is in much danger.'

CHAPTER 61

The London tour guide called them his 'freebies': the people who would secretly slip into his tour group without paying. Because of his engaging and almost theatrical delivery, the rotund American ex-drama teacher from the Midwest had managed to build a reputation as one of London's most respected guides. Over the years, he had become particularly astute at recognising 'freebies'. The differences were almost indiscernible to the untrained eye but were there nonetheless. The movement of the 'freebie' interlopers was subtly at odds to the rest of the fee-paying crowd. Often turning abruptly, they would try to hide behind the main nucleus of the group and would never make direct eye contact. He didn't mind; in fact, he positively encouraged it. With the inheritance money from his father's estate, he was financially independent and, what's more, he had never forgotten the day in Paternoster Square, when a small Scottish lady tour guide had fired his own interest in London history. He had quietly joined her tour, and to this day he still owed her a guiding fee.

He noticed their presence just after he began his daily St Paul's Cathedral tour. As he showed the group the magnificent monument to the Duke of Wellington, one of Britain's greatest soldiers and statesman, he observed something particularly unusual about their movements: they had chosen a position deep within the group yet focused their attention elsewhere. The gaze of the man, who was dressed conspicuously in a dirty crumpled suit, was scanning in all directions. His partner, a pretty but stern Mediterranean-looking woman, was doing the same. At first, he thought they were looking for a lost child, but as time went on he concluded that they were, in fact, hiding from someone. The tour guide tried to follow the direction of their concerned looks but could find no specific focus to their observations. For a moment, he lost his train of thought and realised that he had stopped speaking. He felt the eyes of his tour group upon him, most of them unsure whether his momentary pause was designed for dramatic effect or whether he had forgotten his script. A tangible sense of relief broke out when the guide gave out a loud chuckle and continued on with his commentary.

Sabatini took hold of Blake's arm. Through his jacket, he could feel her hands trembling.

'They've followed us in here.' Sabatini glanced anxiously over her shoulder. 'They could be anywhere. We've got to get to the sanctuary before they do.'

Blake looked up suddenly at the tour guide.

'Did you hear that?' said Blake.

Sabatini was baffled. She hadn't heard a word the guide had been saying.

'Shhhh! Listen!'

'I'm afraid we can't see Wren's floating staircase today, owing to the restoration work of the beautiful eighty-eight steps, but the door is just over there near the main entrance to the cathedral.' In unison the group turned and followed the guide's outstretched arm pointing to a simple wooden door between a large exhibition stand of the cathedral's charitable work in Africa and a sumptuous Christmas tree covered in slowly blinking red lights. By the time the tour guide re-gathered the group at the chapel of St Michael and St George, he noticed the 'freebies' had gone.

From his position high up in the whispering gallery, Denic saw the targets break across the cathedral floor and disappear into a side room close to the entrance doors. He gestured wildly to Crossland, who was hundreds of feet down below. His partner took only a moment to interpret the unequivocal hand signals. As Crossland sped towards the wooden door across the great nave, he slid the safety off the pistol hidden in his jacket pocket.

This time he wouldn't miss.

CHAPTER 62

The visit to the cathedral had been the highlight of her two-week holiday to London. The Danish schoolteacher from the outskirts of Holstebro stood at the bus stop, her mind fixed firmly on trying to keep her hands warm. She had left her gloves on the small writing desk in her hotel room, and now her fingers were thoroughly chilled. Adding to her discomfort was the fact that the number 23 bus, which would have taken her directly to the door of her Westbourne Park Hotel, had just left the bus stop. According to the timetable, the next one wasn't due for another twenty minutes. As she paced up and down trying to keep warm, a black limousine turned into one of the restricted car parking spaces beyond the cathedral steps.

The advanced suspension system of the Jaguar XJ coped easily with the short line of cobbles leading to the parking bay, which was marked off in a rectangle of white paint. The tourist stopped pacing. The previous day, she had spotted a famous British actor conducting a television interview outside the Houses of Parliament. Much to her dismay, her day of sightseeing had left the batteries of her camera completely drained, and she missed her opportunity to capture a picture of the handsome star. Today, there would be no such problem. Her camera had spent the night charging in her hotel room, and the fact that photographs were prohibited in the cathedral meant that the batteries were almost fully charged.

She had plenty of time before the arrival of her bus, so she moved closer to the car and settled for a position next to a phone box. With her camera ready for action in the pocket of her sheepskin coat, she waited expectantly for the doors of the blacked-out car to open. She didn't have to wait long. The rear door closest to the holidaying schoolteacher opened silently as if powered by itself. From her vantage point some ten metres away from the limousine, she peered into the back seats.

Squinting, she strained to differentiate between the brightness of the winter sunlight and the darkness of the car's cabin. She tried to make out the shape of a passenger inside, but all she could see was shadows. She edged forward, her chilled fingers gripping her camera in readiness.

Like the antenna of an insect sensing the air, a walking stick appeared to stab at the space around the open rear door, followed by a pair of lady's legs swinging themselves over the edge of the seat onto the pavement below. The tourist overheard voices. A male driver was imparting instructions to his impatient female passenger about the details of a flight to Tel Aviv.

'Ma'am, I've had word from the captain. He's just getting flight clearance from Ben Gurion Airport. The jet will be refuelled in the next hour. You could be in Jerusalem within seven hours. Arrangements are being made at the Temple Mount.' The driver's voice was controlled and refined, and reminded the tourist of her English lecturer at the University of Copenhagen. The passenger in the back of the car remained silent in the shadows for several moments and then slowly emerged into the light, causing the Dane to take several steps backwards.

The striking woman who sat perched on the edge of the back seat was elegantly dressed in a tailored pinstriped trouser suit. The magenta silk scarf tied high above the collar of her blouse contrasted vividly against her flawless pale skin. The tourist struggled to place her age, her assessment made even more difficult by the dark sunglasses that hid the area surrounding her eyes. At first, she placed the lady in her late twenties, but as the passenger used a walking stick to pull herself up, she realised that she had no idea of her true age. Something about the winter sun low in the sky gave the light on her face a strange muted quality, as if her skin were obscured by an almost imperceptible shadow.

Now that the woman was fully upright, the schoolteacher could see that she was tall, well over six feet, her model-like stature accentuated by the close-fitting material of her suit. The tourist stood excitedly as the lady walked quickly by her side. The walking stick that she thrust forward with every quickening step like the baton of a sergeant major on parade was evidently nothing more than a peculiar fashion accessory.

As the woman climbed the steps, the schoolteacher tracked her ascent through her camera's viewfinder, her finger pressing the shutter release as she went.

Then, the woman's progress was unexpectedly curtailed by someone or something just by the entrance doors.

Mary stared at the figure that had just passed her on the cathedral steps. The dog by her side rose instinctively to its feet, sensing that the atmosphere had somehow changed. All of a sudden, Mary was overcome by a terrible feeling. The foreboding came to her with a force of such unquestionable certainty, she found it difficult to breathe. The tall woman stopped and then slowly looked back at Mary. Even though the woman was wearing dark sunglasses, Mary felt her eyes burning into her soul.

CHAPTER 63

The heavy wooden door slammed shut, and the sound reverberated in the open space of the stairwell. Somewhere on the other side of the door, in the vast interior of the cathedral, two hit men were hunting them like prey. Sabatini scanned the doorframe for a bolt, but the simple oak door had no visible locking mechanism from the inside.

'They know the rod is here. If we don't find it, all will be lost,' said Sabatini.

Feeling her heart pounding in her chest, she steadied herself against the elaborate iron railings surrounding Wren's famous hanging staircase. The metal was cold to the touch, and it only temporarily neutralised the trembling of her hands. She gripped the ironwork tightly, straining to drag Newton's coded instructions back into her mind.

'Descend the eighty-eight stairs and open the stone door, as all will be revealed in a time, times and half a time.'

Without acknowledging his companion's words, Blake moved to the collection of decorating equipment neatly stacked on a chair against the wall. As he hauled its tubular frame towards the door, various-sized brushes and tins and a large plastic torch crashed to the floor. With his foot acting as a fulcrum, Blake tilted the chair backwards, and then, with a series of hard kicks, he jammed the top of the chair securely under the brightly polished brass handle.

'That should buy us some time. We've got to be quick.' Blake's voice sounded detached, as if his thoughts were running three or four moves ahead. He turned towards the stairs and became aware for the first time of the space they were standing in. Wren's cantilevered staircase appeared to hang in mid-air, as each step of the perfectly symmetrical spiral was supported by the step below.

'Descend the eighty-eight stairs and open the stone door, as all will be revealed in a time, times and half a time,' he repeated.

Without warning, the door handle jolted downwards in a frenzy and then a force crashed against the bottom of the door. The chair wedged under the brass handle momentarily slipped backwards on the polished stone floor before securing itself once again under the ornate handle.

Sabatini snatched the torch up from the floor as Blake grabbed her arm. 'We've got to go now!'

Jumping several steps at a time, they quickly descended the eighty-eight steps. The surrounding walls were perfectly smooth with no obvious ornamentation, recess or door to the outside world. Once at the bottom of the hollow stairwell, the two companions soon realised they had run into a dead end. There was no way in or out, apart from the door they had just come through, the same door that was now being forced open by two hired killers.

The only feature in the stairwell was a large circular granite plinth in the centre of the floor. Just over waist high, it supported a platform several metres in diameter. The top was divided into twelve pointed chevrons of alternately coloured black-and-white inlaid marble, like the markings of a compass. At the centre was a small golden inscription: *'On this moment hangs eternity, for no moment is backwards.'*

'It must be something to do with this,' Blake said.

Running along the perimeter of the chevron design was a circular brass track inset flush to the marble's surface. A series of markings were uniformly engraved along its edge, dividing the metal track into regular increments. Sitting on the circular rim of metal was a small brass knob elaborately fashioned into the shape of a beehive.

Blake stared at the beehive design. Something was familiar about it. He wracked his brain, and then it came to him: it was the same design that he and Milton had seen over a year ago in the back of the coded notebook found with Tarek Vinka's body in The Faversham restaurant in Soho, the same notebook stolen from the Cannes residence of Didier Clerot. Before he could explain, Sabatini started speaking.

'Look, it's the sign of the society. The rod must be here.'

'What do you mean?' Blake looked blankly towards her.

'Don't you remember Newton's words in the crimson book? He mentioned a stone door and a lock in the shape of a beehive. In his alchemic writings, Newton used the beehive to denote a secret brotherhood. Like bees, the *brothers* would go out into the world in search of the nectar of God's hidden knowledge. Once found, they would bring it back to the hive for safe keeping.'

Walking around the marble platform as she spoke, Blake positioned himself next to the metal beehive emblem. He reached out and touched the engraved handle protruding about an inch above the flat marble platform. Much to Blake's surprise, the brass knob moved easily under his fingers. He crouched down, his eyeline now level with the beehive insignia, to which he carefully reapplied pressure. He watched it glide effortlessly along the metal track, and as the brass insignia gently came to rest on the metal runners, a sound echoed throughout the empty space of the stairwell. High above their heads, the door handle started to jolt violently again.

'They're coming through the door!' Sabatini's voice was full of terror.

Blake looked up to the doorway some twenty metres above their heads and saw the red glow of Christmas lights through a small gap beside the door. He refocused on the platform and the brass mechanism embedded around its edge. Biting the side of his tongue, he wrestled hard with the questions screaming in his head.

Why would Wren place such a structure at the exact location identified in the map? It must be here. Newton's annotations talked of a stone door, not a massive block of granite.

Blake could taste the tang of blood in his mouth.

'Carla ... the inscription, what does it mean? It must be something to do with the rod's location.'

Sabatini was transfixed on the doorway, her face blanched of colour. Grabbing her shoulder, Blake repeated his question, and the strength of his voice snapped her out of her trance. She glanced down to the gold lettering at the centre of the marble plinth.

'On this moment hangs eternity, for no moment is backwards.' The words stumbled from her mouth. Blake's eyes widened.

'The movement of time. The inscription is about the movement of time. It's a clock! It's a clock! Just like his pocket watch. The prophecy will unfold in a time, times and half a time. The brass handle must be a pointer, like the hand of a clock.'

Blake could hardly get the words out. His heart was beating so fast, he could feel its rhythm pulse along his shoulders and down the insides of his arms. He moved the brass handle back to its original position at one end of the circular track marked by a small engraving of what looked like a bee. As he positioned the beehive knob in line with the marker, he felt a faint click travel through his fingertips from deep within the marble platform. Blake pushed the beehive handle along the track to make a circuit around the marble platform. The brass beehive handle slid easily on its runners, and Blake realised that it was running on ball bearings set within the track. At first, he walked slowly around the perimeter, gently guiding the beehive emblem with his hand, but before long he was propelling the handle forward with a series of hard pushes.

'One circuit complete. That's the time,' Blake spoke through gritted teeth as the beehive insignia crossed the start marker after one complete circumnavigation. 'Now for the times!' Blake redoubled his efforts around the plinth, the handle continuously gathering speed. As he completed another circuit, the handle appeared to be travelling under its own momentum. Fighting to keep up with its progress, Blake was now running around the perimeter of the platform, the insignia's position just out of reach of his outstretched hand. After another entire revolution, Blake lost his footing and stumbled forwards. Trying to keep himself upright, he lost his grip on the side of the plinth and fell towards the wall like a stone ejected from a slingshot. As Blake's shoulder slammed into the solid granite wall, he yelled out to Sabatini.

'Stop it!'

Before Blake's words had time to echo in the empty stairwell, Sabatini stepped towards the platform, her eyes following the arc of the emblem as it travelled around the plinth. Her hand shot out and came down onto the beehive emblem, stopping it dead in its tracks exactly halfway round the disc of marble. A noise like grinding teeth sounded deep within the stone and sent strong vibrations through the handle, causing Sabatini to release her grip. Now sitting prostrate on the floor on the other side of the plinth, Blake's face was frozen in a dumbfounded expression, his gaze transfixed on the dark recess that had opened up at the base of the plinth.

'Carla, hand me the torch. I think we're going to need it!'

CHAPTER 64

Whatever Denic said to the group of school children congregating around the large wooden side door scattered them like chaff in the wind. By the time Crossland had dragged the exhibition board in front of the closed entrance leading to Wren's famous staircase, Denic had assessed the doorframe surrounding the door's lock. He had already tried to force it open, but the door was blocked by something on the other side. Crossland positioned the large stand between Denic and the roaming eyes of visitors arriving through the main cathedral doors. Once the screen had been secured in position, Denic unzipped the dark green canvas bag at his feet. As his gloved hands strained to release the crowbar trapped at the bottom of the bag, the barrel of his Sig Sauer popped out from the opening. He tugged again. Finally, the steel bar was released, accompanied by the sound of metal scraping against metal. The sound was strangely reassuring to Denic's ears.

Whilst his partner was readying himself to attack the doorframe with the crowbar, Crossland became aware of an elderly couple that had just emerged from the main entrance hall. By their irritable demeanour towards each other, he guessed that the husband and wife were in mid-argument. The stick-thin husband was busy mimicking his wife's complaints from his position safe behind her wheelchair. The vertebrae of his neck looked fused in a permanent stoop, as if he were battling against a gale. By the way the man struggled to change the direction of the wheelchair, his wife was of a much larger build, although it was hard to tell exactly owing to the copious blankets packed around her body. Without replying to the woman's scolding, the man engaged the brakes of the wheelchair and set out towards the ticket desk. Now marooned in the centre of the entrance hall, the woman's frustration towards her husband spilled out in a series of exasperated shakes of her head.

The woman gradually became conscious that she was being watched by a huge man standing next to the exhibition stand. From across the hall, Crossland threw the lady a contemptuous stare, which caused her to self-consciously adjust the heavy tartan blanket on her lap.

Finally, the sound of splintering wood came from behind the exhibition stand.

'Max, we're in!'

CHAPTER 65

The torchlight shook wildly on the rough stone wall as Blake and Sabatini hurried their way along the cold passageway. The air temperature had dropped noticeably since they'd crawled their way through the hidden recess at the base of the granite platform, and their breath was like pale smoke in the electric torchlight. The entrance led to an iron ladder some twenty feet further down into the foundations of the great cathedral before connecting to the cramped tunnel that they were now traversing. Without the torch that Sabatini had liberated from the pile of workman's tools near the stairwell door, the space would have been completely devoid of light. The passage was narrow, with a coffin-like shape that allowed neither occupant to stand up fully straight.

They were moving deep within the London clay. Contrary to the pact she had made with herself moments before, Sabatini looked over her shoulder into the blackness. Her breath had become shallow and rapid as she imagined the darkness consuming her. She looked forward again, her hand grasping the hem of Blake's jacket. Just as her fingers secured their grip onto the jacket lining, the direction of the passageway made a sharp turn to the right.

As they squeezed their way around the ninety-degree bend, Blake whispered to his companion, 'Remember the turn marked on the map? We must be moving along the nave towards the great dome.' Blake coughed, sending the torchlight juddering upwards. Sabatini imagined the staggering weight of Wren's masterpiece bearing down on the roof of the tunnel. She began to repeat a prayer her mother had taught her as a child. She could feel her blouse sticking to her back.

Continuing along the tunnel, Blake became convinced of two things. The first concerned their physical location. Although their dark and cramped conditions confused his senses, he was now certain that, since making the sharp turn in the tunnel, they were descending. His second insight was even more alarming. Going by the light's fading intensity against the tunnel wall, he was sure that the torch batteries were about to give out.

Blake came to a stop. The way forward was completely blocked by a stone wall. He felt Sabatini's grip tighten on the back of his jacket.

'Oh my god, we're trapped!' Sabatini's voice was full of panic, and a film of ice-cold sweat began to form on her forehead. She felt the heavy darkness shroud her body, dragging her slowly down into the heavy clay. She dropped to her knees. Blake felt Sabatini release her grip on the back of his jacket, and he struggled to turn his body. The back of his head scraped against the rough surface of the tunnel roof and cut into his scalp. Only after Blake had positioned the fading torchlight in Sabatini's direction did he realise that they had missed a doorway ten feet back down the tunnel, as its location was marked by a large dark rectangle contrasting against the pale reflection of the torch beam from the surrounding wall.

'We passed it. Carla, it's there. The passage carries on over there.' Tracing its dimensions with the light, Blake marked the position of the opening in the wall. Suddenly, the torch made a gentle fizzing sound and then went out.

Standing in the pitch black, Blake felt Sabatini's warm breath against the back of his hand. He shook the torch barrel up and down vigorously. The batteries rattled inside their metal housing and the torch flashed back into life, but with an even weaker intensity than before. Wasting no time, Sabatini scrambled to her feet, and the two companions headed for the doorway in the wall.

As they passed through the entrance, both became aware of a sudden change in the air around them, as if the atmosphere had become electrically charged.

'Vincent, what is it?' The timbre of Sabatini's voice had changed and now echoed all around. Slowly raising the torch beam from the floor, Blake felt a surge of adrenalin as he tried to take in the view before his eyes.

'Oh my god!' said Blake. His stomach turned inside out. 'It's all real: the inner sanctuary, the New Jerusalem ... It's right here, under the dome of St Paul's.'

Crossland took the torch from the canvas bag and slammed it onto the stone floor. The Cambridge job had gone pear-shaped and this one was unravelling before his eyes. He stared at the opening at the base of the granite platform, knowing that it represented the only possible route of escape from the closed stairwell. With his mind imagining the brutality he would unleash on Blake and Sabatini when he finally caught up with them, he watched his partner disappear through the opening at the base of the plinth. Before moving to join him, his attention was drawn back to the canvas bag. He inspected its contents for several seconds before locating an object that caused a malevolent grin to cross his face. Slowly raising the serrated hunting knife to his lips, Crossland imagined blood dripping off its eight-inch steel blade.

The space into which they had just emerged was substantial. To estimate its dimensions, Blake moved the torch beam across the face of each wall, but the light was soon swallowed up in the darkness. Even in the faltering light, he could make out the elaborate craftsmanship of the wooden panelling lining the walls and the shadowy outline of a large, heavy curtain hanging down from the ceiling. Close to the entrance stood a large metal candle stand, a small upturned spike marking the position for seven individual candles. The centre of the space was dominated by a large marble platform, about four feet high and eight feet across. Made from fine white marble, it reflected any light that fell upon it, giving its surface a strange glowing luminosity. Its top surface was engraved with a perfect hexagram. As Blake approached, he could feel the hairs over his body rise.

'Look!' exclaimed Sabatini. 'Move the light to the middle of the platform.' Sabatini pointed at what looked like a roll of material placed at the very centre of the circular platform. Approaching the edge of the pedestal, Blake trained the torch directly on the object, which was a package of mildewed red velvet rolled tightly into a cylinder no more than two feet in length.

Deep under the foundations of Wren's great dome, Blake leant forward and took hold of the bundle in his right hand. Immediately he felt the weight of an object bound within its folds. Its centre of mass shifted as he brought it closer to his body, like a gyroscope pulling against the force of his hand. In the place where the bundle had been, Blake now noticed a small metal object gleaming momentarily in the path of the torchlight. With his free hand, he picked it up and brought it close to his face. It measured about an inch across and by its relative weight, Blake guessed it was made of pure gold. As he rotated the talisman in his fingers, the tips of its six-pointed star design felt sharp on his fingertips. He quickly put it in his pocket and returned his attention to the roll of faded, red velvet. Swallowing hard, Blake carefully began to unroll the parcel. With each rotation, his heart beat faster. After several turns, the velvet material fell away. Letting out an audible gasp, Sabatini stared at the object remaining in Blake's trembling hands.

Measuring about the length of his forearm, the dark cylinder appeared to be made from a piece of twisted dense wood. It was tapered slightly at one end, and its surface was perfectly smooth except for the precious stones inset along its length and a series of symbols carved along its surface. Blake brought it closer to the beam of the torch, causing a large shadow of the rod to rear up on the wall in front of him. As he rotated the rod slowly in his fingers, he became aware that its surface was getting hotter.

'Vincent, the letters!'

For a moment, Blake was frozen to the spot, his brain unable to process the information being relayed by his eyes. The Hebrew lettering running along its length had begun to glow, its brightness now stronger than that of the pale torchlight. Blake released the staff, sending it clattering onto the hard marble surface of the platform. The sound echoed out into the darkness.

CHAPTER 66

Crossland switched off his torch and stared at the diffuse shadows reflected on the back wall of the tunnel. The light source from the opening in the stone passage appeared to be static, but every so often the elongated shadow of a person reared up and then disappeared back into the stonework. He could hear voices clearly through the entranceway. After adjusting the large hunting knife secured on the belt of his trousers, Crossland checked that there was a round in the chamber of his pistol. He would allow himself some fun with these two. Indeed, he would savour the sensation of slicing through the tendons in the man's neck and watching the blood gush from his carotid artery. This job had been fucked up from the beginning, and they would pay for it.

Denic recognised the blood lust in his partner's eyes. He would turn the other way when the time came for him to satiate his hunger. The military psychologist at his court martial had described Crossland as borderline psychopathic, but the truth was that the British Army had nurtured his talents for violence and created a killing machine: a killing machine that needed to be fed. Denic readied himself. It would all be over in a matter of minutes.

A bright flash from the darkness some twenty feet to their rear burst from the barrel of a titanium silencer on the end of a Walther P22. Denic had often wondered what his final seconds would be like: whether the passage of time would slow down or whether the events of his life would be replayed in his mind. The reality of the experience was very different. He managed to turn just enough to see the back of Crossland's head explode in a cloud of red mist. As gritty splinters of bone hit the side of his cheek, he became mindful of a second flash of light from behind. A tenth of a second later, a .22 pistol round exited his left eye socket. As the electrical activity in his brain ebbed away, he had the most dreadful sense that his soul was being dragged down into the London earth.

When Denic's body had finally stopped twitching on the floor, a tall figure emerged from the darkness.

'Too many mistakes, gentlemen. You were just making too many mistakes. Your contract with the Drakon has been terminated.'

The female whisper was as cold as the stone floor. Slowly, the figure moved towards the tunnel opening. It would be tidier this way. All the bodies would be resealed in the chamber and there would be no trace. Before walking through the opening, the Drakon stopped and looked down at the pool of blood now surrounding the two corpses. A walking stick prodded at Crossland's crumpled body, and the serrated edge of a hunting knife was visible from beneath his blood-stained jacket.

Hearing sounds echoing in the tunnel, Blake grabbed the rod from the podium and quickly placed it on the floor next to the edge of the platform as a strong beam of light emerged through the opening leading to the sanctuary. Squinting into the light, Blake tried to make out the shape behind the glare. He took Sabatini's hand and prepared himself for what was to come.

'Thank goodness you're safe,' said the voice.

The words reverberated around the sanctuary and were so unexpected that for a moment Blake's mind couldn't quite take them in. Slowly, the beam of the flashlight was directed to the floor, revealing the face of the figure concealed behind it. The tall and well-dressed woman had a deep frown of concern across her forehead. Strangely, instead of looking directly back at Blake and Sabatini, her line of sight was fixed firmly on the podium. After a long pause, she spoke with renewed urgency.

'My name is Ema Mats. I was a friend of Brother Nathan's. We must leave this place immediately,' said the woman. She beckoned them forward and turned towards the doorway.

'Come quickly, and bring the rod. There is no time to lose.'

As the woman's body turned, Sabatini noticed the strange walking stick illuminated by the flashlight. She noticed its curious carved handle and her expression turned troubled as she tried to hook a memory from deep within her subconscious. Blake stepped away from the podium to get enough space to crouch down and pick the rod up from the floor. Then he heard Sabatini whisper something under her breath.

'There's something wrong.'

As the realisation of where she had seen the elaborate carvings detonated in her mind, Sabatini shouted at Blake, 'Stop. It's a trap. It's Newton's walking stick! She has Newton's walking stick!'

By the time Blake looked back at the woman, he was staring down the barrel of the pistol.

'Where is it?' Mats's voice had a chilling intensity.

'It's not here,' said Sabatini, her voice trembling. She took a step closer to Blake.

'Don't lie to me. It's here. I can feel it,' said the Drakon. For a second time, Mats demanded an answer to her question. 'Where is it?' This time she moved forward menacingly, the pupils of her eyes narrowing like a reptile.

'I will ask you one more time. Where is the rod?' As she emerged from the shadows, Mats's physical frame grew in stature, like a terrible wave rising on the sea. 'Dr Blake, Dr Sabatini, you *will* tell me.' The woman's voice was hard and filled with threat. Her teeth bit through the cold, murky air as she came closer.

Sabatini spoke, 'It's not here. We've searched the—' before she could finish her sentence, the Drakon lashed out in fury, the handle of the pistol smashing into the side of Sabatini's skull. The impact sent Sabatini's body crashing to the ground. Blake stared in horror as a small dark trail of blood seeped from behind Sabatini's head.

'You fool!' The terrifying sound of the Drakon's voice reverberated throughout the sanctuary.

Blake stumbled backwards, recoiling from the barrel of Mats's pistol being driven into his temple. He stared directly into Mats's crazed face. Her tongue stabbed at the air as the sinews in her neck tensed like strings of catgut, straining against the writhing motion of her head. Blake shut his eyes. He felt the cold metal of the pistol move away from his forehead. Was this it? Was he going to die? He tried to drag the memory of Sarah's face into his mind. Then he felt Mats's warm breath against his ear.

'You will tell me. Or soon you will be whimpering like your daughter.'

Blake's eyes slowly opened. 'Sarah?'

A collection of untethered thoughts now snapped into place.

'*You* are ... the Drakon.' Blake's voice faltered, as the name opened up a seismic fault in the bedrock of his mind. Blake now stared down the barrel of the gun into the eyes of the brutal criminal mastermind. 'It was you. *You* were the one who broke into my house and ...'

A mocking grin opened up at the side of the Drakon's face as she sucked in air. 'Who killed your wife? Yes, that was me. I relished every second, seeing her brains spilled out on the tarmac.' She paused. 'But that wasn't the best thing; the best was biting into the flesh of your deformed daughter.' As the words came out of her mouth, her tongue darted between the fingers of her hand. 'Mmm, her young blood tasted so sweet.'

Wild with rage, Blake lurched forward, his chest jabbing into the barrel of the gun, as though he were an enraged fighting dog straining against a short leash.

Mats stabbed the gun hard into Blake's ribs. 'You want to kill me, don't you? I can feel the poison rising up in your blood.'

There was a loud click, and then a pain exploded from the centre of Blake's right kneecap that sent shockwaves reverberating through every nerve ending in his body. Blake's leg buckled backwards and spun him to the ground like a corkscrew. The back of his head struck the stone floor.

Mats stood over Blake's crumpled body.

'Do you think you will prevent me getting what I am destined to possess?' said the Drakon. 'The pain you are feeling now will be nothing compared to the misery you will feel if you do not tell me where the rod is. No one will be able to hear your screams. You are completely alone. Tell me now where you have hidden the rod and I promise your daughter will live.'

As Mats's walking stick pressed down on Blake's shattered knee, an excruciating jolt of pain ricocheted up the side of Blake's body. The intensity of his screams brought a glimmer of satisfaction to Mats's face.

'We are wasting time. Where is it?'

Straining to find his breath, Blake turned his head in the direction of the marble platform and groaned something. His throat choked.

'Again, louder!'

'It's on the floor, aghhh ... next to the platform.' The last word collapsed into a gasp for breath.

The Drakon spun round and redirected the beam of her torch onto the base of the plinth. It only took her a matter of seconds to locate the relic against the marble pedestal. After pulling on her patent leather gloves, she raised the relic triumphantly above her head. Sucking in a long draft of air, she closed her eyes and started to recite an incantation. The intensity of her voice increased with every phrase.

'I claim this rod for you, my Master. With this relic, the dark prophecy will be set in motion. Let your fire be unleashed and let God and all His prophets be thrown down into the stinking pit.' She was now spitting the words from her mouth. 'They will all be consumed in your blackness, and the tribulation will last forever.'

Abruptly, the invocation came to an end, interrupted by the loud groans from the body writhing pathetically on the ground. The Drakon's eyes widened as she remembered the hunting knife, which weighed heavily in her pocket.

With a cruel grin flickering on her lips, she placed the rod carefully on the platform and unsheathed the knife from her pocket.

After all, the occasion did warrant a great sacrifice. The search had taken millennia, and finally it had come to an end. Her master would appreciate the spilling of blood deep under the temple of God.

She would start with Blake, then Sabatini, and end with Blake's precious daughter. Butcher them all like pigs.

She circled Blake's crumpled body. A large pool of dark blood had formed around his leg. The sound of Mats's shoe heels clicking on the stone floor close by jolted Blake back into consciousness. As his vision cleared, he became aware of Mats's silhouette standing above him. A hand reached down and grabbed a clump of Blake's hair, lifting up his head several inches above the ground. The serrated blade of the hunting knife rested against the tendons of Blake's neck. Mats pressed the blade against Blake's pulsing carotid artery and watched as a single drop of blood tracked slowly down his white skin.

Blake tried to fight, but his efforts were useless. Excruciating pain had now been replaced by a heavy coldness that made anything but the smallest of movements impossible. As he stared into the face of evil, he felt the past reach out to receive him.

CHAPTER 67

'Stop! Get away from him.' The Drakon looked up, jolted by the unexpected voice. At first, she struggled to discriminate between the shapes hidden behind the strong light, but as her eyes readjusted, the profile of a woman and a large dog became clear. The strange vagrant woman standing in the doorway to the sanctuary was pointing a pistol directly at the Drakon's head. Mats recognised it as Crossland's Sig Sauer. The Drakon slowly lowered the blade from Blake's throat.

'Thank goodness you're here. My name is Ema Mats. This man and woman are dangerous criminals. They tried to kill me and bury me here. Help me, please!' said the Drakon.

Blake felt his body slump forwards. With his mind moving in and out of consciousness, he tried to focus on the blurred shapes morphing in and out of his field of vision. He felt the dull chill of the stone floor against his right cheek and then heard something like the barking of a dog resonating high in the ceiling. A tremor shivered through his body and then all went black.

Falling to her knees, the Drakon began to sob uncontrollably.

'He said he would tie me up and kill me, cut me into pieces while I was still alive. He said I would feel everything.' Her words could be barely heard through her sobbing. 'Thank goodness you're here.'

Mary looked at the aura shimmering above the head of the figure kneeling in front of her. It was different from anything she had seen before. Like the raised sting of a scorpion, it arched out from the woman's shoulder blades and rose six feet above her head, its surface shimmering as if made of flowing oil. It seemed to possess a quality that distorted the very fabric of the space around her body, drawing the surrounding light into itself. Mary struggled to cock the pistol, which felt heavy and awkward in her hand.

'I know who you are, Ema Mats. It has been foretold,' shouted Mary.

Mats's eyes narrowed, her tears replaced by a malevolent gaze. With the pistol trained on her target, Mary slowly unbuttoned her large overcoat. Shaking the coat from her shoulders, it fell to the ground by her feet. The Drakon inhaled loudly at the design tattooed over Mary's body. Swamped by an oversized vest and skirt, Mary's emaciated body was criss-crossed by a web of lines and symbols tattooed into her skin. At certain places on her arms and shoulders, the intersection of lines was marked with the crude motif of a church. Many of the lines terminated at a single point several inches below Mary's throat. In a circle surrounding the junction, the words 'St Paul's' were etched into her pale skin, their rawness a testament to their recent age.

'Step away from the rod!' shouted Mary.

'The rod needs to be studied as a historical artefact. I have a team of research scientists already assembled in Jerusalem,' said the Drakon.

'It can never be returned to Jerusalem until God has willed it.' Mary's voice trembled at first but quickly took on a hard determination. 'Returning it to Jerusalem will usher in the End Times.'

The Drakon spat back a contemptuous reply. 'What do you know of the rod?'

Mary turned her arm and exposed the inside of her forearm. Running along its length were a series of ten Hebrew characters cut into her skin. The scarring was deep, and by the inconsistency of the texture, each letter appeared to have been made over several different occasions. Mats immediately recognised the sequence of letters as the same as those engraved down the length of the rod. She breathed in loudly through her teeth like a snake tasting the air.

'I see you are aware of the ten symbols of the plagues of Egypt.' The Drakon's words were slow and deliberate. 'Each symbol is the first letter of one of the ten plagues unleashed by your God to force the release of the Jews from their captivity.'

The Drakon walked slowly around the plinth.

'We have both been chosen to find the rod,' said the Drakon.

'Don't move! I have been chosen by God to keep the rod hidden until the allotted time has come, and you ...' A long pause followed. 'You are the Watcher, chosen by the devil himself to wreak destruction on the world.'

'The Watcher? You know nothing of me,' spat the Drakon.

Swapping the pistol from one hand to the other, Mary turned her other forearm into the light.

Three words—'Mastema the Deceiver'—were written, one above each other, in scar tissue along its length. 'I cut your name into my body so that I would never forget your evil. Ema Mats. Mastema. You are the same.'

Mats smiled. 'Just a playful rearrangement of letters. I am known by many names: Ema Mats, Mastema, the Drakon, Abaddon, Haborym, Beelzebub. I have searched for millennia for the rod and now I have found it.'

Trembling, Mary took a step backwards. 'You are the agent of the devil!' she shouted.

Mats's head dropped as if pulled down by an invisible force and then rose slowly to an angle that just exposed the whites of her eyeballs.

'You understand so little.' The sound of Mats's words were now contorted and unrecognisable as coming from the voice of a woman.

'I understand what is written in the Holy Scriptures, about you and your kind,' said Mary.

'My kind?'

'It is written in the Book of Enoch that the 200 fallen angels, known as "the Watchers", were banished to earth at the time of the falling. Taking on human wives and producing children, half-human, half-demon, they had only one reason for living: to seek revenge for Satan's great expulsion from heaven. You are Mastema, the angel of hatred, created by Satan.'

'We are both children of the expulsion,' said the Drakon.

'What do you mean?' said Mary.

'In the beginning, there was only the symmetry of God; a prison of uniformity. His grand purpose was to hold existence in a cage of regularity, His perfect symmetry cancelling out all opposition to His will. You call that heaven?' The words spewed from her mouth, driven out by some demonic force inside her body.

'Then, in the recesses of the universe, the Dark King willed himself into existence, a kernel of disturbance in the perfectly balanced field of your God. Once there, the disturbance grew rapidly, creating ever-increasing vibrations in the fabric of heaven. Eventually, the growing presence of the Dark King threatened to shatter the cage's symmetry forever.'

Mary shouted out, 'You are Mastema, the Deceiver!'

'Don't you understand? Without the disturbance, you and I simply couldn't exist. God's symmetry would cancel out all opposition, all aberration, all instability. But once the disturbance had occurred and the symmetry of his prison had been broken, He had to expel its cause. We exist because God had no choice.'

'God expelled Satan, and he fell from heaven like lightning,' said Mary raising the pistol.

The Drakon took several steps backwards, her body completely vanishing in the darkness. Panicked, Mary tracked her pistol wildly from side to side, trying to pick out any sign of movement in the black void.

The dog at Mary's side snarled loudly, its jaws biting at an invisible enemy. For an instant, two points of crimson light flashed in the darkness like the burning eyes of a serpent. Mary heard the demon chant loudly in a language not of this world, the words swirling upwards like a vortex. Pointing the gun into the darkness, Mary squeezed the trigger. A shot rang out deep below the dome of St Paul's Cathedral but the words continued even faster than before. Mary squeezed the trigger again and then again, the sound of the gun reverberating in the empty void.

Suddenly, the Drakon's body stepped out from the shadows into the light. Terrified, Mary jabbed at the trigger but the weapon just returned a series of hollow clicks. Only then did Mary see the single bullet hole through the Drakon's temple, a line of blood tracking a path down her face. The Drakon staggered forward and then crashed to the floor like a boxer cut down by a killer blow.

Still shaking, Mary moved warily towards the dead body. The Drakon's face stared up from the ground. All of a sudden, the dog's ears pointed forwards to get a fix on something in the darkness. The animal bore its fangs, readying itself for attack, but all was silent apart from the sound of Mary gasping by its side. After retrieving her coat from the floor, Mary ran over to the marble plinth and placed the rod into its heavy folds of material. Then she knelt down next to Blake's and Sabatini's unconscious bodies. With her arms raised, she began to pray fervently aloud: 'By your almighty power, Lord, save them.'

Moments later, Mary and the black dog were moving quickly back down the tunnel.

CHAPTER 68

The first thing Blake saw after regaining consciousness was the sight of Sabatini's face smiling back at him. Initially her outline drifted in and of focus, but within seconds it had stabilised in his field of view. He realised that she was lying on a stretcher next to him wrapped in a silver space blanket. Instinctively, he reached out towards her, but his movement was immediately checked by the hand of a paramedic adjusting the flow rate of the intravenous drip in his arm.

'Slow down, my friend. You will both be fine.' The familiar voice of DCI Milton echoed in the subterranean chamber.

As soon as Milton and four members of the Metropolitan Police's armed tactical response team had arrived at the taxi parked outside St Pauls, its driver, a Gregory Kovac, had directed them to the main entrance. Kovac had jumped out of the driver's seat of his taxi just in time to see his terrified passengers bound up the main steps of the cathedral.

Bursting through the large doors of the packed nave, Milton and his team had been immediately greeted with a torrent of instructions from the most unlikely of sources. The instructions had come from a wheelchair-bound seventy-eight-year-old lady holidaying from the States. She had seen two 'undesirables' force open the door to Wren's floating staircase who she was concerned were 'up to no good.' Her suspicions raised, she had commanded her husband to inform the Cathedral's staff; however, after thanking the senior citizen for his diligence, they had advised him that the two individuals were actually workmen employed on the staircase's restoration. The woman, however, had not been convinced.

Milton crouched to his knees beside Blake.

'I don't know what the hell went on down here, but it's all over. You and Carla are safe,' said Milton as he patted Blake's shoulder. 'But I tell you, you were both very lucky. If it wasn't for a stray dog barking at the base of that plinth showing us the way down here, I don't think we would have found you in time.'

CHAPTER 69

Three Months Later: Tuesday 1 March

As he waited for the consultant to finish flicking through the charts pinned to the clipboard at the foot of Sarah's bed, Blake allowed himself a smile. He had received the call from the auction house whilst clambering into the back of the taxi on the way to the hospital. He balanced his crutches on the seat next to him to answer the insistent ringing of his phone. The call lasted seconds but produced such a feeling of jubilation in him that he punched the back of the driver's headrest, much to the driver's annoyance. The sales clerk rang to inform him that his lot had been sold successfully during that morning's auction. Something of a buzz had been created around the unique twelfth-century Cabbalistic amulet, and the sales price had exceeded all expectations. The auction catalogue had described it as '*the earliest known example of a Jewish amulet displaying the Star of David.*' The final auction price was a record six-figure sum. With the proceeds from the sale, Sarah's ongoing hospital bills would be paid for the foreseeable future.

The consultant returned the clipboard and stood beside Sarah's bed. 'Mr Blake, Sarah continues to make progress. Her level of consciousness seems to have changed since the ... incident.' The consultant shifted uncomfortably as Blake glanced at Sarah's hand and the gap where her little finger used to be.

'When Sarah was first admitted, she was in a very deep coma and completely unresponsive to external stimuli, but gradually she seems to be recovering. There are real signs that her body is becoming responsive.'

Blake listened intently to the consultant.

'The nursing team have reported some very encouraging signs over the last few weeks. Now and again Sarah has partially opened her eyes, and it's really great news about her breathing.'

A smile returned to Blake's face. Today was a special day: the first day in over a year he had seen Sarah's face without the plastic intubation tube. Without it, her mouth looked relaxed. She looked beautiful. Just like her mum.

Blake tried to talk, but his tongue stuck to the roof of his mouth.

The consultant continued. 'Waking up from a coma is usually very gradual. The signs are encouraging but we need to be cautious. Every coma is different. We need to take one day at a time.' The consultant repositioned the stethoscope around her neck and changed the subject. 'So, Mr Blake, how's that knee of yours?'

'It's getting there. I was told that the surgery was a success,' said Blake.

'Very good, very good, and how long before the cast comes off?'

'Two more weeks and then physio.'

The doctor smiled reassuringly.

'They're pretty confident that with time I'll regain most of the movement in the joint.'

'Good.' With that, the medic stood up, shook Blake's hand and left the room.

Before the door had chance to shut behind her a head peered through the door. It was Anje, the Filipina nurse who had been assigned to Sarah's ward.

'Vincent, you want tea?' said the nurse.

'Yes, please.'

'Okay, tea with milk coming up.'

Since their first meeting at Sarah's bedside months ago, Blake and Anje had become friends. She had shown him photos of her family back in Cebu and told him about the money she sent back every month for her sons. She was kind-hearted and had a mischievous personality.

Carefully backing her way through the door, Anje returned with two overfilled mugs of tea. On seeing the magazine tucked under her arm, Blake gave out a loud groan.

'Vincent, you didn't tell me you were so famous,' she said playfully. 'After all, it's not every day I know someone who's on the cover of *The Times* magazine.'

After depositing the mugs of tea on the table next to the window, the nurse recovered the magazine from under her arm and opened it to the inside cover. Blake moved uncomfortably in his seat. With a strained expression, Blake nodded his approval and Anje started reading from the lead article.

'A church has stood on the summit of Ludgate Hill, in the heart of the City of London, for more than 1,100 years. The most recent incarnation of the church, Christopher Wren's baroque masterpiece, vies as the nation's most iconic building. Since its construction after London's Great Fire of 1666, the cathedral has laid witness to some of the most remarkable episodes in the City's history. But the events of 30 November go down as some of the most dramatic in the cathedral's history. Tourists and cathedral staff looked on in horror as an armed tactical response team, led by Detective Chief Inspector Lucas Milton from Scotland Yard's Art and Antiques Section, stormed the cathedral's entrance.

What the police discovered buried deep in the cathedral's foundations has shocked and intrigued the nation in equal measure. Whilst the cathedral's regular thanksgiving prayers were being read to the assembled congregation of holidaymakers and local parishioners, a shoot-out was taking place deep underground beneath the cathedral's dome. The subterranean battle left three people dead and two injured, one seriously. The dead include industrialist Ema Mats, the founder of the celebrated Mats Institute, and two hit men wanted by Interpol. The unconscious bodies of Dr Carla Sabatini, a Vatican official, and Dr Vincent Blake, an art recoveries consultant—a man who is himself no stranger to controversy—' Anje sent Blake a playfully disapproving look, *'were also found at the scene.'*

'Whilst the facts surrounding these sensational events are shrouded in secrecy, the discovery of an unknown network of underground passages and the ensuing gun battle have led some to suspect a hunt for hidden treasure. The presence of Dr Blake, a man who has been associated with the recovery of several high-profile works of art in the past, has only fuelled rumours of buried riches. However, police sources have categorically denied that any such treasure has been found, a fact that both Dr Blake and Dr Sabatini

have corroborated.' Feeling self-conscious, Blake fingered the inside of his shirt collar. Anje read on.

'What does appear to be certain, however, is that the prompt action of disabled senior citizen Edna Smith, holidaying from the USA, undoubtedly saved the lives of Dr Blake and Dr Sabatini. Her suspicions had been first aroused by a man acting strangely outside a doorway close to the cathedral's entrance. On seeing the armed police team storm into the great church, Mrs Smith, now something of a celebrity, took no time in directing DCI Milton and his unit to the door leading to Wren's famous geometrical staircase.'

Blake waved his arm in protest. 'No more, no more!'

Groaning with disappointment, Anje promptly shut the magazine and returned it to the table.

'Vincent Blake, very famous man; a very good and famous man.' The nurse pondered for a second.

'If you not let me read on, then I think I should be able to sign your plaster cast?' Before Blake could say anything, Anje unclipped the pen from the front pocket of her nurse's uniform and bent down to his outstretched leg. She found a small unmarked area of plaster and began to write. After she finished, Blake was completely silent, his gaze fixed upon the words that Anje had just written in thick black ink.

The steps of a good man are ordered by God. Psalm 37:23

CHAPTER 70

DCI Milton looked up from his workstation just as the hands of the large wall clock shuddered forward to mark the end of another day. All was quiet on the third floor of the Central London police station except for the sound of the detective's fingers moving quickly over the computer keyboard. The email that Milton had just composed was characteristically to the point. He rescanned its contents and carefully checked the syntax of the email addresses with those printed on the official Vatican business cards arranged on the desk in front of him. Paying no heed to the voice in his brain recommending restraint, he pressed the send button.

Less than forty-eight hours after the discovery of the bodies under St Paul's Cathedral, Milton had been summoned to the Chief Constable's office in New Scotland Yard. The meeting had lasted no more than a few minutes, but by the end of it Milton had become noticeably riled. Through half-moon glasses, the Police Chief had read out the details of a special access order signed by the Home Secretary herself that gave a forensics team from the Vatican's own police force right of entry to the crime scene. He was to provide them with every assistance and not impede their investigations in any way. The specifics of the order were highly irregular and, notwithstanding Milton's strongest protests, the Chief Constable made it clear that they were to be followed to the letter.

From the moment the three-man team arrived on the scene, it was clear that they were pursuing different objectives from Milton's investigations. To his enormous frustration, his questions were to be referred to a special liaison officer based in Rome and not to the on-site team. Their attention seemed to focus on two areas, first of which was the recovery of a small crimson book that had been in Father Vittori's possession leading up to his murder. The book had apparently been stolen from the Vatican archives and was to be returned at the earliest opportunity. The second area of investigation was a dark angular mark discovered on the crypt floor directly under Mats's corpse. The area of discolouration, some two inches in diameter, appeared to have been imprinted onto the white marble stone. Milton's own forensic team had paid it little attention, assuming that the mark was a remnant from the crypt's construction, but the Vatican investigators' series of chemical and ultraviolet tests seemed to show some other significance.

Milton's email was the fourth formal request for information concerning the results of the Vatican's investigations. As with his previous attempts, he wasn't very hopeful of a response. He stood up and waited for his computer to complete its long shutdown procedure. Before long, the office central heating system would switch off, and the temperature in the incident room would drop significantly. It was time to go home. After collecting his coat from the back of a chair, Milton headed slowly for the lift. His body was exhausted, but his mind wouldn't let go of the case details. There were still too many loose ends. Halfway across the open-plan office, he abruptly changed direction and walked back towards the large incident board that dominated the far end of the room. The board demanded one last inspection before his brain would let him leave for the day.

The centre of the board was given over to two photographs of Ema Mats, aka 'the Drakon'. The smaller of the images, a glossy black-and-white publicity photograph of Mats accepting an industry award, contrasted starkly with its neighbour: a full colour picture of her corpse with a dark red pool of blood behind her head. An elaborate spider web of string, held tight by coloured drawing pins, formed connections between suspect photographs and handwritten notes arranged in clusters around the two pictures of Mats. She had been the centre of it all.

Once her body was positively identified, Milton sent a squad car to her exclusive Mayfair residence to secure the premises for forensic examination. The police car arrived at the address moments after two fire engines from Kensington Fire Brigade had set to work training their high-pressure hoses onto the roof of the building. The luxury town house had been set alight, but the swift actions of the fire officers largely saved the back half of the building from the ravages of the flames. After the building was made safe, it became apparent that the Georgian town house was not all as it first appeared. Concealed behind an unremarkable door in the ground-floor study lay the entrance to a network of underground quarters. The evidence retrieved from this sunken labyrinth of rooms conclusively identified Mats as the mastermind behind the Newton robberies. Blake had been right all along. A 'Dr No' figure had been commissioning robberies to furnish a private collection. The shelves lining the underground library were filled with the stolen material from the previous Newton robberies, including Newton's personal copy of the *Principia* taken from the Wren Library. Mats's interest in the celebrated scientist had turned into a dangerous obsession. Nothing would stand in her way.

The three smartphones retrieved from the corpses in the crypt of St Paul's had also provided a rich seam of evidence against Mats. Once Scotland Yard's e-crime unit had decrypted each device's text messages, the picture had become clear. Mats had commissioned Denic and Crossland to do whatever it took to secure the Newton material, which had included premeditated murder. Blake's landlord, whose body had been found amongst the smouldering remains of his bedsit, had just been the latest victim.

The world would be a better place without scum like that, thought Milton as he drove a bright red drawing pin through the centre of an enlarged CCTV image of Denic taken from the Dover Port Authority cameras. A last waft of air from the overhead heating unit rustled the photographs pinned to the incident board before the slats directing the machine's airflow moved noisily to a closed position.

Milton studied the network of coloured string, which criss-crossed the incident board like the connectors of some giant circuit board diagram. A single picture stubbornly refused to be linked to any other. He stared at the grainy image of what looked like a tramp entering the doorway from the nave of St Paul's Cathedral to the stairwell of Wren's hanging staircase. Despite the imaging department's best efforts, the picture could not be resolved enough for a positive identification. However, Milton suspected that the several fingerprints lifted from the weapon allegedly used to shoot Mats would match those of this mystery figure. Both Blake and Sabatini had reported being stopped by a homeless woman on the steps of the cathedral, but although the picture had been distributed to police stations and homeless shelters throughout London, the search for the suspect had yet to deliver a firm lead.

Milton patted down his inside jacket pocket in search of his smoking inhalator. With some difficulty he retrieved the white plastic tube caught in the silk lining and bit hard onto its end. Another unreconciled fact gnawed at him. It was there, like a seed stuck between his teeth. Both Blake and Sabatini were convinced that Mats and her henchmen had been searching for some Jewish religious relic hidden in the cathedral. Despite a detailed search of the scene, no such object had been found. Whether the object was real was not Milton's immediate problem: the three dead bodies found in a secret crypt under the great dome of St Paul's were. He hadn't the time or the resources to go on some wild goose chase hunting down a myth. Milton pushed the thought resolutely to the back of his mind and took a long suck on his inhalator. With the white plastic tube still between his lips, he headed for the lift.

Milton pressed the button at the side of the lift door and waited. Eventually, the lift stopped with a jolt, and the doors opened with a disquieting rattle. Milton stooped slightly as he stepped into the large metal box. Turning to face the door, he felt the lift's bright ceiling lighting begin to warm the top of his head. Though his car was parked in the basement, Milton hesitated over the button marked with a red glowing letter B. Instead he selected the button for reception.

I'll get a taxi from the rank outside the station, he thought. The notion of going underground made him feel uneasy. After all, he had spent enough time in buried rooms to last him a lifetime.

CHAPTER 71

Mary read the inscription: *Christopher Wren's design for a memorial to the Great Fire of London was finished in 1703.* Squinting against the sun, Mary looked up at the imposing white marble column standing like a solitary oak in a forest of grey concrete office buildings. Looking back at the inscription, she read on. *Known simply as 'The Monument', the great architect sited the world's tallest free-standing Doric column close to the location where the fire started in Pudding Lane ...'*

Mary's gaze was now drawn to the massive plaque set on the west face of the column. Something in its grand baroque decoration fascinated her. Her eyes darted up and down its carved marble exterior, as if attempting to trace a concealed connection between points on its surface. The design was comprised of a strange collection of figures. Whispering down to the dog, she described the hidden geometry that had stayed unnoticed for over 300 years.

'See what the goddess is holding in her hand?' The dog turned its head slightly as if acknowledging Mary's instructions. Close to the centre of the white marble plaque, pointing skywards, was carved the outstretched arm of the goddess Minerva. In her grip was a rod of the most peculiar design. As if summoning down to earth the blessings of heaven, the rod terminated in the shape of a hand, and though the stone had been weathered badly, the outline of an eye carved into its palm was clearly visible.

'My friend, it is the holy rod of Aaron, marked with the all-seeing eye of God.' Mary looked down to the dog and chuckled. 'It has stood here all along without anyone ever realising it.'

Mary gave the dog's neck a vigorous rub. The animal pulled itself closer to its companion, luxuriating in the sensation. As it did so, the dog picked up the scent of something enticing, somewhere deep between the folds of her heavy overcoat. Mary smiled, her face looking suddenly youthful.

'Ah, I know what you're after.' Pushing her hand deep into her coat pocket, she searched for the packet of biscuits she had retrieved from a bin outside Kings Cross Station earlier that day.

Her fingertips walked down the length of the sacred rod weighing down the lining of her coat. Mary felt the distinct shape of the inscriptions carved into its smooth surface. God had entrusted her with Aaron's rod and she would keep it safe until the allotted hour. A homeless beggar and a dog were now the caretakers of God's most powerful instrument on earth.

She smiled and then slowly withdrew her hand from the pocket. The dog's eyes followed the movement, its tail wagging excitedly in anticipation.

'There you go, my friend.' Tilting its head, the dog snapped up the crumbling biscuit from Mary's outstretched hand and looked expectantly for the sign of another. 'No, no.' She chuckled loudly. 'It's time to go.' A pair of glistening eyes stared back up at her. 'You lead the way.'

The dog barked its approval.

'God will speak and reveal His purpose to us, when the time is right … in a time, times and half a time.'

AFTERWORD

The Sotheby's Sale

In March 1936, a large metal trunk was delivered to John Taylor, the Chief Cataloguer of the Books and Manuscripts Department of the prestigious London auctioneer, Sotheby's & Co. The trunk contained a substantial collection of the private papers and personal effects of Sir Isaac Newton, arguably one of the greatest thinkers of the modern age. Since his death in 1727, these papers had been kept hidden from public view at Hurstbourne Park, the family home of the Earls of Portsmouth. Believing the trunk's contents would jeopardise Newton's untouchable reputation, successive heirs of the collection had concealed the papers from academic scrutiny until 1936, when Viscount Lymington instructed Sotheby's & Co. to auction the papers in an open sale as a way to clear substantial death duties.

Taylor was tasked with examining the trunk's contents in readiness for a sale later in July, and within he found a treasure trove of manuscripts and personal notebooks which had sat hidden for more than 200 years. Many of the texts were written in code, some were merely paper fragments only a few lines in length, while others were complete drafts of large unpublished works. Far from being aligned with Newton's standing as a cold, rational scientist, a large number of these papers reflected his secret obsession with biblical prophecy.

From his New Bond Street Office in London, Taylor organised the papers into 331 separate sales lots. Amongst the buyers was the Jewish scholar and businessman Abraham Yahuda, who eventually acquired a substantial personal collection of the auctioned biblical works. Today, an inventory of the papers making up the 331 sales lots of the Sotheby's sale remains incomplete. Substantial parts of the collection are held by the University of Cambridge and the Jewish National and University

Library in Jerusalem, whilst others have been lost to private collections around the world.

Isaac Newton

A display cabinet containing Newton's personal effects is on show at the Wren Library, Trinity College, Cambridge. Amongst the exhibits are his pocket watch, his walking stick and his personal copy of the *Principia*, complete with annotations in his own handwriting.

It has been estimated that out of Newton's surviving writings, 700,000 words are concerned with scientific research, 600,000 words relate to alchemy and 1,700,000 relate to his biblical research.

During his later life, Newton became obsessed with unlocking the secrets hidden within Holy Scripture. Certain of its accuracy, Newton described biblical prophecy as a 'history of things to come'.

Newton was convinced that encoded in the design of Solomon's first temple was some divine hidden knowledge, and he became consumed with recreating the floor plan of the Temple from descriptions contained within the Book of Ezekiel.

Newton's analysis of the prophetic writings of Daniel was published after his death. He believed that the scriptural reference 'in a time, times and half a time' (found in Daniel 7:15 and 12:7, and also in Revelation 12:14) was of special significance.

An inventory of Newton's personal possessions showed that he was obsessed with crimson, the colour of blood.

Newton referred to a Mr F many times in his alchemic writings. To this day, the true identity of Mr F remains a mystery.

As Newton is quoted as saying, *'For the parts of Prophesy are like the separated parts of a watch. They appear confused and must be compared and put together before they can be useful'.*

Christopher Wren

Whilst excavating the foundations for St Paul's Cathedral, Wren's labourers uncovered many historical artefacts, including relics dating back to Roman times.

During its construction, Wren hid the overall design of the cathedral from his workmen and sponsors, keeping many aspects of the full plan secret.

The question as to whether Christopher Wren was a freemason has been the topic of much debate. The first grand lodge meeting of English freemasonry took place at the Goose and Gridiron Tavern in 1717, just metres away from St Paul's Cathedral. Wren commissioned his chief sculptor, Causis Cibber (a head of a freemason lodge), to create the sculpture at the base of the Monument, which was built to commemorate the Great Fire of 1666. The mysterious design incorporates a female figure pointing a rod up to heaven. The rod terminates in a hand with an eye at the centre of its palm, indicating its divine nature.

Peasants' Revolt

The events surrounding the 1381 Peasants' Revolt in England included savage premeditated attacks on the Knights Hospitaller. The Prior of the religious order, Sir Robert Hales, was dragged from the Tower of London during the uprising and decapitated.

The Royal Society

Isaac Newton and Christopher Wren were fellow members of the Royal Society, both serving terms as President.

The headquarters of the Royal Society was at Gresham College in London. Mysteriously, the path of the Great Fire was halted at the edge of its grounds, saving the building from destruction.

The Alignments

In 1185, the Patriarch of Jerusalem visited London to muster support for a new Crusade. He was accompanied by Roger de Moulin, the Grandmaster of the Knights Hospitaller. With them, they carried several sacred objects that had been liberated from the Holy City. During his visit, the Patriarch consecrated St John's Church and Temple Church, the headquarters of the Knights Hospitaller and the Knights Templar in England.

In Jerusalem, the Dome of the Rock, the Church of the Holy Sepulchre and the Cathedral of St James, (the crusader headquarters of the Knights Hospitaller in Jerusalem) form the points of an equilateral triangle.

In London, St Paul's Cathedral, Temple Church and the former location of St John's Church, Clerkenwell (the crusader headquarters of the Knights Hospitaller in London), form the points of an equilateral triangle. Wren changed the axis of the cathedral by 8 degrees to align it exactly with Temple Church.

Vatican Observatory

With its headquarters at the papal summer residence just outside Rome, the Vatican Observatory is one of the world's oldest astronomical research institutions.

Mastema

According to the ancient Jewish book of the Jubilees, Mastema is the chief of the demons that were engendered by the union of the fallen angels ('the Watchers') and their human wives.

BIBLIOGRAPHY

The following works particularly inspired me during the writing of this book:

Ackroyd, Peter, 2001, *London: The Biography* (Vintage).

Defoe, Daniel, 2001, *A Journal of the Plague Year* (Dover).

Defoe, Daniel, 1986, *A Tour Through the Whole Island of Great Britain* (Penguin).

Eve, John, 2006, *The Diary of John Evelyn* (Everyman).

Gilbert, Adrian, 2003, *The New Jerusalem. Rebuilding London: The Great Fire, Christopher Wren and the Royal Society* (Corgi).

Gleick, James, 2003, *Isaac Newton,* (Vintage).

Hebborn, Eric, 1997, *The Art Forger's Handbook* (Overlook Press).

Hebborn, Eric, 1991, *Drawn to Trouble: The Forging of an Artist* (Mainstream).

Hollis, Leo, 2009, *The Phoenix: St Paul's Cathedral and the Men Who Made Modern London* (Phoenix).

Jardine, Lisa, 2002, *On a Grander Scale: The Outstanding Career of Sir Christopher Wren* (HarperCollins).

Levy, Joel, 2009, *Newton's Notebook: The Life, Times and Discoveries of Sir Isaac Newton* (History Press).

Robinson, John L., 1989, *Born in Blood: The Lost Secrets of Freemasonry* (M. Evans).

White, Michael, 1997, *Isaac Newton: The Last Sorcerer* (Fourth Estate).

And finally, a number of the biblical quotations referenced in this novel are taken from *The Holy Bible, New International Version,* 1996, (Zondervan) and from *The Authorized (King James) Version*, reproduced by permission of the Crown's patentee, Cambridge University Press.

ABOUT THE AUTHOR

Duncan Simpson spent his childhood in Cornwall, England. As a teenager he gained experience in a variety of jobs, from working in a mine to doing shifts as a security guard in an American airport. After graduating from the University of Leeds with a physics degree, he spent a year backpacking around the world. On returning to the UK, he embarked on a successful career in business. Along the way,  he became the finance director for a technology company and a partner in a leading management consultancy firm.

His debut novel, *The History of Things to Come* was born out of his lifelong fascination with the relationship between science and religion. A keen student of the history of London, he loves exploring the ancient stories and myths surrounding the city. When he's not writing or consulting, you'll find him playing guitar in a rock band, running by the Thames, or drinking tea with his wife and three children in their home in Berkshire, England.

He can be reached through his website at:

http://www.duncansimpsonauthor.com

ACKNOWLEDGEMENTS

Thanks to my readers and community at:
http://www.duncansimpsonauthor.com and also to my friends on
Twitter.

Thanks to my production team: Gale Winskill, at Winskill Editorial
and Amy Butcher of the Book Butchers for copy-editing and
proofreading; Derek Murphy for cover design; and Jake Muelle at
Creativindie for interior print design. Also a big thanks to Jill Munro
and Kathryn Moore, who did a great job beta-reading the book.

As always, my biggest thank you goes out to Katie, my master editor. I
am constantly in awe of her love, patience and keen eye. Thank you for
allowing me to dream and for riding shotgun on the journey. She is the
brightest star in my sky.

Whitefort Publishing

Thanks for joining Vincent Blake in
THE HISTORY OF THINGS TO COME.
He will be returning in the *DEVIL'S ARCHITECT.*

If you've enjoyed this book, it would be fantastic if you would consider sharing the message with others. Your help in spreading the word is gratefully appreciated.

Here's what you can do next.

- Mention the book in a Facebook post, Twitter update, Pinterest pin, or blog post.
- Recommend the book to those in your small group, book club, workplace, and classes.
- Head over to www.facebook.com/duncansimpsonauthor, 'LIKE' the page, and post a comment as to what you enjoyed most about the book.
- Tweet 'I recommend reading #TheHistoryofThingstocome by @ DSimpsonAuthor'
- Write a review on amazon.com, bn.com or goodreads.com

For more information and updates on new releases, join Duncan's mailing list at: http://www.duncansimpsonauthor.com

Get in touch:
Website & blog: http://www.duncansimpsonauthor.com
Twitter: http://www.twitter.com/dsimpsonauthor
Facebook: http://www.facebook.com/duncansimpsonauthor

CPSIA information can be obtained at www.ICGtesting.com
Printed in the USA
LVOW11s2100300516

490494LV00001B/330/P